BABY

To Stella
With very best wishes,

Marie
P.

Baby
Published by The Conrad Press in the United Kingdom 2016

Tel: +44(0)1227 472 874
www.theconradpress.com
info@theconradpress.com

ISBN 978-1-78301-964-9

Copyright © Marie Campbell, 2016

The moral right of Marie Campbell to be identified as author of this work has been asserted in accordance with the Copyright, Designs and Patents Act 1988.

All rights reserved. This book is copyright material and must not be copied, reproduced, transferred, distributed, leased, licensed or publicly performed or used in any way except as specifically permitted in writing by the publisher, as allowed under the terms and conditions under which it was purchased or as strictly permitted by applicable copyright law. Any unauthorised distribution or use of this text may be a direct infringement of the author's and publisher's rights, and those responsible may be liable in law accordingly.

Book cover design and typesetting by:
Charlotte Mouncey, www.bookstyle.co.uk

The Conrad Press logo was designed by Maria Priestley.

Printed by Management Books 2000 Limited
36 Western Road
Oxford
OX1 4LG

BABY

Marie Campbell

For Steve and Charlie, with my love.

1

The air was thick with the smells of beer and fried food. The post-work crowd jostled for space at the bar, seeking liquid relief from the monotony of long, hard days in the office. Michael Stanton leaned against the sticky wood, a twenty between his fingers, and tried to get the barman's attention.

'Hello, stranger,' a woman next to him said.

He thought she was speaking to someone else; he didn't even acknowledge her, just paid for the drinks and pocketed his change. He knew he'd really have to get going after this one. Then she said it again, 'Hello, stranger,' so close to his ear he could feel her warm breath.

Michael turned towards the voice, and stopped breathing.

It was Anna.

2

She was just as stunning as he remembered her. Her glossy hair, so dark it looked almost black, was cut shorter than he remembered, and fell smoothly to her chin in a shapely bob; *it suits her*, he thought. And the full lips. Lips he'd kissed God knew how many times. The eyes, hazel with flecks of gold. Eyes that had looked into his more often than he could remember; intense eyes that always seemed to be just for him. Her lips, her eyes, and her hands, with their long, strong fingers and ornate silver rings – they were all Anna.

Feeling a sharp twinge of excitement in his solar plexus, he moved away from the bar and, beers in his hands, faced her for the first time in over three years.

She was wearing a silky olive-green dress patterned with tiny birds and black, opaque tights. At five ten, Michael wasn't exactly short, but even in the flat, ballerina-pump shoes she had on, she almost matched him in height. She was wearing smoky make-up around her eyes and clear gloss on her mouth. Michael took a deep breath. She looked amazing. And her perfume: he remembered it so well; Midnight. It was musky, spicy. It acted like a catalyst on his memory, bringing images of remembered pleasure, remembered thrills, dangerous ecstasies that made the twinge feel much, much stronger. She took a sip of the white wine she was drinking and smiled at him.

'Anna. This is a surprise,' Michael said slowly, hearing how hoarse his voice was. 'What… what are you doing here?'

'Oh, you know, just… I was in the area and I wondered if you still came in here,' she said, her voice sounding velvety and determined in his ears, as it once had, as it always had. She started fiddling with the silver chain around her neck. Michael recognised it as the intricate silver knot she'd always worn.

'I thought it would be nice to see you. Catch up.'

'Ah. Well, er, yes, I do. Still… still come in here, I mean. Creature of… well, habit, that's me,' he said. 'So, what brings you here? I thought… assumed… you don't live around here anymore, do you?'

'No, I don't, no. It's just I was in town for a work thing and I was at a loose end this evening and… well. It's good to see you, Michael,' she said, then took a long swallow from her glass.

Suddenly, she laid her right hand on his left forearm. Her skin was cool and paper-dry. The sudden feel of her touch on him again made him dizzy; for a moment he actually wondered whether he was likely to pass out. A memory coursed through his brain like molten lava. Those hands, linked behind his neck. His back against a rough concrete pillar. Her lips against his, their tongues writhing together like battling serpents. He shook his head, trying to clear it.

'It's good to see you too. It's… it's been a while. Anyway, I'd better get these drinks over to the lads. You take care.' Michael turned to go. He felt sweat beads popping up on his forehead. He was breathless.

Her fingers, feather-light at the small of his back, stopped him in his tracks. He closed his eyes against the images that were tugging at the edges of his mind.

'Wait,' she said. 'Michael, I… well, I wondered if we could get together for a coffee, maybe? It would be a shame not to catch up properly, after all this time, don't you think?'

Michael turned back to look at her. Her head was tilted to one side, and she was running a finger absently around the top of her almost-empty glass.

'Listen, Anna, I'm not... actually I'm not sure that's such a good idea. Probably best we don't, eh? I've got loads on at work at the minute, and I'm sure you're busy as well.'

She lowered her face. When she looked up, a single tear was rolling down her cheek. He watched her tongue, pink and cat-like, dart out and catch it at the side of her mouth.

'There was a lot left unsaid between us, Michael, wasn't there?' She raised her hands, palms towards him, as if guessing what he would say next. 'I know, I know – you maybe think it was all a long time ago. But it would be good to just, well, have a chat. Like I said, catch up a bit. Please?' She smiled at him. 'It would mean so much to me,' she said.

Michael looked at her, remembering how one minute, she could be so serious, and the next, a smile would illuminate her face so brightly, it was as if someone had turned on the sun. He was torn – the very last thing he should do was sit across a table from her, raking up a past that should never really have happened. But then again.

'OK,' he said, shocked to hear the agreement coming so readily from his mouth.

'Great,' Anna said. '*Great*. How about Starbucks, on Lothian Road? Tomorrow, when you finish work? Shall we say about quarter to six?'

Michael nodded helplessly, then watched as Anna turned and walked away, swallowing the last mouthful of wine and placing her empty glass on a table she passed, then pulling on the coat that she had draped over her arm.

He kept watching as she slipped easily through the crowded bar and vanished out of the door like smoke. He blew out a long breath and walked over to his friends Gary and Kevin.

He dished out the beers and swigged deeply from his own bottle of Becks, only half-listening as they slagged him off for taking so long at the bar, then returned to their conversation about work and the Celtic match that was about to start on the pub TV. Michael put his empty bottle down and pulled on his jacket. It was time he went home. He could still smell Anna's scent.

3

Normally, Michael went to sleep really quickly. Jill joked that he was the only person she knew who could fall asleep mid-sentence. She said he could go from zero to snoring in less than five seconds. But that night he lay awake, staring into the dark and listening to the rain pounding against the windows.

When the dark was replaced by pale early-morning sunlight, he got out of bed and went downstairs to the kitchen. He'd slept for no more than an hour or so, and his sleep had been haunted by memories of Anna. He flicked on the kettle and made a cup of tea that he didn't really want and sat at the table, throbbing head in his hands.

After rummaging in the cupboard for some painkillers, he swallowed two Paracetamol with a mouthful of tea and went back upstairs to shower and dress.

He looked through the bedroom door at Jill, curled up on her side in their bed. She was making the soft purring noise she always made when she was deeply asleep. She looked so small and vulnerable; he felt a sudden rush of affection for her and guilt at how much he'd been thinking about Anna since seeing her again. He hurried over to where Jill lay.

He pushed her long blonde hair gently back from her face. Normally, she tied it back before she went to sleep, but it had come free from its tie. Her normally golden skin looked pale and waxy. Even though the sickness – the term 'morning sickness', she'd said, was a complete myth, and 'morning, noon and night sickness' would be a far better description – had stopped a while ago, it had really taken its toll.

'Baby,' she'd said the day before, as she'd come into the bathroom to clean her teeth while he was showering, 'when *exactly* is the glow pregnancy is supposed to bring going to appear?' He'd laughed and told her she didn't need any help to glow, she was beautiful enough already. She'd grimaced and started to brush make-up onto her cheeks.

She did look shattered though. Usually, he'd wake her as he left, say goodbye and tell her to have a good day, but she looked so peaceful that he decided to leave her. He checked her phone, made sure her alarm was on, then pulled the sheets over her bare shoulder, kissed her cheek and left the house.

The rain had stopped, but dampness still hung in the air and clung to his clothes. Michael briefly considered taking the car into work; despite being up since dawn he was somehow running late. But finding a parking space would gobble up any time he saved. Instead, he hurried along the street and then broke into a run as the number 42 bus approached.

He got on and sat down, leaning his head against the window and closing his eyes. The painkillers had done nothing for his headache; if anything, it was getting worse, the throb behind his eye keeping time with every bump and pothole on the road.

The day dragged, punctuated by two overly-long meetings and a project update with the management board.

One of the things Michael loved about being an IT contractor was that, as well as being more or less his own boss, no one really bothered to get to know him, thinking he'd soon be off to another company with his spreadsheets and flowcharts. And they were right – his contracts could last anything from a few weeks to several months, rarely more.

He didn't get involved in office politics, tea clubs and collections, and, normally, that suited him just fine.

Today, though, he could have done with a bit of banter. He itched to ring Jill, but then she'd ask what time he was leaving work, and that would mean lying to her, or at least, not quite telling her the truth.

Maybe he should ring Ben, arrange to meet him for a pint later and tell him all about it. No, he'd catch up with him at the match on Saturday. He'd go right home after he left Anna. Get in early. See if Jill fancied going out for a bite to eat, maybe see a film.

He smiled to himself. It still took him by surprise sometimes, how much he actually wanted to go home and see Jill, after all those years when his main objective was staying out for as long and as late as he could.

Michael left the office at precisely five-thirty. The day was still dull and drizzly, and his head still ached. The coffee he'd been downing all day to stay awake had left him feeling jittery, and his stomach felt greasy; it churned unpleasantly as he walked the two blocks towards Starbucks. He'd barely eaten all day, his lunchtime sandwich abandoned after two bites.

His mind was whirling. In his head, he'd gone over and over the reasons he'd agreed to meet Anna. Guilt, over how it had ended. Curiosity, at what she was doing with her life now. And, of course, excitement at the chance of seeing her again. He'd told himself it was complicated. But he knew that it wasn't complicated, not really. He was meeting her because, from that first illicit couple of weeks, he'd never been able to say no. He was meeting her because he couldn't resist. He was meeting her because he wanted to.

Back then, he'd just meant for them to have a bit of fun. Then she'd left Stuart and it had all got a bit more serious. Maybe, if things had been different…

And it was, let's face it, weird, her turning up now, after all this time. He'd thought of her a lot lately, since Jill had got pregnant. Every time someone indicated Jill's neat bump and asked if it was their first baby, every time he nodded and said, yes, it was, he felt a sudden hot flash of guilt. But there was nothing he could do about it. It couldn't possibly have worked out, not in the long term.

As he approached Starbucks, Michael thought, for a second, about just continuing on down the street. And then he pushed the door open and walked into the coffee shop.

The air inside was heavy, and the odours of wet clothes and coffee made him feel queasy. It was busy, and he looked around, not seeing her at first. Something streaked through his mind. Something close to disappointment.

Then he spotted her, tucked in the corner, almost concealed by a man with long ginger hair who was tapping away furiously on his laptop. Michael made his way over to her. She was staring out of the window, fiddling with the deep-red, leather gloves that she'd laid in front of her. She had tucked one side of her hair back behind her ear, and was wearing less make-up than she had been the night before.

'Hi,' he said when he reached her table. 'Can I get you something?'

She stood, smiling, and kissed his right cheek. Her lips felt warm against his skin. She had boots on today, long ones that stopped just shy of her knees, with a heel that made her slightly taller than him. Her perfume, filled his nostrils: the same spicy, musky scent. A scent of danger, a red alert kind of scent. *No, a black alert*, he thought, *it is called Midnight after all*. Anna sat back down and gestured towards the two cups on the table, shaking her head.

'I've got you one already. I assumed you'd still drink cappuccino. You do, right?'

'Yes, yes, I do,' Michael said, even though a cup of coffee was the very last thing he wanted just now; he felt hyper enough already. He pulled off his jacket and hung it on the back of the chair then sat down opposite her.

'I'm glad you came,' she said. 'I thought you mightn't.'

She stirred her coffee slowly then lifted the spoon to her mouth and licked off the foam. Michael broke her gaze and stared down into his own cup.

'Do you know what day it is?' she asked, looking straight at him.

'What? It's Thursday. April the…' he glanced at his watch, '… third. Why?'

'Yes. April the third. Does that even mean anything to you?' she asked. Michael frowned as she paused and took a sip of coffee.

'No, of course it doesn't,' she continued. 'It's his birthday. Or would have been.'

'Whose birthday?' Michael asked. 'Sorry, you've lost me.'

'Our baby. He would have been three today,' she said.

Michael looked down at the table and took a deep breath.

'What do you mean, "He"?' he said, keeping his voice right down. 'How do you know what sex it was?'

Anna met his gaze and gave a shrug. 'I don't. But I somehow feel sure he would have been a boy, not a girl. He would have been your son, Michael.'

Michael just looked at her. 'Oh, Anna, I think maybe this was a bad idea. What's the point of bringing all that up now? Listen, maybe I should just go. It doesn't do anybody any good, dwelling on the past.'

He eased himself up from the chair, and she reached across, wrapping her fingers around his arm. The strength in her grip surprised him.

'I'm sorry. Don't go,' she said.

Michael sighed and wiped a hand across his face. He sat back down.

'Would you, though?' she said.

'Would I what?' Michael asked.

'Change it? If you could, I mean? Rewrite history? We had so much, such potential... you must have known that, and yet, you threw it all away. We could have been good together. We could have been a family. I think about it a lot. The milestones. Just think, he would have been at nursery now, starting school soon. You must think about these things too, surely? You must think about me?'

'*Of course* I think about you,' he said, rubbing a hand across his face. 'And what we had was good. It was exciting.'

'Yes, it was,' she said. 'It really was.'

'But it finished a long time ago,' Michael replied. 'It's been over three years, Anna. A lot of water under the bridge and all that. We've been apart for much, much longer than we were ever together. We were only together for, what, four months? What was it you hoping for today? A catch-up? A big reunion?'

'I just wanted to see you, that's all. I've missed you. I've missed *us*,' she said, her voice suddenly surprisingly small and almost inaudible. 'You must sometimes wish, surely, that things could be the same as they were back then? That we were still together? We had some amazing times, you and me.'

When she looked at him, her eyes were shining. She looked so hopeful; he could hardly bear to meet her gaze.

'Anna,' he said softly, 'we had a good time – a really good time – but it could never have lasted, not really. You know that as well as I do. And some of the stuff you said, did, wanted to do – it, sort of, set off alarm bells in my head. I couldn't give you what you wanted. It had to end. You must know that. Especially after–'

Anna covered her face with her hands and started to cry; gulping sobs that made her shoulders shake with the effort. Michael reached across and put his hand on her arm.

'Come on, now,' he said. The wave of affection he felt towards her was sudden, and unexpected. 'There's no point getting yourself so upset. Hold on, I'll get you some water.'

Michael got up and went to the counter.

4

The night they'd met, she'd been sitting with Stuart, drinking from a bottle of beer. She'd been wearing a strappy top, and tight, dark-blue jeans with high sandals. She'd been fiddling with the silver knot necklace that hung down towards her cleavage as she looked over at him and caught his eye, and that was it. It was exciting, a challenge, a risk.

And it *had* been good. She'd had a way of making him feel like he was the most fascinating person alive. Who could possibly resist that?

He could never anticipate what she would suggest next. She'd turn up and, without saying a word, produce a silk scarf and hold out her wrists to him. Once, she'd given him a gift-wrapped blindfold.

Another time, she'd produced a map of the countryside and insisted he stick a pin in it. She'd suggested they drive to the spot he'd marked 'for a picnic'. Only there was no food and the only scenery he saw was from on his back in the long grass near the car park, with her strong, naked body on his.

But eventually all that had changed. It wasn't all sunshine and rainbows. And that intensity – it couldn't go on forever. And then the serious stuff had come too quickly. Anna getting pregnant, the talk of settling down, being a family. It was too much, too soon. He shook his head. He was too tired for this. He just needed to go home to Jill. When he got back to the table, carrying a glass, Anna was dabbing at her eyes with a cloth handkerchief. Her long, dark lashes were damp with tears.

'Please, just sit with me for a while,' she said, fiddling with a sugar sachet. 'Finish your coffee, please, Michael. It's just brought it all back to me, seeing you, that's all. We *were* good together, you and me. You meant so much to me, you know. It might have only been four months, but it seemed like a lot longer. It was the best four months... anyway. You're right. No point in upsetting myself. Tell me, though,' she cleared her throat, then added, 'can you honestly say you don't have feelings for me anymore? I don't believe you can just suddenly stop being attracted to someone. You can't just flick a switch and turn these things on and off.'

Michael gulped his now lukewarm cappuccino.

'You're a... well, you're a very attractive woman, Anna. You know that. It was only that... circumstances were against us.'

Anna sniffed loudly and nodded, then blew her nose and placed her hands flat on the table in front of her. Michael looked around. Ginger-laptop guy was packing his stuff away. The two women opposite were leaning over a magazine, pointing at and then dismissing a series of wedding dresses.

Michael waited for Anna to speak. She picked up the glass and took a delicate sip.

'I do go to see him sometimes, you know,' she said, looking down into the glass.

Michael inhaled sharply. 'What do you mean? How is that... well, how's it possible? And what you said earlier about the date? You couldn't possibly know when the baby would have been born. And anyway, what you did – we agreed it was for the best. We both *agreed*. Both of us. Remember how much we talked about it? We didn't want to be parents. But... I still don't understand what you mean?'

'You don't understand what I'm trying to tell you, Michael. It isn't the baby's grave I go and see. How could there be a grave, anyway?' Michael put his head in his hands. At the time, he really had thought Anna having the abortion was for the best. She'd been thirteen weeks pregnant when she'd had it. Thirteen weeks. Michael, the night before she'd been due to go into the clinic, compelled by a curiosity he couldn't control, had searched on Google images for what a foetus aborted at thirteen weeks looked like.

He'd vaguely imagined it would be a clump of cells that was hardly recognisable as anything, let alone a child. But that wasn't what the foetus was like. Oh, God, it really wasn't. Instead, it was an almost perfectly formed miniature baby about three inches long. He'd just stared at the image in utter horror.

Anna had gone to bed by then. He'd been close, so close, to waking her up and telling her there was no way he was going to let her go through with it. He knew she wasn't keen to have the abortion anyway, that she was only going through it for his sake. He knew that the moment he said he didn't want it to happen, that would be the end of the matter. But he hadn't woken Anna and told her he didn't want her to have the abortion. Instead, he'd just gone and fixed himself a double whisky and drank it, then another one, alone, in the kitchen until the terrible image of the thirteen-week-old baby faded from his mind. Then he'd got into bed next to Anna, and after what seemed like hours, he'd finally stopped seeing the miniature baby and had gone to sleep. 'It's Stuart,' Anna said, startling him back to the present. 'I go to see Stuart.'

'*Stuart?*' Michael said. 'You visit Stuart?'

'Yes, sometimes. I wasn't really sure if I should, the first time. After all, I was a bit cruel to him, dumping him to be with you. Those few weeks when I was seeing you both... it was cruel, really cruel. But I think he enjoys seeing me now, chatting about old times.'

'I don't know if that's such a good idea. He's... he's not the same now. It's best not to get him wound up.' Michael shook his head wearily. 'I had no idea you were visiting him. He's never mentioned it.'

She smiled, then leaned forward and cupped her chin in her hand. 'It must be our little secret, then,' she said. 'So, what about you? Has life been good to you? Are you happy?'

'What?' Michael said. He felt as if his head was going to explode. He longed to close his eyes. 'Yes,' he said. 'Yes, I am, actually.'

'Good,' she said, nodding. 'Good. And are you with someone?'

Michael gave a slow nod, feeling suddenly intensely uncomfortable about telling her this. 'Yes. I have been for a while now. I live with her. We've been together... a couple of years, nearly.'

She raised an eyebrow. 'That's a long time. For you, especially. I mean, you were always saying you didn't do commitment. And now... you'll be telling me you're getting married next. Or that you and your girlfriend are having a... well, having a baby.'

Michael felt his face redden. He shook his head, trying to clear it. He looked at his watch, trying to focus on the time. The numbers seemed to be dancing around. 'Yeah, well, I supposed I've changed. Yes, I suppose I have. Listen, Anna, I am sorry, you know. About how things worked out. But we've both moved on now. And now, it really is time I went home. It's been a long day.'

'Yes,' she said. 'For me too.'

He pulled on his still-damp jacket and waited as she put on her coat and gloves then followed her to the door. He embraced her awkwardly, brushing his lips against her cheek. He was so, so tired. He felt as if he could barely hold himself up.

'Look after yourself,' he said.

She nodded, and smiled as they stepped out of the door. Michael shivered and pulled up his collar. It was really chucking it down now.

'Can I give you a lift?' she said.

Michael felt he ought to refuse. They'd said goodbye, they should go their separate ways and have done with it. But he was so tired. He knew the choice was stark and simple. He could walk to the bus stop in the rain, and hang about for ages waiting for one to turn up, or he could accept her offer, get in the car and be home in fifteen minutes. 'Yes, well, thanks, Anna, that would be great. If it's not too much out of your way, that is.

'No, no,' she said. 'It's no problem.'

They walked in silence along the damp street, each step he took requiring more and more effort.

'I've got the same car,' she said, gesturing towards the olive-green Volvo parked up next to a meter. It was the same car that she'd driven back then, he remembered. It had seemed ancient even then. She'd told him many times, though, how much she liked it – said it was almost a classic, and could go on forever. He'd joked that she liked it because there was plenty of room in the back seat.

He sat down heavily on the passenger seat, another rush of memories spilling into his brain. Reversing the car one summer evening along a road that was barely more than a track. They'd parked. She'd taken his hand and led him outside. The moon was so bright, he remembered. And the rustling hedges and distant gunshots – just farmers shooting rabbits, she'd insisted – had freaked him out. But not enough to refuse to do exactly what she suggested. And it had been thrilling, it really had, doing it there in the warm evening; her tall and supple and lovely and strong body all his, and he all hers, like he was her possession, it had seemed to him. That had thrilled him too.

Michael leaned his head back against the seat. He could barely keep his eyes open. He thought maybe he would close them, just for a minute. As he drifted off, he wondered if Anna knew where he lived.

5

Jill glanced at the clock. Twenty past eight. It wasn't unusual for Michael to be late. It wasn't even something that bothered her.

In the early days she'd faked irritation, joked with him that he shouldn't keep a lady waiting. But really, she'd always loved his 'life's too short to be early' attitude. She'd never been a great one for time-keeping herself. She was the one whose friends often told her they were meeting half an hour earlier than they actually were, to give her a chance of being on time.

It drove her sister mad, she knew. Louise had never been late for anything in her life. She'd even insisted on breaking the time-honoured tradition and had actually been early for her own wedding. Jill made a mental note to ring Louise later on; it had been a few days since they'd spoken to one another.

Jill shrugged. She'd tried to wait, so they could eat together, but hunger was getting the better of her, so she dished up a bowl of the pasta that was already starting to dry out. She filled a second bowl and put it in the microwave, grimacing at the faint fishy smell as she opened the door. Michael insisted on eating kippers on a weekend, even though the smell lingered for days.

There was something she had read about, to get rid of it. Lemon juice, or something. She'd look it up later.

Jill carried her bowl through to the living room and sat on the sofa. The *EastEnders* theme tune was starting up as she flicked on the TV. She was ravenous.

That was how it seemed to work now. One minute, she'd not really be hungry, and the next, starving. Her body went from one extreme to the other. Or she'd be watching TV, thinking about nothing in particular, then seconds later, be in floods of tears. As she ate, she rested her free hand on her stomach, spreading her fingers wide. It seemed unreal, that there was a tiny person inside of her, eating, sleeping and growing.

Jill put her bowl on the floor, leaned over the side of the sofa and hauled up her handbag, fishing in it for her diary. She opened it and took out the small plastic wallet she kept there. In the grainy black and white picture, the baby was lying on its back, shadowy arms and legs floating above it, tiny bubbles trailing from its mouth.

She closed her eyes and remembered lying there, trying to ignore her full bladder, which she was sure would burst at any minute. She'd felt sick with anxiety. Even though she'd known she shouldn't, she'd spent hours online, searching for information on abnormalities and diseases. There was so much that could go wrong.

She'd clenched her stomach muscles as the sonographer had squirted on the icy gel and then started rubbing the scanner gently over her barely-noticeable bump. And then, there it was. Their baby. Their perfect, healthy baby. *'Look, it's waving at us!'* Michael had said. They'd both cried as the woman pointed out the face, the kidneys, the white bones of its spine. The sound of its tiny, beating heart had filled the room.

'Last chance,' the sonographer had said. 'Are you certain you don't want to know the sex?'

'Yes, thanks,' Michael had replied before Jill had a chance to speak. 'We're sure. There aren't many surprises in the world. Let's make sure this is one.'

Jill smiled as she gazed at the picture now. She stroked a finger across it then closed the wallet and put it back in its place. She dropped her bag back to the floor and pulled up her legs, so she was lying flat on her back.

Their baby. Even when she looked at the evidence – the picture, the bulge where her waist once was, the piles of clothes that no longer fit – she still couldn't believe it. In the middle of the night, she'd wake up, sweating and shaking, sure there had been a terrible mistake; that someone would tell her, no, actually, she wasn't pregnant at all, she'd been imagining things. She wouldn't believe it, really believe it, until the baby was here and in her arms.

She'd done it again, she realised, as she sat up and stretched. Fallen asleep. Her back protested and her left foot tingled with pins and needles. It was another of the pregnancy side-effects that seemed to have crept up on her; the overwhelming need to sleep, often at entirely inappropriate times, like in the middle of the afternoon, at work. She'd sit there at her desk, thoughts of a thick, soft mattress filling her head. She'd even fantasised about just sliding from her seat onto the dusty grey carpet underneath her desk and laying her head on the floor amongst the biscuit crumbs and discarded paperclips.

Jill forced her eyes open, and stood up, narrowly avoiding the bowl of congealed pasta sauce. It was dark now, shadows dappling the walls. She groaned as she straightened her stiff limbs, and walked to the window.

The clock on the mantelpiece told her it was just after eleven, and there was no sign of life in the street. The streetlights glowed through the misty night. Michael must have gone upstairs, she assumed; he'd not have wanted to wake her, she thought, as she drew the blinds closed.

She picked up her mobile from the side table as she passed. A missed call from Lisa. She must call her back and have a catch-up. She'd let things slide since she'd been pregnant.

Going out to bars and watching her friends gulp back Pinot Grigio while she sipped an orange juice that would no doubt give her heartburn had kind of lost its appeal.

Her legs just felt so heavy. Even though so many people had told her pregnancy was exhausting, she'd had no idea she would be this wrecked. She'd planned on still hitting the gym at eight months, in some sort of designer maternity wear. Fat chance of that. She'd cancelled her membership weeks ago. Even the thought of putting on her gym gear was tiring. Hopefully, at some point, she'd get the surge of energy that she'd heard about.

Jill walked into the bedroom. Instead of the messy sheets and heavy snores she'd been expecting, the sheets were smooth, the pillows and cushions exactly in place. Frowning, she looked in the bathroom. No sign of him. No puddle of toothpaste around his toothbrush, no wet towel flung across the side of the bath. A pair of checked cotton boxer shorts lay half in the laundry basket, where he'd thrown them the previous night. She pushed them over the side.

'Where are you, Michael?' she muttered. Her phone was still in her hand, ready to plug into the charger by the bed. She dialled his number. It went straight to his voicemail. She rang again. The same thing happened again.

'Hi, it's me. Just wondering where you are. If you've decided to sleep on someone's sofa, let me know, if you're still conscious. I'm going to bed now. Speak to you soon.'

She put her phone on her bedside cabinet and started to pull off her clothes. She really should fold them, she thought. And she should cleanse her face and brush her teeth. But she was so tired. Just this once, she told herself as she climbed into bed and pulled up the covers. She looked at the blank screen of her phone again before lying back on the pillows.

He'd done this before, and as she'd been on the verge of calling in the emergency services, he'd come bursting in in the early hours with a tale of a one pint too many and a lost mobile. No doubt he'd have crashed at one of the lads' houses, or be up talking and forgotten the time.

At least there'd be no snoring tonight. He'd have to change though, when the baby came. Then again, she didn't really want him to. He was the Michael she'd fallen for. Why would she want him to be someone different? She smiled as she drifted off to sleep. Pregnancy was making her soft.

6

Jill jolted awake as the alarm sounded the next morning. The sheets were barely creased – she must have lain in the same position for eight solid hours – yet she still felt so tired, as if she hadn't slept at all.

She reached over and picked up her phone to switch off the alarm. The relief that it was Friday at last quickly faded when she remembered that Michael hadn't come home last night. Or this morning. She'd had no missed calls or texts. She dialled his number again – still straight to voicemail. Her stomach clenched. Even though she knew his phone was probably dead, he should have made some sort of contact. Even if it was just to let her know he wasn't lying in a gutter somewhere.

She felt a rush of annoyance, and held onto it, hoping that it would paper over the worry that was creeping through her bones.

Jill walked to the bathroom and stepped into the shower, then closed her eyes as the hot stream pounded down. She rubbed herself dry on a thick white towel and wrapped another around her head, then dressed quickly.

As her waistline expanded, her outfit options shrunk and the black trousers with their adjustable, elastic waistband were her staple item. She was already sick of the sight of them. No doubt she'd be ready to burn them by the time the baby came.

Jill had promised herself she wouldn't be one of those women who slobbed about in leggings and their partner's shirts but now, she was starting to see why that could be tempting. The stripy top she pulled from the wardrobe stretched snugly over her bump. She pushed a pair of silver hoops into her ears and ran a hand through her hair, then headed downstairs to the kitchen. She toasted a slice of bread, buttered it and cut it in half. As she stood against the worktop eating it, she made herself a cup of the decaffeinated coffee that she'd been drinking ever since she'd read that caffeine wasn't good for developing babies.

After a couple of gulps, she gathered her bag, phone and keys and pulled on her coat. Her still-damp hair clung to the back of her neck, making her shiver. She reached back and pulled it into a loose bun as she walked down the path and onto the street.

She glanced at her phone again before shoving it into her bag. Still no word from Michael. She wanted to stay home, wait until he turned up, looking for a clean shirt and his phone charger, and give him a lecture of how not to be so thoughtless.

'Morning,' said Christine, as Jill walked into the office and headed for her desk. 'No offence, but you look worn out.'

Jill shrugged off her coat and looked across at the woman who, as well as being her line manager, was a good friend. Christine was immaculate, as usual, in a close-fitting dress the colour of ripe cherries. Her nails were painted the exact same colour, and as she moved, her expertly-highlighted brown hair swung in a shiny arc around her head.

'I am worn out,' Jill replied. 'I'm always worn out, or starving, or needing to pee.'

Christine laughed. 'Just make sure you do those pelvic whatsits. Or else *needing* a pee'll be the least of your worries. Believe me, I wish I'd done them. We were at a party last weekend and their kids had a trampoline. I didn't dare risk having a go.'

Jill laughed as Christine went to switch on the kettle.

Christine had had her kids young, and they were teenagers now. She adored children though, and had been almost overcome when Jill had told her she was pregnant.

She'd confessed to Jill once over a glass of wine that she wished she'd had more children. She had shed a few tears, even though, she said, at forty-six, she had to be realistic and accept that it wasn't going to happen. She'd just live in hope, she said, that her son and daughter would reproduce early so she could give up work and be a glamorous granny, staying at home surrounded by babies.

Jill pulled her mobile from her bag and dialled Michael's number. Voicemail, again. She scrolled through her address book for his office number. He moved offices so often, she hoped she'd remembered to save the latest one.

'Hello,' Jill said, when the receptionist answered. 'I'm trying to get in touch with Michael Stanton. Could you put me through to him please?'

'One moment, please,' she said, and then Jill sat with the phone to her ear, listening to the awful tinny 'hold' music.

'Yes please,' she mouthed, as Christine gestured to her with an empty cup.

'There's no reply at that extension,' said the receptionist when she came back on the phone. 'Would you like me to put you through so you can leave a message?'

'Erm, no, it's OK. I'll try again later.' As Jill replaced the handset, a feeling of unease twisted in her stomach.

'What's up?' Christine asked, putting a mug of tea down on Jill's desk.

'It's Michael,' she said, taking a sip. 'He didn't come home last night, and I can't get in touch with him.'

'Have you tried his work?'

Jill pushed her hair back from her face and nodded.

'Yeah, he's not there. Something's not right, Christine. He's stayed out before, the odd time, but that was ages ago. When we were first going out. He'd never do something like that now. I'm... I'm a bit worried, to be honest. Actually more than a bit. He's always at his desk by eight, if not earlier, and it's–' Jill glanced at her watch, 'half nine now.'

Christine frowned. 'Have you tried your home phone? In case he's there, crashed out or something. Maybe he's lost his mobile.'

Jill shook her head. 'He never answers the land line. Actually, it hardly ever rings, just sales calls and my sister. You're right, though, there'll be some explanation. I just wish I could get hold of him.'

Christine nodded. 'Men. So bloody inconsiderate at times. Let me know if you hear anything.' She turned and headed back into her office, a small glass-fronted area at the top of the room.

Jill switched on her computer and started ripping open the pile of envelopes in front of her.

'How are you doing?' Christine asked.

Jill looked up from the file she was reading through. She was trying, and failing, to decide whether the figures that were floating in front of her eyes actually added up.

'Fine,' Jill said.

'Any word from Michael?'

Jill sighed. 'No, nothing. I can't tell you how frustrating it is, not being able to get in touch with him.'

'Listen, why don't you take the rest of the day off?' Christine said. 'It's nearly lunchtime anyway, and Friday afternoons are always quiet in here. I bet Michael will be there when you get in.'

'You're sure you don't mind me going?' Jill asked. Christine was always so good to her, and she didn't want to take advantage.

But she felt too jittery to just sit at her desk. And it wasn't as if she was doing any worthwhile work.

'Of course. Just go. Give me a ring to let me know everything's OK. Because it will be, obviously.'

Jill pushed the papers on her desk into a pile and dumped them in her drawer, then pulled on her coat. She hurried out of the building and onto the damp street just as the bus was approaching. She collapsed onto a seat, trying to catch her breath as she pulled out her phone, willing it to ring.

Even though she knew his phone battery really must be dead, she kept dialling his number, again and again. It gave her something to do with her hands. The journey was painfully slow, the bus stopping at every stop and then sitting for long minutes at yet more road works. She got off two stops early and walked the rest of the way, unable to bear the delay a second longer.

'Michael?' she called as she opened the front door. 'Are you in?'

There was no sign of him. Upstairs, the bed was made, the shower dry.

Jill walked slowly down to the kitchen and sat at the table, the screen of her phone still annoyingly blank. She opened up its address book and searched for Ben's number. Michael was always chatting to him – Jill joked that she'd never known two men be such gossips. It was nice though, that he was so close to his best mate.

Ben answered after a few rings, and she could tell she had interrupted him at work. He hadn't heard from Michael, he said, and didn't expect to see him before the match that weekend.

'I hope he comes home soon,' Ben said. 'I'm sure he will.'

Jill scrolled through the address book again and rang anyone else who she thought might possibly have heard from Michael. He'd say she was being ridiculous, over-the-top. She had to do something, though – it made her feel slightly better than sitting and doing nothing at all.

Jill pulled a pad towards her and tore off the half-written shopping list. She scribbled down the names of everyone she called and whether they'd answered or if she'd left a message. There were a couple of people she didn't have numbers for. Gary, that bloke he went for a drink with after work. And there was another one. She couldn't remember his name.

She called Michael's office again and eventually got through to Gary. He said he hadn't seen Michael since he left work the day before.

Jill put the phone down on the table in front of her and leaned forward, resting her head in her hands. She was still in her coat and no further forward. Her stomach churned; she felt suddenly, overwhelmingly scared.

She wished she could ring her mum. Wasn't that what women did, when they had a problem or just wanted a bit of reassurance? They rang their mothers. She was being ridiculous, she knew.

She could ring her sister, but Louise would be all business-like and try to tell her what to do. Anyway, she knew what she should do, but really, really didn't want to do it.

The number was easy enough to locate but Jill's hand was shaking so much that it took three attempts before she could punch in the digits in the correct order.

'Hello, Edinburgh Royal Infirmary, can I help you?'

But not one of the four people she repeated her story to could help. Jill thought her heart had stopped beating when one nurse disappeared to have a look at an unidentified male who had been brought in before her shift. But it turned out he was at least sixty, bald, and didn't speak any English.

The relief she felt quickly faded when she realised she didn't know what to do next. She opened up the laptop and searched for other hospitals. Two hours later she had rang everywhere, from A&E in Glasgow to the tiny village hospitals that didn't even have emergency departments.

Bladder bursting and head pounding, Jill stood up and almost lost her balance. She held the back of the chair, closed her eyes and tried to push down the panic that was rising in her chest.

There has to be an explanation, she told herself. He'd walk through the door, any minute, and she'd be so, so mad at him, and he'd be saying 'You won't believe what happened…' and she'd cry, and punch at his chest with her fists and they'd go to bed and he'd kiss her all over in the way she liked so much and everything would all be fine.

The landline started to ring. Jill almost tripped over her feet as she scrambled to answer it.

'Hello?' Jill said.

'Ms Talbot? We've been trying to contact you,' said the voice at the other end.

'You have? What's happened? Is it Michael?'

'It's about your PPI, madam. Did you know–?'

Jill slammed the handset back into the base unit. She thought she might be going to be sick. She went back to the kitchen and turned on the cold tap. She held her wrists under the flow and took some long, deep breaths.

The clock on the wall told her it was five o'clock. Somehow, a whole day had almost passed. She was overreacting. There'd be an explanation. Of course there would.

7

As Jill sat, watching the clock and waiting for the phone to ring with some news, Michael opened his eyes. There was nothing but blackness. He tried to move, but he couldn't. His mouth felt sandpaper dry. He ran his tongue over his teeth, trying to unglue them.

The air was ripe with the sharp stink of sweat – his own, he knew – mixed with a heavy floral scent. Some sort of cleaning product, he thought. He coughed as it caught the back of his throat.

'Hello?' he said, shocked at how weak and broken his voice sounded.

There was no answer. His breath came in ragged gulps, and he tried to slow it. Focus, he told himself. Stop panicking.

He could feel a slight pressure at his temples, some sort of fabric against his skin. A blindfold? Or bandages? What if he was blind? He swallowed that thought down, and tried to concentrate on the rest of his body.

He could also feel the rise and fall of his chest, and he knew he was lying on his back, covered in something. Blankets, or some sort of bedclothes anyway. He was in bed, then. Hospital. He must be in hospital.

He concentrated hard, and found that he could wriggle his fingers. His legs felt stiff and leaden, but his toes moved. He couldn't be paralysed, could he, if his toes moved? Maybe he'd broken his legs. But he'd broken a leg once before, years ago, playing football, and it had been agony. He didn't seem to be in any pain, now.

He tried to think, to remember what had happened. He'd left Starbucks with Anna, accepted her offer of a lift. He vaguely recalled getting into her car. But after that, nothing.

They must have been in an accident. Maybe he wasn't even awake. Maybe he was dead already. He screwed up his eyes, trying to stop the pounding in his head, the fizzing in his brain. His mind raced, fearing, and believing, the worst.

'Hello,' he said again, his voice a little louder this time. He cleared his throat. 'Please. Anyone. Is there anybody there?'

Maybe no one could hear him. Maybe he could only hear his voice inside his own head. He'd seen that in films. He was so thirsty. Surely that was a good sign? He couldn't be thirsty if he was dead, could he?

'Hello?' he called. But there was no reply. He held his breath and strained his ears, but there was nothing other than a faint dripping sound.

Michael felt himself floating. He was lying on a cloud, a thick, velvety cloud. He tried to move and felt himself sink further. A sound over to his left, feather-light but undoubtedly footsteps, brought him slowly back to reality.

There was a sudden movement in the air and he flinched as something – a hand, he was sure; a cool, dry, hand – was lain gently on his forehead. He opened his mouth to speak then felt something on his lips. A straw. He sucked greedily, the cool water like nectar on his parched throat.

'What happened to me?' he said, when the straw was moved. 'How bad is it? Has anyone let Jill know? Is she here?' He spluttered over the words spilling from his mouth, his throat thick with emotion. 'Can you hear me?'

'Ssh,' he heard. A soft, soothing voice. He waited, sure there was more to come. He felt a sharp sting in his arm and then, nothing.

A damp sensation on his cheek dragged Michael back to consciousness. Someone was there, wiping his face. He tried to move as he felt a wet, rough cloth being rubbed down his arms and under his armpits. He smelled soap. Someone was washing him. Another, dry, towel followed, and then he felt the bedcovers being pulled further up onto his chest.

'Please,' he said. 'Tell me what's happened to me.'

But whoever was there remained maddeningly silent.

Michael had an itch, just above his left eyebrow, when he woke up again. He tried to lift his arm to deal with it, but it felt too heavy to move. What if he was dreaming? Maybe he wasn't even in hospital, but lying at the side of a road, drifting in and out of consciousness, with no one around to help?

And Anna, she'd been driving. She must have been hurt as well. Dead, maybe. Maybe that's why they weren't telling him anything. They must think he wasn't up to hearing bad news about her. They'd have assumed she was his girlfriend or something.

He knew he desperately needed to phone Jill, to tell her he was OK. The need to see her was an actual, physical pain, high in his chest. He ground his teeth together and tried to get his mind to think straight.

He needed to let Jill know where he was. More than anything, he needed her to know that he hadn't run off and left her. But she'd know that, wouldn't she? He'd promised her again and again.

He knew she hated being so insecure, and he hated himself for making her that way. But he was certain she knew he would never again abruptly just leave her. She knew. Of course she did. If he could just get in touch with her, then he could remind her of that himself.

He'd gone about it all the wrong way, before. He should have talked to her, behaved like a grown-up, sorted things out.

It was easier, though, to pack a bag and walk out of the door and sit drinking beer and not thinking. He'd come so close to losing her for good. He'd been an idiot. But it had scared him, how he felt about her. He'd never felt like that in his life, and it was terrifying.

He'd never leave her, ever. She'd be so worried. And the baby. She shouldn't be on her own. He just needed to get someone to contact her, so she could be here with him. If he could just *think*. And speak to someone.

'Listen,' he said, as the footsteps approached again. 'Please, will you listen to me?'

There was no response. Michael lifted his head from the pillow, ignoring the rush of nausea, and blurted out the words what had been whirling around in his brain.

'I know you're probably trying to keep something from me. Is it because the girl I was with has been badly injured? You don't need to worry, I mean, it's awful if she's hurt, or... worse. But you can tell me. She's... she's just someone I used to know. I need you to contact my girlfriend for me. *Please.*'

'I've seen this sort of thing on TV, where hospitals keep bad news from people,' he continued. 'But it's fine, really. Just tell me. Tell me what's wrong with me. And contact Jill, Jill Talbot. Her number's in my phone. Do you have my phone? Please, can someone call her? She'll be so worried, and she's pregnant and it can't be good for her, to be anxious. And I'd really like to know what happened to Anna? That's who I was in the car with.'

He lay back, straining his ears, waiting for a response, realising that he was speaking gibberish. They'd think he was having an affair or stringing two women along. He needed to explain. He took a deep breath, ready to speak again. But then he heard footsteps fading away and the sound of a door closing.

'Wait,' he called. 'Please, talk to me. Somebody, please. *Talk to me.*'

8

It was less than three days since Jill had seen Michael, but it seemed to her like a century. She tried to pretend this was just a normal Saturday. But a normal Saturday would involve them lying in bed late, debating about whose turn it was to go out for bread and papers, then spending at least part of the day together. Maybe he'd go to the match and she'd go to the shops, or meet a friend for coffee or a glass of wine. They might see a film at some point, or go out for food. Meet friends for drinks.

So what she was doing now – sitting at the kitchen table at six-thirty in the morning, nursing a cup of coffee that she didn't want and staring at a phone that didn't ring – was far from normal.

An unopened magazine lay on the table in front of her. She pushed it away and dragged herself up to the bathroom.

Jill put the phone on the side of the basin while she took a shower. Most of the people she'd left messages with the previous day had called back or texted throughout the evening. Not one of them had anything useful to tell her.

Someone – an old school friend he rarely saw, Cameron, she thought his name was – had suggested posting a message on Facebook, but Michael hated social media. He'd always said he would never set up an account, had ranted about people posting pictures of their dinner, or bragging about their kids.

Christine had rung, a few times, and insisted Jill call her if there was anything she could do. Ben had called as well, made sympathetic noises and assured her Michael's disappearance was as much a mystery to him as it was to her.

Jill had also rung her sister and listened as Louise listed all the things that could have happened and suggested she get a train down to Newcastle and stay with them. Jill had politely declined. She loved her sister, she really did. After all, she was the only close family member she had. It was just that she loved her more when there were over a hundred miles between them.

Half an hour later, Jill was back in the kitchen, dressed and gazing out of the window as the garden brightened up. She tried to think of the last time she hadn't heard from Michael for a whole day, and drew a blank. Even when they'd been having problems, or if one of them had been on a weekend away or a work trip, they'd always checked in, at least once a day.

It might just be a quick text, but there was always contact. Always. She dialled his number, knowing before it even rang that it would go straight to answerphone.

She ran a hand through her hair and picked up the cup of cold coffee. She opened the microwave door, intending to heat it up, rather than making a fresh cup. The bowl of pasta she'd put aside for Michael the night before sat inside, and she picked it up and dropped it, bowl and all, into the bin.

She sat down, coffee forgotten, and gave in to the thought that had been nagging in her brain as she'd lain awake most of the night. *The police. I need to call the police.* But still, she hesitated. That would make it all too real. It would change things from him not coming home after a few drinks, to being an actual missing person.

9

Jill's stomach lurched, and she leaned against the wall, then took a deep breath and picked up the handset.

It was only when she held the phone in her hand that she realised, beyond dialling three nines, she didn't know how you actually went about contacting the police.

After a wasted ten minutes of searching, she finally found a number. A call centre, no doubt, she thought. Her fingers danced above the keys, but she put the phone down without dialling. She quickly used the bathroom, looking away from her anxious face in the mirror, then picked up her bag and headed out of the door.

Sitting with the phone at her ear, working her way through a series of automated options and then waiting in a queue to speak to a real person was unthinkable. She needed to look someone in the eye and ask them to help her. And anyway, if she went out, maybe he'd be home by the time she got back.

'Yes?' said the officer at the desk, glancing briefly at her. His skin was pink and doughy and Jill could see flakes of dandruff clinging to the greasy roots of his hair as he leant over a pile of paperwork, pen in hand. His shirt collar looked too tight, and Jill found herself wondering how he could bear to sit through each day being almost strangled by his uniform.

'Hello,' Jill said. She could barely speak through the tightness in her chest. 'It's... it's probably nothing, but I, I want to report someone missing. My partner. His name's Michael Stanton. He didn't come home on Thursday night and I'm worried that something has happened to him. He went to work before I woke up but everything was fine when we went to bed on Wednesday night and I'm... I just don't know what to do.'

'Right,' the policeman said, reaching for a form. 'What's your name, please?'

She gave him the details he asked for then sat on one of the orange plastic seats beneath a toughened-glass window. As she waited to be called, she crossed and uncrossed her legs, desperate to get up, pace about, do something. Anything.

She stood and walked over to the noticeboard and stared at the posters about crime prevention and drug abuse without taking in a single word that was printed on them.

'Jill Talbot?'

Jill turned and saw a slim woman, probably in her thirties, in black trousers and a loose cream blouse, calling her name. Her dark hair was pulled severely back and she had a biro tucked behind her ear.

'Yes,' she said. 'Yes, that's me.'

'This way, please,' the woman said, as she turned and opened a door to a long corridor.

As they walked, the police officer introduced herself as Sergeant Morton, then led the way into a small, windowless room. The only furniture in it was a desk and a trio of chairs, arranged so two were at one side and one at the other. The matte grey walls did nothing to lighten the airless, claustrophobic atmosphere. Jill wrinkled her nose at the smell of stale coffee; her mouth filled with water and she swallowed the urge to be sick.

'Right, then,' said Sergeant Morton, as she freed the biro and pulled the lid off with her teeth. 'Boyfriend's gone missing, has he? Let's get some details.'

Jill sat down on one of the chairs. 'Maybe I'm overreacting.'

The sergeant didn't answer. She just frowned and started firing her way through the list of questions in front of her, barely looking up as she nodded and scribbled down the answers Jill gave her.

There were questions about medical conditions, mental health issues, relatives. Debts. She wanted to know where he went and who with. His bank details. A photograph. Jill noticed the way the sergeant's eyebrow raised, just for a second, when she told her that yes, they had split up in the past, and yes he had left, once. But that was different. Nothing like this.

'I think that's it, for now,' said Sergeant Morton. 'The best thing you can do is go home and wait to hear from us.'

'That's it?' Jill said. 'I just feel so helpless. I even looked through all his pockets in the middle of the night, in case I could find anything. A clue. It's just so... it's agony, just waiting. He hasn't taken any clothes. He hasn't even taken his toothbrush.'

The sergeant gathered her papers and gestured towards the door.

'Chances are he'll be in the house when you get there, tail between his legs,' she said. 'That's what happens, in most cases like this.'

Jill walked out of the police station and onto St Leonard's Street, feeling empty and sad. She shoved the pile of leaflets she'd been given into her bag and let her body sag against the wall.

Her mind whirled. People walked past her, mostly students heading out or in, making the most of their weekends. An old man in a scruffy blue three piece suit sat down on a bench, taking delicate sips from a can of cider, his long white hair blowing in the breeze.

Normally, when she was in this area, she loved to stop for a moment and take in the view of the wild landscape and Arthur's Seat looming above her. But now, as she looked up at the heavy grey sky, Jill felt like opening her mouth and screaming, as long and loud as she could. But she pulled herself upright and set off down the street, towards home.

Jill walked on autopilot, reaching the front door without remembering a second of the journey. She put her key in the lock but stopped before turning it, closing her eyes and hoping, *hoping*, that he would be there.

But the house was as silent as she had left it. There was no one home. She sat down on the bottom stair and let out the wail that had been building up inside her. She was still sitting there as the daylight faded, the sound of her noisy sobs echoing around the empty rooms.

10

Michael opened his eyes. It was Monday morning, and he should have been at work, but he had no idea what time, or day, it was. Nor did he have any idea that, two days previously, his girlfriend had reported him missing to the police.

He blinked, squinting at the pale light in the room. *I can see*, he realised. *I can see.* Whatever had been covering his eyes was gone. He reached up, feeling for wounds or stitches, but his face seemed unmarked.

He pulled himself up on the bed into a sitting position. It wasn't the metal hospital bed he had expected, but a white wooden framed one with a vertically-slatted headboard. It looked like something from Ikea, not the NHS. And the covers weren't the heavy blankets and starched sheets he'd imagined, but a thick duvet in a pale-green and white striped cover.

He felt sluggish and disorientated, with that sickly feeling you get after waking suddenly from a deep sleep. He pushed the covers further down and went to swing his heavy legs from the bed, then cried out as the thick metal chain that was attached to his ankle cracked against the joint.

He slowly put his feet onto the floor, wincing as a sharp pain shot through his heels. He was wearing grey, jersey shorts and a plain white t-shirt, clothes he didn't recognise and knew weren't his own. He wasn't wearing his watch. He thought he had to be dreaming. This couldn't be real.

He examined his feet. They were bare and pale and both heels were covered with bandages, strips of tape holding them in place.

And the chain. He closed his eyes, sure that when he opened them, it would have disappeared. But it was still there, shiny and heavy and attached to some sort of cuff. A shackle, he thought it was called, although he had no idea why he knew that. Two padlocks fastened it firmly in place. The chain snaked across the floor, coming to an end at a long iron floor-to-ceiling pipe.

He stood up and stopped to take a loop of the chain in his hand, then walked across to the pipe. His stomach twisted as he realised it went beyond the top of the room and was sunk into the concrete of the floor. In other words, there wasn't even a millimetre of give in it.

As he looked closer, he saw that to make escape totally impossible, the chain had been wound around the pipe several times and secured with several padlocks. He counted six of them. He ran his hands through his hair, swallowed down the growing panic and turned to look at the room properly for the first time.

It was large and rectangular, without windows, but with a narrow alcove that he assumed led to a doorway. The light was coming from a floor lamp in the far corner, but he could see several spotlights on the ceiling as well. The walls were painted in a pale shade of green, similar to the stripe in the duvet. A couple of Jack Vettriano prints hung on the walls; he didn't recognise one of them but the other was his favourite, *In Thoughts of You*. A leafy plant in a ceramic pot stood on top of a white side table against the back wall. A slim, black TV set was positioned on top of a chest of drawers, in the same wood as the table, beyond the end of the bed. A table-football game was pushed up against one of the walls and a slim bookcase full of paperback novels was in the corner along from the bed's headboard.

It must be some sort of private hospital, he tried to tell himself.

But then his brain screamed: *The type of hospital where they chain you to the wall?*

And why wasn't anyone here?

Maybe it was some sort of prison. Had he got caught up in something? There had to be some mistake. Did someone think he was dangerous? Had he drunk too much and hit someone? But none of that made sense. He'd never been in trouble with the police in his life.

He looked around for some sort of buzzer or intercom, but there was nothing. There was, though, a lens in the corner of the ceiling, trained on the bed. So someone *was* watching him, he thought.

He was desperate to pee, and he moved slowly across the room, walking on his toes to avoid putting any pressure on his painful heels.

A door in the corner, adjacent to the bedhead, opened outwards and revealed a tiny bathroom with a white toilet and basin and a small, glass-fronted shower cubicle. When he moved forward, he found that the chain was just long enough to allow him to pass the toilet and basin and get into the shower, with barely an inch of give. He shivered as he realised that someone must have put a lot of careful planning into this, this *arrangement*, whatever the hell it was.

A single green hand towel hung from a plastic hook – the type you pressed onto a wall with a sticky pad that always fell off eventually – and a pump bottle of antibacterial soap sat on the edge of the basin. A mirrored tile was stuck to the wall above the basic – when he tapped it with his fingers, he realised it was made from acrylic.

He urinated and washed his hands then turned and hobbled back to the bed. He stood beside it and set about testing how far he could walk in the other direction. Not as far as the TV, he found. Even stretching his arm as far as he could, it remained out of reach. So he could basically reach the bathroom, and the end of the bed, and along to the bookcase, but that was it.

He sat on the edge of bed and leaned forward, elbows on knees and head in his hands. He was exhausted. What the hell was wrong with him? And why wasn't there anyone here to tell him, to give him some answers?

* * *

'You need to rest. Don't try to talk.'

Michael tried to open his eyes, to clear the fog in his brain. He was sure he recognised that voice. His eyelids felt so heavy.

'Jill?' he said.

'Hush, now,' the voice said.

He almost let himself drift off. Then he remembered. He shook his head and pulled himself up. A figure was standing at the end of the bed.

Michael's head felt thick; he must have banged it. That was why he was imagining all of this. He blinked, taking in the crisp blue cotton top, the upside-down watch pinned to her chest. The glossy dark hair. The smile playing on her full lips. It couldn't be. Could it?

'Anna?' he said, relief flooding over him. 'Thank God. Please, you have to find out what the hell is going on.'

She crossed her arms and looked at him. She was wearing a blue top, fitted snugly over her slim, athletic frame, and matching, loose trousers. A uniform. Her nurse's uniform.

'Hello,' she said. 'Did you sleep well?'

'I can't tell you how good it is to see you!' he burst out. 'You have to find out what's happened! You have to help me get out of here! There must have been some sort of mistake, or accident. Look,' he pointed at the chain. 'They've even chained me up.'

'Don't worry,' she said. 'You're probably feeling a bit odd at the moment. That'll be the sedative, but it'll wear off soon.'

'*What?*' he said.

'Never mind. Just try to relax.'

'Please, just tell me what's happened. Has anyone contacted Jill?'

'All in good time. You just need to rest, now,' she patted the duvet. 'Take it easy for a while.'

'But... there's so much I need to ask you. I mean–'

She held up her hand, silencing him, and smoothed her hands across the front of her top, still smiling that funny little smile.

'We'll talk more later,' she said. 'We've got a lot to talk about. But for now, you just need to relax.'

He saw the glint of the syringe, a gleaming pearl of liquid spilling from its pointed end.

'What? No–' he began. But then his lips turned to rubber and his mouth wouldn't work. His eyes slipped closed. Maybe sleeping for a while would clear his head. And then they'd talk and she'd explain what was going on. Maybe Jill would be here by the time he woke up.

11

The following day, before Michael had even woken from his drugged sleep, Jill eased herself up from the padded bed in the midwife's room at the surgery and smoothed her top down over her stomach. She sat, legs dangling towards the floor, and scratched at a stain she had just noticed on her trousers.

'Everything looks fine,' the midwife said as she rolled up her tape measure. Jill had assumed she'd see the same midwife every time she went to the clinic, but so far, it had been a different face every time. This woman seemed pleasant enough though. Efficient. And old enough to have plenty of experience and know what she was talking about.

A couple of the girls she'd seen when she went for her scan had looked too young to have left school. She didn't want to cause offence, but nor did she want to be a part of someone's training.

'No problems at all,' the midwife continued, as she scribbled down some notes. 'But you haven't put on much weight. I'd have expected you to be heavier at the thirty-three-week-week stage. Did you suffer badly with morning sickness? That should have stopped ages ago though, unless you're one of those rare cases unlucky enough to get it the whole way through.'

Jill nodded. 'I was sick quite a lot at first, but I haven't been for ages. And... maybe I've forgotten to eat properly over the last few days,' she admitted.

The midwife looked up at Jill, her head tilted to one side. 'Well,' she said. 'That won't do. You need to make sure you look after this baby. And yourself, of course. You need to eat properly. Plenty of good calories. Lots of fruit and veg. And iron. Actually, I'm going to arrange a prescription for you. You could do with taking some iron tablets. You don't drink or smoke, do you?'

Jill shook her head. 'No. I've never smoked, really. Just the odd one when I was young and daft. And I've not had a drink since I found out I was pregnant.' Although I really could do with one, she thought.

'Good, good. And are you getting some exercise? Nothing too strenuous, but it helps to keep active.'

'I... I go for walks, sometimes. I meant to go to those yoga classes and stuff, but, well, I just haven't got round to it.' Jill could feel her face reddening. There were so many things she'd meant to do.

'You could try some gentle swimming; that's good when you're pregnant. You might even enjoy it. You'll probably find you're getting more tired now. You should rest when you need to. Listen to your body. Are you still working?'

'I'm... I'm having some time off at the moment. Dealing with some personal stuff.'

The midwife raised an eyebrow but, mercifully, didn't ask for further details. Instead, she busied herself, testing the urine sample Jill had provided and updating details on her computer screen. The printer kicked into life and started to spit out documents.

'You didn't find out the sex, did you? At your twenty-week scan?' she said.

'No,' Jill replied. 'We decided we'd like it to be a surprise. There aren't many surprises in life, are there? So we thought we'd make this one.'

She looked down and fiddled with the cuff of her top as tears threatened to spill over her lower lids.

'Hmm, that's nice,' the midwife said, running a hand through her dark hair. 'You're right. Not many surprises in this life. Now, I think we need to keep an eye on your weight, so I've made you another appointment in two weeks. And I'll make sure it will be me you see every time you come in from now on. It gives us both some continuity. In the meantime, you take care of that baby.'

'OK,' Jill said, as she stood and pulled on her coat. 'I'll see you in a couple of weeks. What was your name, again? My memory is shockingly bad at the minute.'

'Elizabeth,' the woman said, handing Jill the folder full of paperwork that seemed to be an essential part of pregnancy. 'I'll see you soon.'

Jill walked out into the waiting room of other women, a few of them accompanied by partners, in various stages of pregnancy. Shel headed down the stairs to the surgery's reception area. She was so heavy and slow; her legs felt like lead. Her breasts, although never exactly small, now seemed to be the size and weight of melons. They ached constantly and threatened to spill out of any bra she attempted to put on.

The urge to pee was coming on again, and as she walked to the surgery's cramped toilet, she wondered how that could that even be possible. She'd drunk nothing for well over an hour, and she'd given that sample to the midwife when she arrived.

But all of these pains and niggles, they were nothing compared to the ache in her heart. Nothing at all.

12

This was meant to be the happiest time of my life, Jill thought, as the surgery's automatic doors slid open and she walked out into the damp afternoon. But instead, she'd never felt so sad. It just wasn't fair.

She'd tried not to dwell too much on the fact that, with her own and Michael's parents dead, the baby wouldn't have grandparents. She'd told herself that even though her only relative, her sister, lived miles away, it didn't matter because they could visit whenever they wanted. She'd convinced herself that their friends would make up for the lack of family. But now that the baby's dad was missing, it was all just too much to bear.

She couldn't believe Michael had been gone for less than a week. It felt like he'd been gone for ever.

She knew she'd been so upset she couldn't even properly remember what she'd done in the days since he'd vanished, six days, other than field calls from concerned friends and fend off visits from anyone who offered to call round. Her insistence that she was fine hadn't worked every time though, and she felt slightly ashamed that she'd hidden in the kitchen and ignored the doorbell when she'd seen her friend Natalie's car pull up the previous day.

Jill felt that if she couldn't be with Michael, then she just didn't want to be with anyone else, no matter how well-meaning and concerned they were. She didn't want company, or advice, or sympathy. She was sure that unless someone could tell her where Michael was and when he'd be back, there was not one thing that they could say or do to help her.

Jill had read that, apparently, unborn babies could tune in to their mothers' emotions, just like they learned to recognise her voice and the music she played. She put a hand to her stomach as her eyes filled with tears. *Stop it*, she told herself. If what she'd read was true, she'd be giving birth to a baby that never stopped crying.

13

Jill let herself into the car, but instead of switching on the engine, she closed her eyes and leaned her forehead on the steering wheel.

When she'd first found out she was pregnant, back in September, it had been the most exciting, terrifying, amazing moment of her life. She'd been sure the test would be negative; she was only one day late and she didn't feel any different.

She'd read on forums about women who knew, just somehow *knew* that they were pregnant from the moment of conception. But she and Michael had only been trying for a baby for a couple of months, and she knew the chances of getting pregnant were tiny in that time. So she couldn't believe it when the two blue lines actually appeared.

Michael had already left for work, and she'd sat on the side of the bath for ages, torn between ringing him, and thinking it would better to tell him face-to-face. She'd decided to wait, and tell him when he got in that night.

She'd gone into the office as usual, then not done a scrap of work all day, just pushed papers around her desk and ignored the ringing phone. She'd even volunteered to do some filing, a task everyone hated, so that she could stand in the deserted storeroom and gaze into space, her hand on her stomach, imagining the tiny life that was growing there.

All Jill had been able to think about that day was the huge secret she had inside her. When it was finally time to go home, she'd dashed into Boots and bought three more tests, just to be sure. They were all positive. Then she'd sat down at the kitchen table with all four tests in a plastic freezer bag and waited for Michael to come home.

She'd found it impossible to sit still, and had cleaned out the fridge, rearranged the tins in the cupboard and cleaned the worktops, even poking into the corners with cotton buds, before he'd strolled in, kissed her on the cheek and headed to the fridge to get a beer.

She'd said no when he asked if she wanted one, then asked him what he fancied for dinner. He'd shrugged and said he'd have whatever she wanted. 'Well,' she said, 'I'll have anything, really. As long as it's not blue cheese, or rare steak. Or runny eggs.'

He'd looked at her, a frown creasing his brow. 'What are you on about? Since when have we had boiled eggs for dinner?'

Jill had passed him the bag of white plastic sticks. 'What's this?' he'd said, a look of utter confusion on his face.

And then, at last, he'd realised.

He'd picked her up and swung her off her feet, then put her down and kissed her, again and again. 'We're going to be a family,' he'd said. Then he'd insisted they go out to celebrate.

Jill smiled as she remembered that night, toasting their unborn baby – her with sparkling water and him with a bottle of Peroni – as they ate pasta and joked about potential names, inspired by the menu. 'Gamberoni' and 'Tagliatelle' sprang to mind. She missed him so, so much.

14

Jill switched on the car engine, shaking her head to try and clear the memories. She needed to focus on the present, the here and now. The sound of Manic Street Preachers filled the car. She reached forward and turned off the radio, unable to bear the noise invading her thoughts.

She navigated out of the car park and headed towards home. Usually, she'd be grateful for the quiet roads, but she found herself yearning for traffic. She wanted to be surrounded by people, instead of driving alone back to the empty house.

Being alone in the house had never been something that bothered Jill, before. She'd lived on her own for a lot of her adult life.

She'd had boyfriends of course. Some of them serious; most of them, not so. She'd only ever lived with one man before Michael. Paul. She'd barely thought of him in years.

They'd lived in the same block of flats and often ran into each other, then one thing had led to another and they'd ended up getting together. He'd moved into her place, and looking back, it had been far too soon. He was obsessed with going to the gym, and would fill the fridge with weird-smelling shakes, and the bedroom floor with foul-smelling unwashed sportswear. Jill and Paul only rarely went out, and he was so obsessed with keeping fit and basically increasingly indifferent to anything else that she'd gradually realised that she was living with a middle-aged man in a fit, young man's body. They'd stopped having sex, and soon stopped doing anything at all really except arguing. Before long he'd moved out. That was more than ten years ago, she realised suddenly. A lifetime ago.

Before Paul, the only time she'd shared a flat was for the couple of terms she'd been at university. She'd hated sharing; her flatmate – an extremely strange girl called Bonnie who kept the curtains closed day and night and mediated in the middle of the living room floor – spent hours in the bathroom and stole her bread and milk, and despite the fact that she rarely spoke, made an extraordinary amount of noise when she brought various even stranger men home for sex.

It was ironic really – Jill had been desperate to move out of her parents' place and go to university; desperate to get away and grow up. And then they'd died and she and her sister had suddenly become responsible for selling the family home, the place they'd lived all of their lives. They'd both bought flats with their share of the proceeds of the sale. Dad had drummed into them from an early age that putting your money in bricks and mortar was a good thing. He'd been a builder; bricks were his currency.

She'd dropped out of university shortly after that, to take the supposedly temporary job in the Civil Service that she was still doing all these years later. She remembered a boyfriend around that time telling her how lucky she was, not having to pay rent. She'd given him a scathing look and told him, yeah, it was really lucky, being orphaned at seventeen, and maybe he'd like to ask his parents to die in a car crash to save him a few quid in rent.

She had to admit there had been a lot of good things about living alone, though. Lying in bed all day at weekends, only getting up when it was time to go back to the pub. Taking long, scented baths, with Eighties classics playing at full volume in the background. Wandering naked around the house while her fake tan dried. Always having somewhere to go that was her place, her sanctuary.

But all of that stuff seemed so trivial now. A world away from what was currently happening. She would give anything – *anything* – to never live alone again, and to spend every one of her days with Michael.

15

The sound of her phone ringing brought Jill back to the present. She leaned over awkwardly to the side, keeping one hand on the wheel as she tried to scoop up her bag from the passenger footwell. It was just out of reach, and she sat back up, banging her palm against the steering wheel in frustration as the ringing stopped.

She looked for somewhere to pull over, but there was a bus lane to her left and she could be home in the time it would take to find a parking space. The lights ahead of her changed to green and the driver behind tooted at her to get a move on.

Ten minutes later, she pulled up outside of the house, undid her seatbelt and reached for her bag. The screen on her phone showed the number of the call she had missed. It wasn't one she recognised, but the caller had left a message and she jabbed through the options until she heard the policewoman, Sergeant Morton, asking her to call back.

Jill had contacted her daily since Michael vanished, but all she ever said was Jill should just wait to hear from her. Jill rang her now, barely able to breathe as the phone rang and rang. An answerphone clicked into life. 'Hello,' Jill gasped, feeling clammy and sick. 'It's Jill Talbot, returning your call. If you could ring me back as soon as you can please. Please.'

She ended the call and held the phone tightly in her hand as she got out of the car and made her way into the house.

She fumbled in her bag for her keys and opened the front door, holding her breath. She started to do so whenever she entered the house, ever since Michael had vanished. But all there was to greet her were a few envelopes on the hall table.

She closed and locked the door, then leaned against it and dropped her bag to the floor where she stood.

This place is a mess, she thought, looking around. The floors needed cleaning and there was a film of dust on the surfaces. She normally did the housework at some point over the weekend, but she'd been unable to summon up the interest or energy to do so. Old newspapers and flyers littered the kitchen table and there were used cups everywhere.

Her mother would be horrified if she could see the state of this place, Jill thought sadly, picturing the plastic covers for the dining chairs, and the tea-towel that had to be placed, just-so, over the handle on the oven door. Her mother had been able to spot from twenty paces if one of her precious china ornaments had been moved from its crocheted placemat.

Jill shook her head and walked through to the kitchen.

She couldn't possibly wait for the police to call back. With shaking fingers, she unlocked her phone and dialled again, holding her breath as the phone rang and rang.

'Morton,' the sergeant said abruptly when she picked up. She sounded harassed and breathless.

Jill gave her name. 'It's about my partner Michael. You left a message, asking me to call. Have you found something?'

'Hang on,' the sergeant said. Jill heard the clunk of the handset hitting the desk, then the shuffle of papers. She put her hand to her chest, trying to ease the feeling that her heart was about to burst through.

'Right,' Sergeant Morton said, coming back on the line. 'Here's the problem. Sometimes... well, people disappear for their own reasons. You know that, right?'

'What do you mean?'

'Well, like I said, people have their own reasons for their actions, for how they behave...'

'I don't... I don't understand what you're saying. Have you found something out?'

'All we can do, the police I mean, is go on what we do find out. What we discover.'

She paused. Jill felt like screaming. 'And what is it, this thing you've discovered? Please,' Jill's voice started to break. 'Just tell me what you know.' She licked her dry lips and swapped the phone over into her other hand.

'You remember when you came in,' Morton said. 'I asked you to bring in phone details, bank information, that kind of thing?'

'Yes,' Jill agreed. She'd gone back to the station the following day and handed in an envelope. She'd written down details of his friends, his workplace, which bank he used, who provided his mobile.

'Well, like I told you, we do some checks. Activity. Phone calls. That sort of thing.'

Jill walked through to the kitchen and sat down. *I don't want to hear this,* she thought.

Sergeant Morton cleared her throat. 'All I can tell you, Miss Talbot, is that following our enquiries, we've come to the conclusion that there's, well, not really a case to investigate. There's no easy way to say this, Miss Talbot, but maybe you should just move on, let things lie, as it were...'

Jill could sense the discomfort in her voice. The *pity*. She was telling her, in her roundabout way, to get over it.

'But... but he's still missing. Why wouldn't there be a case? What have you found? Please. Please tell me.'

'Listen, Miss Talbot. Jill. Can I call you Jill?' Again, Sergeant Morton went on speaking, as if she didn't have time to wait for Jill to respond. 'All we're supposed to tell you in a case like this is that we can safely assume he's OK.' She lowered her voice. 'He's used his credit card. And his mobile phone. From what we've learned about him, he was a bit of a free spirit, in the past. Sometimes… well, people just don't want to be found. I'm sorry. I know this isn't what you wanted to hear.'

'But… *none of this makes sense*. When I try his phone, it's switched off. He hasn't taken any of his clothes. His friends –,'

Morton cut in. 'You'll drive yourself mad, trying to analyse it. We can never really know what's going on in someone's head.' She laughed, a short, sharp bark. 'It would make my job a lot easier if we could.'

'So that's it? But he could be *anywhere*. In danger, hurt, lost. And that's it? The police aren't interested?' Jill tried to blink away the tears of frustration leaking from her eyes. '*I'm pregnant, and… and he loves me*. We're going to get married, after the baby's born. He wouldn't just leave. He wouldn't.'

'I'm sorry,' Sergeant Morton said. 'If anything else comes to light, or if anything changes, you let us know. You know,' she continued, 'nine times out of ten, they come back. Like I told you before, most people don't stay missing. They just take a bit of time out, turn up when they're good and ready. He's been gone less than a week. There's every chance he'll just turn up of his own accord. There's nothing more we can do at this stage. I really am sorry.'

'Right. Thanks,' Jill said, her voice cracking as she ended the call and dropped the phone onto the table.

This isn't right, she thought, *they have to help me. They have to find him.* There's no way he's just vanished. No way. She got up and went to the window. She gnawed at the skin around her nails, gazing out at the drizzly afternoon, without seeing a thing. She felt horrified that the police believed that Michael, the man she loved, and who loved her back, had just wanted to clear off and leave her.

16

As Jill ended her call with the police, Michael opened his eyes and found that he wasn't alone in the room. There was a faint sound of music playing – he couldn't quite place was it was.

'Anna?' he said. She was standing at the side of the bed, arms folded.

Michael pulled himself up and sat on the edge of the bed, all too aware of the cumbersome chain he dragged with him.

'Have you found out what's going on?' he asked. 'Just tell me. Tell me what's happened.'

Anna remained silent as she reached towards him and placed her fingers on his warm skin. He could feel the thrum of blood in his veins as she took his pulse. Her eyes were bright and wet; she looked to Michael as if she was about to cry. She lifted her hands, covering her face for a moment, then fixed her gaze on him.

'Sorry,' she said, brushing the tears away from her cheeks. 'It's a bit overwhelming.'

Michael put his hand on her arm. 'What is it?' he said. He was starting to panic now.

'Nothing, nothing.'

Anna stood and moved to the end of the bed. 'There's so much we need to talk about. I'm... I'm just so glad you're here.'

'Just tell me,' he said. 'Just be straight with me. Are we in some sort of trouble? What happened after I got in the car with you? I've been trying to remember, but my brain... I dunno, I just can't think. And I'm chained to the wall! I keep thinking this must be a dream and I'm going to wake up and–'

Anna shook her head. 'No, Michael. We're not in trouble. I know this might seem a little dramatic, but it was the only way I could think of doing this. Don't worry, things will be normal soon. Think of this as a, well a sort of settling-in period.'

'What do you mean *a settling-in period*? I don't understand.'

'It might seem a lot to take in, but once you get your head around it, you'll realise this all makes sense.'

'I'm sorry, Anna. None of this is making any sense to me whatsoever. I remember getting in your car, then nothing until I woke up here. I'm *chained up*, Anna! You have to get help; go and find someone.'

This can't be happening, he thought. He was sure he must be hallucinating. Anna had moved to the tall chest of drawers and was placing piles of clothes and towels into them.

'I know this must be confusing for you, Michael. But you're not in any trouble or danger. And you're fine, medically. Your feet got a bit scraped but they'll be fine in a few days, really. I hope they're not too painful now?'

'What? No, they're a bit sore, but it's nothing. Anyway, this isn't about my feet. Just tell me everything you know. Please.'

Anna pulled a folding plastic chair up to the end of the bed.

'OK. OK. Now remember, like I've already said, some of this might be hard to take in, but it will all make sense eventually, I promise. Right. From the start. I'm afraid I slipped a little something into your coffee, in Starbucks.'

'What?'

'I think it's best if you just listen, for now.' Anna paused and raised her palm to silence him. 'And then I'll answer your questions. So, as I was saying. The drugs kicked in properly in the car and you were asleep before I'd driven to the end of the street.'

She ran her hands over her face before continuing. 'I was quite nervous, in case you didn't accept my offer of a lift. But you did, and we drove home and I got you out of the car – I've got a special chair for doing that sort of thing – and into the house. Then all I had to do was get you onto the lift to bring you downstairs – it's one of those stair ones, I had it fitted specially – then onto the bed.'

Michael just sat, staring at her. He was aware that his mouth was hanging open. He had a million questions, but what came out of his mouth was, *'You carried me onto the bed?'*

'No, silly. Aren't you listening? I used the chair. It's called an evacuation chair; I bought it online. It has wheels. And are you forgetting that I'm a nurse? I know all about this sort of thing. Although I admit I didn't quite have you in it properly when we came up the path. I'm sorry. I must have forgotten how tall you are. That's how your heels got a bit scraped.'

'But why?' he said. 'None of this makes any sense. What did you do that? Why did you *drug* me?'

'I knew that it was very likely you'd walk away, if I tried to explain everything to you when we met for coffee. I needed to get you here, so you'd understand better. And the chain, the sedatives – they're all just precautions, and only for a little while. Once you settle in and feel more at home–'

'What?' Michael exploded. 'No. I don't need to settle in. I need to get home, to Jill. Where are we, anyway? What is this place?'

Anna stood and gestured around the room. 'This?' she said. 'This is our *home*.'

17

Michael shook his head. Enough was enough. He didn't know what kind of mess he'd gotten into, or what sick joke he was involved in, but it needed to be sorted out. Right now.

'Anna,' he said slowly. 'I'm not going to pretend for one second that I understand what the hell is going on here, but you need to stop messing about. I don't live here, I live in a house with Jill. She's the girlfriend I told you about before. And she'll be worried sick.'

'Well, yes, she probably will. I know this will be a bit hard for her, but only for a little while. Wait until you see this house properly. It took me ages to find it, to find the perfect place with everything we needed. You'll love it, really, you will. You just need to put Jill, and that part of your life, out of your mind now. Just think of it as a chapter that's closed. That life you had with her is all over now. We're going to be *so* happy here.'

'*Please,*' he said. 'Stop messing about. Just tell me where I am, and help me to get home.'

'*This* is your home now, Michael. Our home. Yours and mine. We can keep talking about it, but I need to be sure that you understand. We live here now.'

Michael glared at her.

'What are you saying?' he gasped. 'We? There is no "we". Do you mean you've taken me *prisoner* or something? Are you insane? That's the craziest thing I've ever heard.'

'Prisoner?' Anna frowned. 'That's a little dramatic, don't you think?'

'What the hell else is it? What are you thinking? You can't keep me here, like some sort of caged animal. You have to let me go. Come on. A joke's a joke, and all that, but you can't seriously expect me to believe that you knocked me out, brought me here and chained me up in a basement? Just let me go.'

'Let you go? Let you go where? Like I said, this is your home now.'

Michael rubbed his knuckles in his eye sockets. He felt as if he were struggling to breathe. He could feel his mouth hanging open but he didn't seem to be able to close it. This could not be happening.

'But where are we? What is this place?'

Anna sighed. 'Are you not listening to me? This is our *home*. It's in a lovely secluded area, nice and private. And quiet; that'll be ideal for when the baby comes.'

Michael could feel a pounding behind his left eye. 'Baby? What baby? What are you on about?'

'*Our baby*, of course.'

He watched as she took something from her pocket, and then proceeded to fill a syringe from a small bottle of clear liquid.

'You've really lost me now,' he said. 'I think you're getting confused. We didn't have the baby, remember.'

'You know, I'd hoped I wouldn't need to sedate you again, but I think this has all been a bit much for you. Everything will make more sense after a good sleep.'

Michael went to stand as she came towards him, but she was too quick. She grabbed his wrist in her strong, firm grip and no matter how much he shrank away, muscles rigid, he couldn't avoid the point of the needle as she plunged it into his bicep.

'You can't possibly think you'll get away with this,' he mumbled as he fell back onto the bed.

'Shh, now. You need to rest. There'll be plenty of time for talking later.' She turned and walked away. The last thing he heard as he drifted off was the sound of footsteps retreating up the stairs, then the slam of a heavy door.

She was in the room again when he woke up, folding a pile of clothes into neat squares.

He stretched, and yawned so widely that his jaw cracked.

'How long have I been here?' he demanded.

'What does that matter?' she said. 'You've nowhere else to be.'

'Just tell me,' he said. 'How long? Days? Weeks? Please.'

'Six days. You've been here for six days. I've been taking good care of you though, don't worry. It was a bit weird, actually. Taking care of you like a patient, I mean. Especially putting in a catheter.' She smiled. 'It's almost like *you're* my baby at the moment. But anyway, I wanted you to have a proper rest and I needed to get a few more things sorted in the house.'

Michael clenched his hands and swallowed. *It's almost like you're my baby at the moment!* He thought he might throw up.

'Six *days?* Don't you realise people will be looking for me? Jill will have called the police. She'll be beside herself.'

Anna stopped folding and crossed her arms. Michael could see a muscle twitching in her right cheek.

'Think about it,' she said. 'A grown man decides not to go home one night. He was never the settling-down type. Everyone will just imagine that you got cold feet.'

Michael gulped, trying to swallow the desperate rage surging through him. He had never felt more helpless. The thought that what she was saying made perfect sense poked at his brain. Even if there wasn't a grain of truth in it.

Of course they'd be looking for him. Jill would be frantic. And he spoke to Ben practically every day; Ben would notice if he suddenly went missing. So would his other mates. And work. Surely they would think it was suspicious.

'Anna, the police will most likely be involved already. This is serious. You need to let me go, before this goes too far. Please. I won't report you. I can make something up, I won't mention you, I promise.'

'Listen,' Anna said, sighing heavily and leaning her hands against the end of the bed. 'You really need to get your head around the fact that, as I keep saying, *this* is your home now. This is where you belong.'

She sat beside him on the bed and laid a hand on his thigh. Her touch was feather-light but he recoiled as if her palm was full of snakes.

'I don't see why the police would see your disappearance as a problem. Like I said, a grown man decides not to go home. What's to investigate? They'll make a few checks, maybe, but the police are always dying to file cases away, shove them to the bottom of the pile. The first things they'll do are look at your phone records and see if you use your bank card. And I've taken care of all that, so there's nothing for you to worry about. No one's looking for you. You need to calm down.'

She lifted her hand and went to caress his cheek. He swatted her away and she wrapped her arms around herself. She looked on the verge of tears.

'You know we were good together,' she said quietly. 'You can't deny that. And we'll be like that again. This room, it's just for now. You'll be much more comfortable upstairs. I know it's a lot to take in but the sooner you accept things, the better. Everything needs to be sorted by the time the baby comes along.'

'What are you on about?' he said. 'What is this baby you keep talking about? Are you pregnant?'

She frowned at him. 'Well, no, obviously. I'm talking about the new baby. The one Jill is having for us.'

Michael just stared at her, his mouth open. '*What*...? I didn't even tell you about the baby, did I? And you can't mean... you can't possibly think that you can just take a baby? You must be out of your mind.'

'You need to just stop and think before you jump down my throat. This is our chance to be parents, be a family. I've had a lot of time to think about things, over the years. When Stuart told me about the baby, I knew. I just knew. This is your chance to put things right. It'll all work out just fine. Now, I'll leave you to rest. I'll see you later.'

She walked from the room. Michael pulled at the restraint at his ankle until his body was slick with sweat and he couldn't stand the pain for another second. He had to get away from here, from this madness. He just had to.

18

Normally, at eleven o'clock on a weekday morning, Jill would have been at work for a couple of hours and be hoping that someone would make a cup of tea soon. But it had been the early hours before she'd managed to fall asleep, just like it had been on every one of the eleven nights since Michael had disappeared, and she'd slept away most of the morning.

Jill walked down the stairs in her bare feet, clutching the thick woollen cardigan around her. She couldn't get warm, even with the heating on. She wished she'd put on some socks but even the thought of going back upstairs and searching for a pair was exhausting, so she continued through to the kitchen, curling her toes at a patch of stickiness on the unwashed tiles.

She wrinkled her nose. Pregnancy had turned her into a bloodhound. She could sniff out a greasy burger van from half a mile away, the stench making her gag.

Now, walking into the kitchen, the scent of neglect that filled the place hit her like a train. She looked over at the sink, full of dirty dishes. Plates she'd filled with food and then discarded, physically unable to go through with the act of eating. The dishwasher was full, although she had no idea if what was in there was clean or dirty – it was easier just to leave the door closed.

Jill flicked the kettle on and huddled on one of the kitchen chairs while it boiled. She went to the fridge, and recoiled. The milk was no longer liquid, and the plastic bottle was swollen out of shape. She couldn't even remember buying it. There were bowls on the top shelf that she didn't want to look in.

She pushed the door closed and poured boiling water into one of the remaining clean cups. The coffee jar stood empty on the worktop, so she threw in a tea bag and then searched for a spoon to fish it out with. Finding none in the drawer, she speared it on the prongs of a fork and dropped it next to the sink.

She looked around at the piles of dirty dishes, the old newspapers strewn messily across the table, the bowl of blackened bananas. She scratched a nail against a hardened spot of candle-wax on the table. She didn't want to think about the last time she'd sat at the table, eating dinner by candlelight, Michael opposite her.

She'd tidy up, soon. She'd never lived like this; it was disgusting. She always kind of enjoyed donning rubber gloves and spraying cleaning products; she liked the smells of bleach and lemons hanging in the air. But now, it was just too much and too trivial to consider.

She sat down at the table and pulled the pile of leaflets from Sergeant Morton towards her. They'd lain there, taunting her, since the day she went to the police station. *Organisations that can help you; Financial Matters; What to do when someone goes missing*. Jill closed her gritty eyes, inhaling the steam rising from the cup.

The ringing doorbell startled her. She ignored it and laid her head down on her folded arms. The ringing continued. If it was a delivery man, he'd give up soon and take whatever he had back to the depot. If it was the window cleaner, he'd want to chat. She stayed where she was, waiting for whoever it was to give up and leave her alone.

'I'm not going away, so you might as well open the door,' Louise called though the letterbox.

Jill sighed and rubbed at the spot between her eyes, which seemed to throb, constantly. Anyone else would eventually walk away. But not Louise.

She got up and moved stiffly along the hall, looking away from the dirty floor and her discarded trainers. She opened the door and squinted at the light. Louise walked in, bringing a gust of chilly, fresh air. Jill shivered and followed her sister along back towards the kitchen.

19

'No offence, but you look terrible,' Louise said, putting down her bags and wrapping her arms around Jill. Jill breathed in the heady, rose scent of her perfume, then pulled away and shrugged. She knew she looked a state – she hadn't bothered with make-up for days, and her hair was in desperate need of a wash – but she had more important stuff on her mind right now.

'I've been so worried about you,' Louise continued. She slipped off her coat and looked for somewhere to put it down. She opted to smooth it over the back of one of the kitchen chairs.

'You didn't need to come. I told you I was fine. Did you drive here?' Jill knew Louise hated driving long distances. She also knew that she hated to admit it even more.

'Yes. I'd have come sooner, but I thought it was best if I came on my own. I had to sort out someone to look after the kids. Peter's away for days at a time now, so I had to wait until he was back.'

'How is everyone?' Jill asked.

Louise cleared a space on the table and put down two hessian shopping bags. 'Oh, fine, fine. All good. Busy as usual – I feel like I do nothing but drive those two from activity to activity. And then there's the school stuff, and the parties, after-school stuff... anyway, I've brought you a few bits. Just some basics. I thought you might need a few groceries. Bread, cheese, some fruit and things.'

Jill nodded as she watched Louise produce an oddly shaped loaf in a brown paper package, thick slices of pink ham wrapped in cellophane and hunk of cheese. Her manicured hand dipped in again and again, bringing out tomatoes, bananas, chocolate brownies in a cellophane wrapper.

'And cake,' Louise said. 'I brought cake.'

I'm definitely going to be sick, Jill thought, as she watched the fresh coffee, orange juice and milk being lined up on the table. She breathed deeply through her nose and cleared her throat.

'Louise,' she said, wrapping her arms around herself. 'You didn't need to do this. I'm fine. I... I just need to be on my own at the minute.'

Louise folded her shopping bags and stood, smoothing out imaginary creases. She pulled her long dark-blonde hair back and secured it in a thick ponytail with a band she took from around her wrist. Jill had always envied her long, straight locks, with never a hair out of place. She lifted a hand and pushed her messy curls back from her face.

'So,' Louise said, 'I take it there's no news, then?'

'Not really, no. The police... well, they're not going to do anything.'

'Really? What on earth for? What did they say?'

Jill looked down. She really didn't want to have this conversation. It was easy to gloss over the details on the phone, but much harder when Louise was sitting in front of her.

'Oh, just something about his phone and bank account. They seem to think he's *chosen to* disappear.'

'What would make them think that?' said Louise, as she rummaged under the sink. She emerged clutching a roll of black bin bags. She pushed up the sleeves of her top – today she was in navy and white Breton stripes over dark-blue skinny jeans. Louise always looked as if she had stepped out of the Boden catalogue. In fact, so did Peter and the kids. Jill doubted there was a single pair of jogging bottoms or an old t-shirt anywhere in their house.

She watched as Louise peeled a bag from the roll and threw in the bunch of dead chrysanthemums that had sat, dripping petals, on the windowsill. Jill felt like gagging as the stench of the fetid water in the bottom of the vase filled the air.

'Well, they said they keep a check on things like bank accounts and telephone usage,' Jill said. 'They seem to think there's been some sort of activity, and so that makes everything all right. Which it's not, of course.'

She watched as Louise opened the fridge and raised a rubber-gloved hand to her nose. She starting clearing out the contents, throwing the rancid stuff straight into the bin bag.

'So what they're saying,' Louise said, pausing as she wiped the shelves, 'is that he's used his account and made some calls? That does sort of change things, though, you've got to admit.'

Jill shook her head. 'But none of it makes sense. I've rang at all hours of the day and night and his phone's switched off. Maybe someone's stolen his phone, and his cards. Why aren't they looking into that?'

Louise placed a plate of buttered toast and a mug of coffee in front of Jill. Jill could feel bile rising up her throat. She tore off a crust and fiddled with it. Louise sat down opposite her at the table, absently arranging the papers strewn across it into orderly piles.

'Well,' Louise said, 'all I can think is that something is making them – the police I mean – somehow sure that he's OK. That he's chosen to disappear. Maybe... I don't know... maybe they've spoken to him.'

'Don't be ridiculous. They'd tell me. Of course they would! They couldn't keep something like that from me.'

Louise stood and started to empty the dishwasher. So the dishes were clean, Jill found herself thinking. She thought of Michael, and how he would absentmindedly start the machine off on another cycle, rather than emptying it. Or place his used glass into the sink, as if a fairy were going to appear and deal with it for him.

She looked at Louise, waiting for her to speak. There was no way she'd have driven for over two hours and not say her piece. She'd want to sort Jill out. Fix her. It was what she did. But Jill felt far too broken. There was a long silence, the only noises the clatter of plates and the ticking clock.

'Look,' Louise said, as she placed glasses into the cupboard. 'I think maybe you've got to start moving forward from this. I know it hasn't been long– '

'Eleven days. It's been eleven days,' Jill said.

'I know, I know, not long at all, but you can't just sit here, moping around the house, hoping that he's going to walk in.' She took a sip from her coffee cup. 'Why don't you think about going back to work? Try and get a bit of routine. Some normality. He can get in touch with you wherever you are, and it can't be good for you, being on your own all of the time.'

'Normality? What the hell is normal, now? Michael's missing. No one believes me. If I go to work, I'll be the crazy woman who won't accept that her boyfriend's left her. Anyway, you can talk. How many years is it now since you last worked? I just need to be here, at home. There's so much think about. So much to do.'

'*So much to do?* You're sitting here, rotting in your own filth. And don't bring up me not working. That's a totally different situation. Look at the state of you, Jill. When did you last even *wash*? You need to take care of yourself. You need to take care of the baby.'

Jill's eyes swam with tears. Her hand went to her stomach. She thought of nothing *but* the baby. And how she needed to find its father.

20

'I really could do with a bit of support here,' Jill said quietly. 'I know you mean well, but can you not try to understand, just a little bit? Remember when you thought Peter was having an affair? I was there for you then. Can't you do the same for me now? Just believe me? Believe that Michael hasn't left me?'

'But... it's just so hard to understand. Do you not think maybe there's a bit of truth in what the police are saying? I know it's hard to believe – really, really hard – but maybe he got cold feet. It's a big thing for a man, becoming a father. Maybe he just realised he wasn't up to the responsibility. That sort of thing happens all the time. And I mean it's not like he hasn't got previous for this sort of thing. Just try to see it from my point of view. It's not as if he hasn't done something like this before.'

Jill glared at her sister. What did she know about relationships? She'd only ever had one. What did she know about anything that didn't fit into the boundaries of her perfect life?

'Your point of view?' Jill hissed. 'This is nothing like before. *Nothing*. We had problems then. It's different now. We'd sorted things out. We're having a *baby*. We'd even talked about getting married. Just the two of us, with some strangers off the street as witnesses. Tell everyone afterwards. We even made a list of who we were going to invite to the party. There's no way he would just walk out and never come back. No way. He hasn't even taken a change of underwear.'

Jill clenched her hands and rubbed her balled fists in her eye sockets. 'So don't come in here, talking about cold feet and all that crap. I really don't need this at the minute.'

Louise opened her mouth to speak, then turned and walked from the room without another word. Jill listened as she climbed the stairs and moved from room to room.

She sat back in the chair and stared at the clock on the wall, watching as the minutes ticked by. The vacuum cleaner started up. She pictured Louise ramming it across the floor, muttering to herself. She shook her head. The leaflets were still in front of her on the table. She scrunched the top one in her fist and threw it. She was still sitting there, staring into space, when Louise came back into the kitchen.

'I've run you a bath,' she said. 'Look, I'm sorry. It's just horrible seeing you like this. I thought maybe a few... I don't know... home truths might help. Cruel to be kind, that sort of thing. It's hard enough, being pregnant, without having this to worry about as well. Seriously though, what are you going to do?'

'I don't know. Find him.'

Jill sighed and followed Louise upstairs and into the bathroom. The taps were gleaming, the toiletries standing to attention, and she could actually see through the glass walls of the shower cubicle.

She had always loved this room, even though people had told her she was mad to sacrifice a bedroom so that she could have the huge bath and walk-in shower that she dreamed of. But she'd explained her vision to the builder, and she'd never regretted it, not for one minute.

She watched as Louise leaned against the doorframe, smiling to herself at the order she had restored. 'I'll go and put a wash on,' she said, and left Jill to it. Jill slowly removed her clothes, wincing at the sharp tang of body odour. She looked at the round ball of her stomach, her heavy, blue-veined breasts.

You should be here, Michael, she thought. *You should be here, with me.* She climbed into the tub and immersed herself in the pleasantly hot water. The air was heavy with the scent of lavender. Jill shook her head. Obviously Louise thought it would calm her down. It did feel good though.

Jill allowed her eyes to close and listened as the vacuum cleaner started up again. As it stopped, the washing machine started its noisy spin cycle. She lay, listening to the familiar, comforting sounds of someone else being in the house. She dipped her head under, so that everything but her face was submerged then pulled herself up and squeezed a dollop of shampoo into her palm. She was massaging it into her hair when Louise reappeared at the door.

'So come on. Tell me what you're going to do,' Louise said, sitting down on the closed toilet lid and pushing her hair behind her ears. 'Just keep sitting in the house? Not eating, making yourself ill?'

Jill closed her eyes. Louise just couldn't help herself. 'Yeah, something like that,' she said, hating the sound of her childish, petulant voice.

'Actually, I'm going to work out what the hell is going on. The police aren't interested. None of his friends have heard from him, or so they say. As far as his work is concerned, they just think he must have decided to end his contract a couple of weeks early. So, seeing as no one else is bothered, it's up to me.'

'But–' Louise began.

'Think about it, will you? Just think about it for one second, instead of being so *righteous*. Why would he just leave? Go to work one morning and then never come back? I must be missing something. He could be hurt. In trouble. Maybe... maybe he's had an accident and lost his memory. There has to be a good reason.'

Louise shook her head. 'I don't know. It's... it's awful, Jill, really awful, I know that. But... well, you read about stuff like this, don't you. Sometimes people do just disappear. I know you don't want to think about this, but maybe he just wanted a new start, or he's met someone else. I don't know. I know you don't want to hear it, but—'

'Will you just listen to yourself?' Jill exploded. 'Why do you always think you know best? Do you know what I did yesterday? I went to see the midwife. And before you say it, I know loads of people go to the midwife on their own. But I so *so* wanted to tell him about it. To get excited together, about how before long, the baby will be here. Do you have any idea how that feels, to think what he's missing? I'd really like it if you would just go now.' She climbed from the bath, and raised a hand as Louise started to speak. 'Just go, will you. Get out of my house.'

Jill wrapped a towel around herself. Suds from her hair ran down her back. She watched her sister retreating down the stairs, then turned and walked to the bedroom, leaving a trail of damp footprints on the carpet. She closed the door and leaned against it, listening to the sound of Louise gathering her things.

Moments later the front door opened and closed. Jill heard the car engine starting up and then fading away as her sister drove along the street. No doubt she'd already be on the phone to Peter, telling him about the state she was in. Peter would just listen, having learned long ago that it was the best thing to do for an easy life.

Weren't big sisters meant to be there for you? Look after you, no matter what?

Jill pulled off the towel and climbed into bed, pulling the covers over her still-damp skin. She rubbed her eyes, the skin there dry and delicate, ravaged by the tears; at first a non-stop river, but now an unpredictable stream, likely to start flowing randomly, at any time of the day or night.

Sadness had settled into her, a solid thing to be carried around wherever she went. Her chest ached and even her bones felt sore. She'd stopped looking in the mirror, no longer wanting to see how old and haggard she looked. New lines had seemed to appear almost daily. The grey hairs at her temples that she was normally so fastidious about dying aged her even more.

But the thought of dealing with any of it – it just seemed so trivial. So pointless, when there were so many other things she had to think about.

Jill sat up and hugged her knees. The house had fallen back into its new, silent state.

Before, there was always noise. A radio left on in the bathroom competing with another in the bedroom, usually on some sports station she had no inclination to listen to. The clatter of cooking. The TV, usually turned up far too loud. The normal, domestic sounds that made a house a home.

The ringing landline at the side of the bed startled her, but, against every instinct, she ignored it and left it to ring. It would undoubtedly be Louise, calling before she hit the A1, wanting to know if she should come back.

When the ringing stopped, she picked up the handset and dialled 1471. Her suspicions were confirmed when the electronic voice relayed Louise's mobile number – the only one, other than her own and Michael's, that she knew by heart – into her ear.

Jill felt a surge of anger. Why wouldn't anybody believe her? These people – their friends, her sister, his work colleagues – why didn't they share her concern? Why wouldn't they help?

Yes, maybe her mates were willing to come round, drink coffee and sympathise, but she knew from their calls and texts that they saw it as just another break-up. And the police? This stuff about his card being used – there must be some mistake, or it could be an automatic thing, a payment long ago set up that just so happened to go through recently.

She threw back the covers and climbed back out of bed, her mind too busy for her body to be still.

She walked back to the bathroom and pulled out the plug. As the water drained away, she switched on the shower and stepped in, rinsing the shampoo from her hair. She rubbed a handful of conditioner through it and ran a razor under her arms and up her shins, then stood under the water, letting it stream over her face, for a long time, then got out and dried herself.

The deodorant can she took from the cupboard was empty. She picked up Michael's and gasped as the familiar scent sprayed from it. She stood for a moment, closed her eyes and breathed it in. Back in the bedroom, she pulled on a pair of black leggings and a long grey sweatshirt, and then walked downstairs.

Jill switched the kettle on and made tea. She sat down at the table, hands wrapped around the mug. The kitchen was immaculate.

She picked up a piece of the cold, hard toast and chewed until she felt she could swallow it. She got up and opened the washing machine and pulled out the pile of clean, wet clothes, dumping them on the worktop. A stray sock, too big to be one of hers, fell to the floor. She picked it up and held it tight in her fist. She felt the tears welling up, and looked up to the ceiling to stop them falling from her eyes. There had to be something she could do.

Jill sat for a long time, looking at nothing and turning memories over in her mind. She walked into the living room, and stood by the window, looking out down the street.

There was no sign of anyone, bar the neighbours' fat ginger cat. He was sitting on the driveway, licking his paws. Not a care in the world. Jill picked up her mobile to check it.

There was a text from Christine, asking if she was OK, and could she ring, please. No missed calls. She sat down, flicked on the TV, and clicked through the channels, stopping when she came across an old episode of *Grand Designs*. She turned the volume down low and picked up a magazine from the pile by the chair, then threw it back down.

She thought about ringing Christine, but couldn't bear to hear the pity in her voice. So she sat and stared out of the window, with absolutely no idea what to do next.

21

Three days had passed since Jill had fought with her sister, and as she sat at home, frustrated, angry and afraid, Anna appeared at the end of Michael's bed.

'I've got a surprise for you,' she said. She had her hands clasped like an excited child, eager to spill a secret. Michael looked at her through half-open lids. 'I just wanted to make sure you were awake.'

Michael shifted uncomfortably and pulled himself up into a sitting position. The air was thick and soupy, and the sheets were damp beneath his skin.

'Ta daah!' she trilled, as she brought her hand from behind her back and produced a sleek black TV remote control.

Michael's eyes widened. His fingers itched to reach out and snatch it from her. Anything to break the monotony. Sometimes when she came into the room, she would bring a radio, and she'd left a pile of paperback books and magazines by the bed, but he couldn't concentrate on the words for more than a few minutes at a time. Ever since he'd realised, when he'd first taken in his surroundings, that the TV was out of his reach in its position beyond the foot of the bed, he'd pretty much ignored the fact that it was there.

'I know you must be bored, and it's not for much longer, I promise,' she said. 'I would have given it to you sooner but there was a problem with the connection. And anyway, it's quite appropriate that I'm giving you this today. It's a sort of two-week anniversary present.'

Michael looked down at the quilt and scrunched the fabric in his hand.

'Oh and there's something else,' she said.

She stepped into the alcove that led to the stairs and came back carrying a fan on a tall stand. She plugged it in at the far end of the room and stepped away as it began to circulate the stale air.

Michael shuffled across the bed and into its stream. The relief was instant. He closed his eyes as the breeze stirred his hair. He could almost forget where he was, just for a second.

'It's the full package, sports, movies, everything. And I hope you don't mind, but I used your card to pay for the fan. I've used it a few times since you've been here; I thought you'd be OK about contributing to our household. It'll also stop the police or anyone snooping about; they'll know you're OK if you're using your card, so I managed to kill two birds with one stone.'

Michael sat on the edge of the bed. He could feel panic worming up through his chest as he took in yet another example of the extent she'd gone to. Using his card; making sure everything that had even the slightest potential as a weapon was maddeningly out of reach; the soundproofed walls; the stair lift; the plastic cutlery. If it hadn't been so terrifying, he'd be almost impressed by her ingenuity.

He'd spent hours fiddling with the chain and its fixtures, trying in vain to find a weak spot. He'd lain or stood in every possible position trying to reach something. Anything that might help him to escape or use as a weapon. He had stretched until his shoulders screamed with effort, to try and reach the drawers, or to pull a piece of wood from the bed. The bookcase, he had found, was secured to the wall. He'd paced the floor over and over again, as if the solution to escaping from here lay in knowing the precise number of steps he could take in every direction.

And besides, he knew that even if he did, by some miracle, knock her out with a plant pot or a thick crime novel, that didn't mean he would be free. It wasn't as if a set of keys to the locks was going to miraculously appear and skitter across the floor into his hands. It was clearly apparent from the tight fit of her jeans that she didn't carry them around in her pockets.

Anna sat down next to him, so close he could smell the fresh, soapy scent of her skin and the lingering shampoo on her hair. She'd always smelled so good, he remembered. One of those people who walked past you and left a scented cloud in their wake. He shook his head angrily, cursing his brain for storing such memories.

She was frowning and muttering under her breath as she fiddled with the buttons on the control, tuning in channels and saying something about signal strength.

A memory flashed, unbidden, into his head. Anna, naked, insisting that he bind her wrists and cover her eyes. She'd always taken sex very seriously, as seriously as she seemed to take everything else. There was no banter, no chat.

On that first night, when they met in the club, he'd left and she'd made her excuses to Stuart and followed him. He remembered the fizz of excitement as, without a word, she'd led him up the deserted back lane, where he'd pushed her up against the rough stone wall, the acrid smells of piss and stale lager in the air. The heady, almost dizzy feeling that overtook him as she unzipped his flies and lifted up her skirt.

Michael opened his eyes and shook his head again, more vigorously this time. He wished there was something he could do to wipe his brain clean of every memory he had of her. He didn't want to remember, think, feel. She was the only thing coming between him and his real life. He hated her for doing that; but in a strange way he felt admiration for her, too. After all, he thought, she'd dreamt all this up, and she'd made it all happen. So far, he realised with horror, everything was going according to her crazy plan.

22

'There,' Anna said. 'All sorted.'

She turned to look at him as she handed over the remote control. 'Are you all right, Michael? You look a bit flushed.'

He breathed deeply. Maybe at some point he could catch her off guard, get her to think like a normal person. If he kept at her, maybe she'd see reason. Realise how mad this whole thing was.

Yelling, spit flying from his lips as he thrashed and raged, had proved pointless when she calmly showed him the invoices for the soundproofing she'd had fitted before the walls and ceiling were plastered. She'd told the builders it was going to be a music studio, she'd explained to him, looking pleased with herself.

The last thing he wanted was for her to start stabbing him with one of her bloody syringes again. It freaked him out, the thought of being there, out of it. So he just stayed quiet, most of the time. Tried to get his head around what it was she was planning to do, and figure out some way he could stop her. But he was running out of options; not that he'd even had any options in the first place.

'Anna, please,' Michael said, standing and facing her. 'Why don't you just let me go? You could take me somewhere, anywhere, and just leave me. Knock me out, drop me off in a car park, or a lay-by. A field. Anywhere. I won't tell anyone, I promise. You needn't worry about getting into trouble. We can just end this, now. Nobody need ever know what you did.'

She looked at him, the crease on her forehead deepening. Two spots of red had appeared high on her cheeks.

'I mean,' he went on, 'if you stop and think about what you're planning to do, you have to realise how cruel, how unfair, it is. Taking a baby from its mother? You must be able to see that?'

Without warning, she lifted her hand and slapped him, hard, across the face with the back of it. 'Unfair?' she hissed.

Michael gasped and recoiled, then sat heavily on the bed, cupping his stinging cheek in his palm.

Anna stood and looked down at him. A nerve pulsed at her jaw. 'You don't think making me kill *my* baby was unfair? That sweet, tiny, miniature person? And taking away my chance to ever have another? Wasn't *that* cruel?'

'But Anna, we weren't ready to have a baby. That wasn't what we were about. What we had... it was exciting, and we had a good time, but settling down? Having a family? Come on, you know as well as I do that wouldn't have worked. And anyway, what do you mean, taking away your chance?'

She continued as if he hadn't spoken, and lowered her voice to almost a whisper. Michael had to strain to hear her.

'Every day, I see them. Smoking, drinking, and worse. It's obvious they don't care about their babies in the slightest. Half of them don't even know who the father is! And then they come in, expecting me to look after them while they squeeze their babies into the world, when all they're thinking about is how soon they can sneak out for a cigarette. Can you believe that? One of them actually said to me the other day, '*Hurry up with those stitches love, I'm dying for a ciggie*'. What kind of life are they going to give the baby? We would have been so, so much better parents than that!'

Anna paused, wiping away her tears with the back of her hand.

'Do you have any idea how hard it is, knowing what a different life I could give them?' she said. 'How, if I could just scoop them up and take them away, everything would be so much better for them?'

She turned away, eyes glazed over, gazing at nothing. 'It's not fair. Every day, I see more and more women taking babies home that they're barely capable of caring for. I stand at night, watching them, sleeping, content and full of milk and innocence, and think how easy it would be just to pluck one from its cot and walk away.'

'But that's the thing, Anna. No matter how much you've thought these things, you've never acted on it. Because you know, deep down, that it's wrong. You're their nurse, their midwife, or whatever. Not some sort of baby-thief.'

She looked at him, shaking her head. 'Don't you see? It was because I was meant to wait for this baby. Not just any random one. This one. Yours. Ours.'

Michael could see the muscles of her jaw, set tight. Her lower lip jutted forward. He rubbed his sore face, then reached forward and grabbed her hand.

'Anna, it's not,' he said quietly. 'The baby is mine and Jill's. Jill is its mother.'

'Michael, just think about it. What's happening is what's best for everyone. This is... it's the perfect solution. Every day, I see evidence showing that just because a woman gives birth to a child, it doesn't mean that the best place for that child is with her. I have to run antenatal classes sometimes, did I tell you that?'

Michael shook his head. She'd told him that she'd retrained as a midwife – she'd been a general nurse when he'd known her, before – but she hadn't gone into a lot of detail.

Her eyes shone as she continued. 'Can you even begin to imagine what it's like, sitting there surrounded by women, their bellies full of babies? They listen to me spouting off about breastfeeding and bathing, about pain relief and immunisations, and they look at me as if I know it all. And that's because *I do*. I will be so, so good at this. I know I can be the best mother there ever was.'

Anna moved closer to the side of the bed and looked straight at Michael, her head tilted to one side. He looked away. He couldn't bear to think that he'd kissed that mouth, ran his hands over that body.

'You know,' she said, 'for a long time, I thought I'd never forgive you. When I saw Stuart, he'd tell me stories about you, but I had no idea if what he was saying was true. Sometimes he'd tell me something about you, and I'd switch on the TV later and see it acted out on the EastEnders omnibus.'

She walked over and leaned against the chest of drawers and continued.

'You never settled down though, and I took a bit of comfort from that. I really believed that maybe we were both still alone because we were meant to end up back together eventually. And then, one day when I was visiting him a couple of years ago, Stuart mentioned a woman you'd met. I didn't take a lot of notice at first – like I said, a lot of what he says is total fantasy. It was a while before I had a chance to go to see him again, but when I did, he mentioned her again, this *Jill*.'

She rubbed at an imaginary mark on the TV screen before going on.

'Even then, I wasn't too concerned. But that all changed when Stuart mentioned that your Jill was having a baby. I was *so* angry with you. How could you want with her all those things that you didn't want with me? You didn't want a partner, a baby, a family. You wanted to live alone, be a free spirit. Some free spirit you are. It's not fair, Michael. What gives you the right to have a happy ending? And then I realised, maybe you were just confused. Maybe it was karma, or something. You get the chance to put things right. And we get the chance to be happy.'

Michael gasped. He could barely believe that a conversation with Stuart had set all of this madness into motion. His brother hadn't even seemed to acknowledge the fact that he was going to be an uncle, yet he clearly retained more than Michael had thought possible.

'But what about Jill? You can't do this to her. She's not like those women you see at work. She's going to be an amazing mother. And maybe... maybe you'll meet someone, have a baby of your own one day.'

Anna looked at him, her eyes wet with tears. 'That's the thing though, you idiot. I won't. I can't. Because of you.'

23

'What? You mean you... can't have children?'

She lifted her hands and slowly started to clap. 'At last, he gets it,' she said. 'No, I can't. It wasn't as straightforward as you seemed to think it was, getting rid of our baby.'

'What do you mean?'

'Something... something went wrong. I won't bore you with the details, but they had to take away everything. All my... Anyway, there's absolutely no chance, not even a tiny, miniscule chance of me giving birth. But that doesn't have to mean I can't be a mother.'

'I'm sorry. I had... I had no idea. I am really, really sorry that you can't have a baby. I can't imagine how you must feel. But you can't blame that all on me. We talked about it, and you agreed. You agreed, Anna. I didn't take you to that clinic and force you to do something you didn't want to do.'

'You made it clear it wasn't what you wanted,' she said. 'A family. A baby. I could see the look of utter terror in your eyes when I told you. But what happened between us... what we had, it's bound us together. So when I heard from Stuart that you were having a baby, I knew it was fate, serendipity, whatever you want to call it.'

'But there are so many other ways you could have a baby. You could foster, adopt. You can't just *take* a baby.'

'You make it sound so harsh, so callous, when really it's just going to be two people who love each other, bringing up a child together. Don't you see? This is a way for us to have a baby together. The only way.'

Michael wanted to scream. He made fists with his hands and drove them into the mattress where he sat, and shook his head.

'How do you think you'll get away with it?' he said. 'How can you possibly think that this will all work out?'

'It just will,' she said. 'You're over-thinking it. Of course it will work out.'

'Then how will you explain a baby to your friends? Your family?'

'You don't need to worry about that. Friends are easy to lose. And as for family, my mother died years ago. My dad's in a care home in Bournemouth. Moved there with his new wife, but she soon dumped him when he started to lose his marbles. He has no idea who I am, let alone whether or not I have any kids. I was the only child of two only children. No siblings. No aunts and uncles. No cousins. Just me.'

She stood and walked towards the way out of the room. Clearly, she'd decided the conversation was over.

'And now,' she said, turning to look at him full in the face before she disappeared from view. 'I'll have a family of my own at last.'

Michael just stared at her.

How was he supposed to try and reason with her? 'Please,' he said. 'Please, let's end this now. Today. Just let me go.' She looked away for a moment, and stood, drumming her fingers on the wall. Please, he thought. Please.

She looked back at him, eyes flashing.

'Don't be ridiculous,' she said. 'I don't know if you're joking with me, but this sort of talk needs to stop. This is where we live. There is nowhere else for you to go. The sooner you stop thinking about wanting to go, the sooner you'll start to realise that you want to stay.'

Michael slumped back onto the bed and lay, staring at the ceiling. His head was pounding and he could feel his heart beating a drum in his chest. He wanted to grab her, shake her stupid ideas right out of her head. He'd never felt so helpless in his life. He opened his mouth and howled.

Anna rushed over to his side. 'Oh, Michael, don't get so upset. All I want is for us to be happy.'

She stood, ready to leave, then turned back and quickly, before he even knew what was happening, curled her hand behind his neck and kissed him lightly on the cheek.

24

Somehow, he slept after she left the room. When he woke up, mouth dry and head aching dully, he felt dizzy and disorientated. He sat up slowly, and looked at his bare, pale legs. He felt naked in the shorts and plain t-shirts she gave him to wear.

Ever since he'd woken up here, the shorts she produced every day had press-studs along the inner leg seams, like something a baby would wear. He had to open the studs until the shorts resembled some sort of skirt, and then pull them off over his head. There was no other way, with the chain, she'd explained. As if the chain was a mild inconvenience and not something she'd come up with herself.

His skin looked pale and dry, and he was sure his limbs looked thinner. He should do sit-ups and press-ups, he thought. Keep his strength up. Was that what prisoners did, he wondered? Or did they just lie and stare into space and hope for a miracle?

He walked slowly to the bathroom and turned on the shower. He noticed that Anna had replenished the shower gel and left two fresh bath-towels. He'd taken to showering twice a day; lying on the bed for most of the time left him feeling hot and grimy. And it broke the monotony – at least he got to be in a different room for a while.

He took his time showering, then dried himself, then rolled deodorant under his arms and used the tiny nail clippers she'd left him. As he made his way back to the bed, he stopped and looked around the room. He wished he knew where this place was. He'd strained his ears for the sound of trains or traffic, anything that might give him a clue. Nothing did, of course, and even if the room wasn't soundproofed, and he heard ten lorries a day, what help would that be? Anna could have driven for ten hours or ten minutes to get here. He could be anywhere. Literally anywhere. How was it that just a short time ago, he'd been with Jill, planning their future, and now this?

'Good, you're awake,' she said, coming into the room. She was carrying a laden plastic tray. 'I brought your dinner.'

She was in jeans and a tight, grey short-sleeved t-shirt that showed off her perfectly toned arms and her small, firm breasts. He wondered briefly where she found the time to work out. Michael had to admit it to himself: she might be crazy but she looked terrific.

Michael picked up the plastic plate and started to eat.

25

Less than six hours after Michael finished his dinner at Anna's, Jill lay in bed, wide awake and staring at the ceiling. She checked the time on her phone - almost one in the morning. She switched on the lamp and climbed out of bed. The air in the room was thick and stale.

Normally, they kept the window open on all but the coldest nights of the year. Michael would lie on his back, naked and uncovered, but she liked to be snuggled under the duvet, with just a foot or a shoulder exposed, relishing the coolness.

Since Michael had been away, though, she had kept the windows firmly closed. She didn't want to hear the sound of cars driving along the street, people chatting and laughing. She wanted the house sealed up, away from the outside world.

She felt a sudden fizz of rage. All she wanted was some support. Real support, not concerned calls from friends who were dying to report back on how mad she was. She was being unfair, she knew she was – people cared, of course they did.

Even Lisa, once her closest friend, had hinted that she should start moving on with her life. And she hadn't spoken to Louise since her visit to the house. Louise had rang, left loads of messages and sent texts daily. Jill had ignored them all. She just couldn't face replying.

If only Louise would behave like sisters were supposed to, and be on her side, without hesitation? It didn't matter what Louise said now, she couldn't take back what she'd said already. Jill sighed and went to the window. The anger had slowly drained away, leaving the heavy, sad feeling that she carried around in the pit of her stomach.

She wished her mum was here. She wished that almost every day, of course, and had done for the last twenty years; it was just something she had to live with. Was this another thing she was going to have to live with, she thought? Michael never coming back?

If her mum had been alive, she could ring and ask her what to do. Not that she'd ever done that when she *was* alive; she'd never had the chance. Her mum had died, Jill realised, before she, Jill, had the chance to realise that she didn't, like every teenager believed, actually know it all.

Jill drew up the blind and watched as a couple she vaguely recognised as neighbours got out of a taxi. The woman stumbled as she made her way up the path to their house, either drunk or unused to the heels she was wearing. The man caught her around the waist and set her back on her feet.

Jill watched as, huddled together, they went through the door. She choked back a sob as she imagined them laughing, falling into bed together. Or maybe they were sitting at the kitchen table, eating toast and bitching about the friends they had just left. 'Enjoy it while you can,' she muttered, wiping at her eyes with the sleeve of her grubby robe.

She looked at the messy bed, and considered getting back in. What was the point, though? Her mind whirled and her stomach churned. What she *should* do was whip off the sheets, creased from the hours of tossing and turning.

Instead, she went to the drawers and pulled out the first clothes that came to hand – the stretchy yoga pants that she wore around the house and a black hooded sweatshirt. Finding underwear was too much effort, and anyway, most of the stuff that still fit was sitting damp on the kitchen worktop where she'd dumped them after dragging a load from the machine. She put on the clothes and two mismatched socks that were lying on the floor, then walked down the stairs and slipped her feet into her trainers, discarded by the front door.

She stopped at the round mirror hanging just inside the door and looked at her bare, pale face. She ran her tongue over her dry, bloodless lips. Her hair was wild and matted from where she had left it to dry, uncombed, after her earlier shower. There were smudges of shadow under her eyes. Even they looked dull, the usual hazel faded to a sludgy green. She looked more like sixty-five than thirty-five.

She shook her head and put on the padded coat that hung on the bannister. She opened the door and stepped outside, then stood on the path for a moment, breathing deeply. Turning left, she headed along the street and out onto Mayfield Road. She shoved her hands into her pockets, wishing she'd brought gloves. She hadn't though, and she wasn't going back for them.

26

Some people called Edinburgh the Windy City. It was certainly living up to its name now, Jill thought as she walked on, litter blowing around her feet and her hair whipping around her face as she headed towards Causewayside.

A glow was coming from the Good Day, and as she passed it, she saw the staff inside, enjoying an after-hours meal. The smell of hot food hung in the air, and her mouth watered.

She couldn't remember the last proper meal she'd eaten; she'd force herself to pick up a piece of fruit, then take one bite and put it down again. Or she'd nibble on slices of cold toast, made hours earlier and left to sit in the toaster. The thought of eating sickened her; she didn't seem able to swallow. And mealtimes only served to remind her that Michael was still missing. As if she ever forgot.

She convinced herself that the baby was getting all the nutrition it needed from her body. She was sure she'd read that, somewhere. She would start eating properly, she told herself. She'd make herself a proper breakfast.

She wondered what he was doing, right now, at this minute. Was he sleeping? Or like her, did he spend his nights awake, in turmoil?

She walked on, the occasional glow of a light from one of the flats taking her by surprise. She felt as if she were the only one awake. When she was alone in the house – the house where once she had felt so safe, so content – she felt like she was the only one not cocooned in sleep, taking respite from the day and preparing to face up to a new one. Time stretched out, with no clear definition anymore between day and night.

Jill strode on as the wind blew harder, stealing her breath. She passed a homeless man, curled up in the entrance to an alley way. She'd seen him before; by day, he pushed a bike around, with bags and boxes strapped to the seat and handlebars. He wore so many layers that it was impossible to know his true size and shape. He'd tried to speak to her once, and she'd hurried away, repulsed by his rotten-fruit breath and the lines of dirt encrusted on his hands.

Now as he lay there, surrounded by his belongings, the bike wheel pressed against his cheek, she felt an absurd urge to curl up beside him.

She continued on, past shops and cafes, shutters down and bins out. Taxis and delivery vans passed her, and every so often, the sound of a siren filled the air. She walked past pubs, doors closed and staff long gone. A teenage boy, earphones on and head down, walked past her without a glance. It was funny, she thought, how you only noticed these things when you were alone. And she had never felt more alone than she did now. She glanced in the direction of the Pleasance, and thought of her and Michael, laughing and a little bit drunk. The first August they were together, they'd set themselves a challenge of seeing seven shows a week during the Festival. They'd watched some total rubbish, but that had made it even funnier. She couldn't imagine ever laughing like that again, doubled over, unable to stop. She lifted her hand to her face to brush away her hair, and was surprised when it came away damp. She hadn't even realised that she was crying.

Her feet ached as she walked down the Mound and looked at Princes Street before her, lights still blazing in the shop windows. She closed her eyes and pictured the last New Year they'd spent here, running it through her head like a film.

She had been so happy then, as they'd stood there, arms around each other, watching the fireworks, and then dashing back to the pub to warm up. She'd allowed herself a tiny sip of champagne, to toast in the New Year and the new life growing inside her. Even that mouthful had given her dreadful heartburn, she remembered.

It felt as if her heart was breaking in two. She grasped two spokes of the iron fence in her hands. Come on, she told herself. This has to stop. He has to come back. He would come back. She glanced behind her, suddenly sure that someone was there, and thinking for a crazy, ridiculous moment that it was him. But she was still alone.

Jill took a deep, shaky breath and walked on. She felt warmer now, but the cold had made her nose run and her eyes sting. It was freezing for the time of year. There was still a frost and just last week, a faint flurry of snow lay on the paths when she opened the blinds each morning.

She decided to turn right and headed past the station. The rumble of trains, usually drowned out by traffic and tourists, rose up the stairs. Jill walked past the hotel entrance, remembering the time they had gone in and drank over-priced mojitos in the bar to celebrate his new contract. She'd nearly passed out at the bar bill, but he'd laughed and ordered another round. It must have been, what, maybe six months ago? It felt like a lifetime.

She would find Michael, she told herself, again and again; she just had to keep looking. He'd be back. She mustn't give up. Even though she knew it was ridiculous to think that he'd be walking around the town in the middle of the night, she couldn't give up.

There had to be clues somewhere, she just had to find them. She tried seeing the city through his eyes. He loved Edinburgh.

So did she, of course – that was the reason she'd stayed in the city when she dropped out of university.

But it was different for him, as he liked to remind her. He was born here, he'd say. The city was in his blood. He loved to point things out, share an anecdote, tell her where so and so used to live. 'That's the route I used to walk to school,' he'd say. He'd shown her the shop he'd delivered newspapers for; the pub where he'd collected glasses. They'd been walking along a street one day when he'd announced that this was where his first love, Janice Thompson, used to live. 'She used to show me her bra and bring me oranges from her dad's shop,' he'd said.

She knew so much about him. She knew the flats where his mates had lived as students, smoking joints and watching Blockbusters on TV. She knew the house his mum had lived in when she split up with his dad. She knew where he bought his underpants, which coffee shop he thought was the best. She knew how ridiculously generous he was, but how he hated to be ripped off.

Like the time he saw her fingering a butter-soft Mulberry handbag, only to go back and buy it and present it to her for her birthday, months later. He didn't mind taking her to lovely restaurants and paying a fortune for a bottle of wine, but he hated paying over the odds for a pint.

The only thing she didn't know was where he was. Jill suddenly felt so tired, so weary that putting one leg in front of the other was like wading through treacle. She thought about hailing a cab. That would mean speaking to someone, even if it was only to give her address. No, she would walk on, and maybe then, she'd be so tired that she could sleep. Maybe.

It was almost four o'clock when Jill turned into the street. The wind had eased and everything was still. A skinny fox padded across the road and stopped to stare at her, as if she was intruding on its patch. Jill shuddered and hurried into the house.

She eased off her trainers, then walked slowly upstairs and sat on the bed. Although she'd hardly left the house since he'd disappeared, whenever she did go out, she clung to the hope that he'd be there when she returned.

Sitting in the kitchen, lying on the sofa, asleep in bed. Saying, 'You won't believe what happened,' as she clung to him. He never was, of course. The house was every bit as still and silent as when she had left it.

She rested her palms at her sides, stroking the soft cotton bedding with her rough, sore hands. She lifted them closer to her face, shocked at the state of them. Remnants of ancient nail polish clung to the beds of her nails, and the skin around them was red and torn. She had never bitten her nails before. Now she found herself constantly chewing at the raw flesh around them.

She lay back on the crumpled duvet. It was the palest grey, with lines of tiny silver sequins. They'd picked it together, and she'd teased him about his unhealthy interest in interior design furnishings. He'd laughed and asked if it was time to go and look at paint charts yet. It was important, he'd said, that the bedroom was just right.

And it was. Tranquil, calm. A few photographs, a cluster of candles. A white-painted wooden carving of the word 'Love' on a shelf above the bed - he'd bought her that for a Valentine's present one year. Two cushions that she used to remove from the pillows at night and put back every morning.

But the calm, the tranquillity; it was gone now. Her bones ached and her eyes burned, yet she couldn't switch off. If only she could swallow some pills and lose herself in a sleep as artificial as her days. 'Please,' she said. 'Please, just let me know what the hell is going on.'

She must have fallen asleep, because when the doorbell woke her the next morning, she struggled awake, feeling sick and groggy. Her mouth tasted vile and her eyes were sticky and sore. She was still wearing the clothes she'd put on last night, and as she moved, the odour of her unwashed body filled her nostrils.

She thought about staying there, ignoring whoever it was. But it could be news. She went to the door and turned the key, then hesitated before turning the handle, reluctant to open the door to the outside world. She pushed her hair back from her face, and pulled the door towards her.

'Delivery for Stanton,' the man at the door said, handing her a parcel and holding out a device for her to scrawl an electronic signature. Jill watched as he hurried back to his van. She turned and placed it carefully on the side table, then changed her mind and ran her finger under the cardboard seal, slowly unwrapping it.

It was a thick, hardcover book, a manual on Project Management. She unfolded the invoice, smoothing it carefully and looking for the order date. It was dated March thirty-first. A few days before he went missing. He wouldn't have ordered a book from Amazon if he was planning to leave. She picked up the phone, thought about ringing Sergeant Morton, telling her about the delivery.

What was the point, though? She'd have an explanation, an answer. Jill placed the phone back in its cradle. She sank down onto the bottom stair and put her head in her hands. 'What am I going to do?' she said aloud, the sound of her voice echoing around the hall. 'What am I going to do now?'

27

As Jill signed for his delivery, Michael had just finished showering and was rubbing his hair on a towel. Three days had passed since Anna had told him he'd been with her for two weeks. He scratched his chin; he was desperate for a shave. He had asked Anna to bring him a razor and some foam, but so far she hadn't.

He'd never had a beard in his life; he'd been curious, a few times over the years, and had considered growing one, just to see what it was like. But now he knew what it was like – itchy and uncomfortable, and it looked ridiculous.

'Hello, Michael,' Anna said.

She was sitting on the bed; he hadn't heard her come into the room and had no idea how long she'd been sitting there.

'I've got a treat for you,' she said. 'Sit down.'

She took his hand and led him to the chair she'd set up by the side of the bed. He sat down and looked at her quizzically.

'What's going on?' he said.

'Wait and see. You just sit there.'

He watched as she carried an empty plastic bowl to the bathroom. He heard the tap running, then it stopped and Anna came back and placed the bowl, steam rising from it, at his feet.

She picked up a towel and a large soap-bag from where she'd left them, against the wall. She draped the towel across his chest, tucking the edges into the neckline of his t-shirt.

'You're going to shave me?' he asked, incredulous.

'Yes. You were saying how much you wanted to shave. I thought I'd do this for you.'

His eyes widened as she produced a cut-throat razor and shaving brush from the bag, and a block of shaving soap in a circular tin. He recoiled as she started to lather up his face.

'Just sit still and relax,' she said. 'I have done this before, you know.'

He closed his eyes, wondering briefly exactly who she'd shaved in the past. The bristles of the brush felt good against his skin, as she worked them into the thick hair around his chin.

He held his breath as she made the first scrape of the blade against his cheek. She rested her other hand against the base of his throat, moving it from time to time to guide his face into the position she wanted. He was sure she was going to slip; he waited for the sudden rush of pain that would confirm his fear.

Still not daring to open his eyes, he listened to the splash of water as she dipped the blade in to clean it, before starting again. Her face was so close to his now, he could hear the gentle sigh of her breaths.

'Lift your head a little bit,' she said.

He opened his eyes. She had the razor in her hand and was staring intently at him.

'I just need to do this bit,' she said. She traced a finger lightly above his top lip.

His throat was dry, too dry. He couldn't take his eyes away from hers.

'Nearly done,' she whispered, as she ran the blade beneath his nose. He could still feel the imprint of her finger on his flesh.

'There,' she said, and dipped the blade into the water again. She rubbed it across her denim-clad thigh to dry it, then reached into her bag for a facecloth. She dipped it into the water then squeezed out the excess moisture before placing it onto his face.

He gasped at the feel of the hot cloth against his tender skin. She placed her palms on top of the cloth, then lifted it and gently wiped away all traces of the shaving soap.

'That's better, isn't it?' she said, dropping the cloth to the floor. She reached forward and cupped his face in her hands, then rubbed her own cheek against one of his.

'So smooth,' she said.

'Thanks, Anna,' Michael said softly. He reached for the towel around his neck and pulled it loose as she walked back to the bathroom to empty the bowl.

She came back and placed all her equipment into the soap-bag. She put that and the bowl at the archway to the stairs then turned and came before him. She took his hand and led him to the bed, then folded the chair and returned it to its spot at the back of the room.

She knelt on the floor in front of where he sat and took his hands in hers.

'I'm glad you enjoyed that, Michael. I just wanted to do something nice for you. So that you know I'm serious about all of this, about us being together.'

Michael wondered what to feel. He just didn't know. He wanted to hate her for imprisoning him, but he found he couldn't.

What's happening to me? he thought. *What the hell is happening to me?*

28

As Anna shaved Michael's face, Jill stood at the open doorway of the spare room and sighed. She felt like crying at the sight of how desperately untidy it was. It seemed even worse than when she had started on it the previous day.

Even though they were always saying they'd clear out the room, spend a full weekend at it and get it into some sort of order, in reality, it had always been so much easier just to keep the door closed and ignore it. Out of sight, out of mind, and all that. Besides, didn't everyone have a place like this in their house? Admittedly, it was usually a drawer, and not a whole room.

She'd slowly started to work through the chaos she'd allowed to build up in the house. She needed to keep busy. The laundry basket was no longer overflowing. She'd tidied out wardrobes, taking old stuff to the charity shop and putting Michael's jackets in to be dry-cleaned.

The piles of newspapers and magazines that she'd spent mindless hours flicking through without taking in a word had been recycled.

She'd left this room until last, though. It had always been a project they were going to tackle together. She had no idea they'd let it get into such a state.

When the piles of unopened post on the table disappeared, she'd assumed it was because Michael had got his act together, and dealt with his mail. Even though she wasn't the most organised person in the world, she could at least lay her hands on all the important stuff.

'I knew you were messy,' she muttered as she found another pile of petrol receipts from 2007, 'but *really?*'

He must have actually *packed* these and brought them with him when he moved in. She shook her head at the sound of her voice; she'd been talking out loud more and more often.

Her life was so full of silence. Before, it had been filled with chat and conversation. There was always music, or the TV, usually too loud. One of her friends had once joked that the way to torture Jill would be to send her to one of those silent retreats.

Now, there was so much quiet and stillness. She needed it, though. To focus. Any distractions might mean she missed a vital thought or idea.

She'd hoped, when she started this, that he had a system of some sort. It had quickly become obvious that he didn't. It was chaos.

Carrier bags of paperwork vied for space with box files bursting with newspaper cuttings. She'd found a clear plastic folder stuffed full of foreign currency, most of it no longer legal tender, and another containing car insurance documents dating back at least twelve years.

Piles and piles of receipts for everything from lunches he'd bought to jeans he had long since got rid of. And that was before she'd even looked at the letters. There appeared to be hundreds of them, spilling from each of the three briefcases she'd come across.

So much of it was rubbish – junk mail, offers of loans, ancient credit card bills, reminders about his tax return. She'd tried to sort it into piles – stuff to shred, stuff to read, stuff to action. Then she'd put it into folders, organised it a bit, so that he could look through it all when he came back.

When Jill had come into the room the previous day, at first, it had all been just too much and after less than an hour, she'd stood, papers fluttering like confetti around her ankles, walked out and closed the door. She'd lain on the sofa for hours watching reruns of *Friends* on TV.

She'd started awake in the early afternoon. *Friends* had finished, and she absently flicked through the channels. When she realised she had been watching an enthusiastic blonde with perfect teeth and an American accent demonstrating a piece of exercise equipment for ten minutes, she turned the TV off with the remote control and went back to get on with what she'd started.

She was getting somewhere, though. Filing cabinets, she thought. That's what they needed. She'd order some later on. Although, soon, the cot would be in here. She shuddered and clutched her bump, thinking of the solitary shopping trips, the choices she'd have to make.

No, she told herself, he'd be back. He'd be back to choose the cot, the pushchair. The baby's name. But she was over 34-weeks pregnant now. The baby could, theoretically, come any time. She tucked her hair behind her ears and forced herself to set to work on the next pile.

The handful of smooth, creamy envelopes stood out from the rest of the rubbish. She didn't like opening his mail; they'd never opened each other's post. Although to be fair, Michael rarely opened his own, never mind having the inclination to open someone else's. She thought of putting them to one side, maybe even in a folder of their own.

They were difficult to ignore though. Maybe they would have some sort of clue, she thought. She took one of them and slit it open with her thumb and unfolded the single sheet of thick paper. *Pear Tree Lodge,* it said on the header. It sounded like an old folks' home. She couldn't remember him mentioning anyone he knew in a home.

Dear Mr Stanton, she read,

I'm not sure whether you received my email, and I haven't been able to reach you by telephone, so this letter is just to confirm that your visit is arranged, as usual, for Thursday afternoon. Stuart has been a little confused over the last few weeks and hopefully your visit will settle him, as is often the case.

We look forward to seeing you.
Regards,

Vanna Conroy

Stuart? Jill thought hard. She couldn't recall Michael ever mentioning a Stuart. And what was Pear Tree Lodge?

She reached for the phone that was never far from her side and did a quick internet search. So it was a residential home, as she'd thought. Just not one for the elderly. It was a place for people suffering from mental illness. Jill ran a hand through her hair, recoiling at the thick, greasy feel of it.

She reached for another of the letters from the pile and opened it. It was a similar letter, confirming a date for a visit. Jill frowned and tried to make sense of it. Before she could change her mind, she dialled the number at the top of the letter.

'Hello,' she said, when a cool, clear voice answered almost immediately. 'I'd like to speak to Vanna Conroy.'

29

Two days later, at just after nine in the morning, as Jill drove towards a residential home to meet a woman who she hoped could give her some answers, Michael opened his eyes after a night of patchy sleep.

The light seemed different. Softer. He sat up and looked around. Fat, cream candles flickered around the room. They were on the floor against the wall, on the TV stand, by the bedside.

'Hello, Michael,' Anna said.

'Hello,' he replied. 'What's going on? Is there a power cut?'

Anna laughed. 'The candles? No, I just wanted to create a nice atmosphere for us. There's something special about candlelight, isn't there?'

'What are you up to?'

'Don't worry. You're going to enjoy this.'

Michael watched as Anna took an iPod from pocket and plugged it into a small speaker she must have brought down with her and placed in front of the TV. She fiddled with it until the gentle tones of Marvin Gaye filled the room. She turned the volume down. Michael recognised the opening bars of *What's Going On?* One of his favourites. But of course, she knew that. They'd often listened to Motown music together, back then. Or at least had it on it the background while they were in bed.

Michael watched, speechless, as Anna walked to the end of the bed and started to undo her jeans. Without taking her eyes off his, she slid them down her legs and stepped out of them. She moved towards the side of the bed, in her underwear and slim-fitting black t-shirt.

'I hope you don't mind,' she said, gesturing towards her discarded jeans. 'They're so restrictive, and it can get a bit warm.'

Michael couldn't take his eyes off her. Her body, unchanged in the three and a half years since he had seen it, was firm and toned. The tattoo on her hip, just poking out from the edge of her lace knickers; that was new, though. She bent forward, seemingly to search for something she had left on the floor, and then placed a small glass bottle on the bedside cabinet.

'Take your top off,' she said.

'What? Why? What are you doing, Anna?'

'Just take your top off. Or do you want me to do it for you? You've been so tense recently. I thought a massage might help.'

'What? No. There's no need. I'm fine. Just... no.'

'I'm not taking "no" for an answer. I want you to relax. You need to start enjoying being here, rather than thinking you're in some sort of prison. I want to do this for you. Anyway, isn't that what couples do, do nice things for one another? Come on, you'll enjoy it.'

She reached for the bottom of his t-shirt. Michael brushed her hand away and lifted it over his head. Anna pushed it to the floor then took hold of his bicep and started to push him. Reluctantly, Michael turned over, until he was lying on his stomach, his head to one side on the pillow and his arms by his sides.

Michael closed his eyes. If he just went along with it, it would soon be over. It felt so wrong, so intimate. He heard her open the bottle, and then the rasp of her palms as she rubbed them together. The oil she was using had a soft, spicy scent.

He gasped as he felt her hands on his shoulders, warm and slick. She began to knead his flesh, gently at first, then harder. A moan escaped his lips as she worked her fingers into the knots down his back.

'So tense,' she murmured.

The pressure changed as she ran the pads of her fingers, feather-light, up and down his arms and across the back of his neck.

His eyes fluttered open as she stopped. She had her back to him and was pouring more of the scented oil onto her palm.

He shifted his weight and allowed his eyes to slip shut again. In the background, Marvin Gaye had given way to Stevie Wonder.

'What are you doing?' he gasped, as he felt her climb onto the bed and then onto his back.

'Ssh,' she said. 'I'm just getting into a better position.'

It was impossible not to relax at her touch; gentle, firm, almost painful, then gentle again.

The scent of the oil filled his nostrils. The flickering candlelight danced beyond his closed eyelids. He felt her hands travel lower, and she lifted herself up from his as she pulled his shorts down low across his buttocks, then repositioned herself, so that she was sitting on the exposed skin of his lower back. She massaged his skin, again and again, with her oily hands. His skin felt hot and tingly. He could feel the heat of Anna through the thin layer of lace that separated their skin. He moved his arms up from his sides and clenched the pillow in his fists, burying his face in it.

Still, she probed, seeking out the tightest muscles until the agony was almost unbearable, but then she would move, and relief flooded him.

He turned his head and opened his eyes as he felt her slip from on top of him. She had her face beside him.

'Turn over,' she said, eyes blazing.

This time, he didn't even begin to protest. Anna picked up the chain and carefully rearranged it as he moved to lie on his back.

'Close your eyes,' she whispered.

He felt her hands on his face, tracing across his forehead, then his eyelids and cheeks. He moaned softly as she traced a finger across his lips.

Her hands moved to his chest, kneading, stroking, and then, she was astride him again. He felt breathless and light-headed. Without knowing he even moved them, his hands found her hips and cradled them. He could feel her hipbones beneath her smooth skin.

She stopped massaging and took his hands away from her body, back onto the duvet.

'Stop,' she said. 'This is about you. No touching.'

Michael licked his lips. They tasted of the oil. His whole body felt overheated, on fire. He watched as she concentrated on his chest. Her face was shining, damp with sweat from her efforts.

She looked up and smiled as she saw him watching her.

'There,' she said. 'Are you feeling relaxed now?'

Michael nodded. He felt a lot of things. Relaxed, exhausted. Aroused. He sank back into the mattress.

Anna pulled the duvet up over him and wiped her hands up and down her arms. Her skin glowed in the candlelight. She looked magnificent.

'I'm going upstairs now,' she said. 'I'm going to have a bath and get changed, and then I'll be back down. You should drink some water.'

She reached to the floor and picked up two plastic bottles of water. She handed him one, then unscrewed the other and drank deeply from it. She wiped away the beads of moisture on her lips with the back of her hand.

'See,' she said. 'It's not so bad being here, is it?'

Michael tried to speak, but his reply was unintelligible. He closed his eyes. He could still feel her hands on his body, as if she had left imprints on his skin. He listened as her bare feet padded across the floor. He heard the whisper of breath as she blew out some of the candles. He lay there, in the almost-darkness as she walked away and locked the door.

30

Jill pulled the car into a generous space outside of Pear Tree Lodge and looked at the imposing grey stone building in front of her. Her stomach clenched as she got out of the car and walked off across the crunching gravel.

With its manicured lawns and tasteful potted plants, it could be a luxury hotel. The hedges were trimmed to perfection. There was even a fountain. But as she stood and looked up at the meshed glass windows, and took in the security pad at the door, she knew this was no holiday venue.

She pressed the intercom and announced her arrival. Seconds later, the door opened and a young woman, all glossy dark hair and dazzling teeth, beckoned her in and directed her to the squashy leather sofas before retreating to her glass desk and shuffling through a pile of papers.

Jill picked up a magazine from the low glass table in front of her. It was the latest copy of *Tatler*, she noticed. Not like the usual waiting room fodder. That day's papers lay, fanned out, on another side table. They looked as if they'd been ironed.

A fish tank bubbled away in the corner, tiny, jewel-coloured fish swimming about in the turquoise water.

Jill's mouth was dry and she thought about filling one of the little plastic cups from the cooler in the corner, but decided against it. She'd already had to pull in and hurry into a Tesco on the way here – and she didn't want this meeting to be interrupted by another dash to the bathroom.

Anxiety bubbled inside her. She'd thought, when she started clearing out the spare room that maybe she'd find some evidence of debts, or even maybe that he was having an affair.

But this? This was something else. She couldn't take it in at first; even now, she couldn't understand it. All those conversations they'd had about family. How they didn't want their baby to be an only child. When she thought about it though, had he really had much to say? Or had he just agreed with her? She wished she could remember.

There had to be a good reason – a really good reason – for him to neglect to mention that he had a brother. A brother who lived in an institution and was unlikely ever to leave. When they had spoken to her on the phone, Vanna Conroy had been reluctant to go into details, but she had made that particular point about Stuart

Jill looked up as the sound of heels on wood signalled Vanna Conroy's arrival. She was small and trim, with Oriental features. Her thick chestnut hair was smoothly bobbed and a pair of thinly rimmed glasses perched on top of her head. She looked every inch the business woman, in her navy blue skirt-suit and flesh-coloured tights. Even her shoes gleamed.

'Jill?' she said, offering her hand. 'I'm Vanna.' Jill nodded and stood to take it. Her palm was cool and dry.

'Did you bring the paperwork I asked for?'

'Yes, here it is.'

Jill handed over the bills and letters showing Michael's details, as well as her own driving licence. The other woman put on her glasses and scrutinised them, a tiny crease forming between her eyes.

'Good,' she declared, passing the documents back to Jill. 'We can't be too careful. I'm sure you'll appreciate we have to protect our residents. I couldn't go into a lot of detail on the phone, and obviously I can't discuss Stuart's medical history with you. I take it you haven't had any news on Mr Stanton?'

Jill shook her head and clenched her hands together. She wasn't going to lose it, not now.

'It's good for Stuart to have visitors,' the other woman continued. 'It perks him up no end. He can be very lucid at times. At other times, it can be like trying to reason with a four-year-old.'

Jill nodded, unsure what to say. She followed Vanna away from the reception area and along a series of corridors, pausing only when the other woman stopped to swipe a slim white card to grant them access to whatever was behind each of the locked doors.

'He has his own room, as do all of the residents, but he spends a lot of time in the communal area. He likes the company, I think.'

'Who... who pays for this place? Does Michael...'

Vanna cut her off. 'No, all his fees are met by the local authority. That's what happens in cases like his, so there's no need to worry about that.'

Vanna stopped and opened a final door. Now this *is* what I had expected, Jill thought. Staff in crisp white outfits seemed to float around on almost silent footsteps. A row of doors, some ajar, led to unseen rooms. There was an underlying scent of urine and disinfectant, and Jill gulped down the bile that rose suddenly up the back of her throat.

Vanna gestured towards the large communal area at the other side of the reception desk. There were people everywhere, in groups, in pairs or alone. Reading, watching TV, playing cards. A woman in the corner was painting on a large easel, dipping the end of her long ash-grey plait into the pot before smearing it across the canvas. A tall man sat in the floor in the far corner, rocking gently from side to side. As Jill approached the open door of the large room, she was struck by the hum of noise; babbling and whispers and the occasional manic screech of laughter.

'This way,' said Vanna. 'He's over here.'

31

Michael was sipping the last of the water when Anna came back into the room. She switched on the lamp in the corner, and he could see that her hair was damp and she was wearing black stretchy trousers and a vest top. Apart from the fact that she quite clearly wasn't wearing a bra, she looked as if she had just done a yoga class.

'Hi,' he said. 'Did you enjoy your bath?'

Michael drained the water. He barely had the energy to lift the bottle to his mouth.

'Yes, thanks,' she said. 'How are you feeling? Massage can have *such* huge effects on people.'

'Good,' he muttered. 'I feel good. Tired. Exhausted in fact.'

She nodded. 'Sometimes you feel energised. Or emotional. Or just really, really relaxed.'

'How do you know so much about it?'

'I did a course, once. At a hospital I was working at. They paid for us to choose a course, something touch-feely that was supposed to relieve stress at work. Anyway I opted to learn about massage. I'm pleased it's come in useful. You seem much more relaxed now.'

'I feel as if I can barely keep my eyes open.'

She walked to the empty side of the bed and sat down, then shuffled down until her head was on the pillow.

'It's so lovely, having you here. Being able to do nice things for you.'

Michael mumbled a reply. He knew he should try to sit up and clear this light-headed feeling, but he stayed where he was and allowed his eyes to slip closed. He jolted awake as he felt her hands on his face, cupping his cheeks.

'Ssh, you sleep now. You look as if you really need it.'

He closed his eyes again and felt her fingers gently massaging his scalp as she lifted his head onto her lap. Several minutes passed as they lay like that, in silence, then he felt the whisper of her lips on his forehead as she kissed him.

'Sleep well, darling. I've got some things to be getting on with. I'll see you when you wake up.'

As she got up to leave, Michael felt himself sink into the mattress. He finally gave in and allowed himself to fall completely, blissfully, asleep.

3 2

Jill gasped and swallowed hard. There was no mistake. There could be no doubt. He was so like Michael, it took her breath away.

His face was softer, as if his skin had melted and then settled slightly off course. But he had the same features; the same thick, dark hair. His hands, resting on the table, were broad, with Michael's short, strong fingers. He looked up at her with Michael's navy gaze and smiled, creases forming around his eyes.

'Hello,' Stuart said. His voice was soft and childlike.

'Hello, Stuart,' Jill said, in a voice so thick she barely recognised it as her own. She swallowed again. She couldn't get upset, not here. She had no idea what effect it would have on Stuart if she did.

'Stuart, this is Jill. She'd like to sit with you, chat for a while,' said Vanna. 'Would that be OK?'

Stuart frowned and looked down at the table. He closed the book he was reading – a paperback copy of a David Bowie autobiography – marking his place by turning over the corner of the page. Something else he shared with Michael. Stuart nodded.

'Good,' Vanna said. She turned to Jill. 'Just let any of the orderlies know when you're ready to leave. Or if he gets agitated.'

She turned and walked back across the room, the click of her heels ringing out in the sea of rubber-soled shoes.

'Stuart, I'm... I'm Michael's girlfriend. Your... brother.'

Stuart nodded again. 'Yes. Jill.'

'Yes, that's right. Jill. I live with Michael. He didn't tell me about you. I wish he had, so we could have met sooner. Michael's... gone away for a while. Have you seen him?'

Stuart looked up at the ceiling, frowning. He didn't speak for a while.

'Is he coming today?' Stuart asked. 'My brother. Is he coming today?

'No, not today, I don't think. Can you remember when you last saw him?'

Stuart put his head down, as if he was concentrating hard on the cover of the book in front of him. Jill looked around the room. The walls were painted a pale, muted yellow. She imagined it was supposed to be soothing. It made her feel queasy.

'Stuart,' she said. 'I don't know where Michael is. Can you remember when he came to see you last?'

'Michael?'

'Yes, Michael. I've... I've sort of lost him. He's been gone for two and a half weeks. I thought you might know where he is.'

'Lost?'

'Yes, lost. But I'm going to find him. I... I was wondering why Michael has never brought me to meet you. I would have liked to know you sooner.'

Stuart shrugged. 'Dunno.'

He clenched his hands in front of him and looked down at them.

'Michael and me, we're having a baby. Although you can probably see that.' She laid a hand on her rounded stomach.

'If he comes to see you, maybe you could tell him I was here? Tell him that Jill came to see you and she's very worried. And ask him to get in touch with me. We could bring the baby to see you, when it arrives, if you'd like that.'

Stuart started to pick at his sleeve. He moved his head slowly from side to side.

'No,' he said. 'No, no, no.'

She put her hand on his arm. He shrugged it off; his flesh was doughy yet she could tell there was strength in his limbs. An orderly, casually watching from by the window, raised an eyebrow at her.

'It's fine,' she mouthed. 'Stuart? I'm sorry. I didn't mean to upset you.'

Stuart didn't respond. She wondered if he even knew she was still there.

'This looks like a nice place. Are you happy here?' She cringed at her pathetic attempt at small talk. Maybe this was a bad idea.

'Anna's cross,' Stuart said suddenly.

'Anna? Who's Anna?'

'Anna's my girlfriend.'

'And why is Anna cross?' Jill said, leaning closer to him.

'Baby. Baby. Baby.'

Stuart's voice was rising. Jill flinched as he formed a fist with his hand – the hand that was so like Michael's – and started to bang it, gently at first and then harder and harder against the plastic table-top. The orderly came, placed a hand on Stuart's shoulder.

'Hey, Stuart, what's up mate?' he said.

'Anna. Michael. Lost,' he muttered.

The orderly looked over at Jill. 'I think maybe he needs a lie down now. I bet he'd like to see you again, though, wouldn't you Stuart?'

Stuart sat, a tremor moving his body. His mind was obviously elsewhere now. Jill stood.

'Is he OK?' she asked. 'He was talking about an "Anna" when he got upset. Do you know who she is?'

'Sorry, no idea,' the orderly replied, taking Stuart's elbow as he helped him to stand. 'I'm new to this wing. One of the guys on the desk might be able to help you though. And don't worry, he'll be fine. It's just, well, the way he is, sometimes.'

Jill stood, watching as the man lay a hand at the small of Stuart's back and steered him out of the room. As she watched him walk away, with his broad shoulders and thick, muscular legs, it was all she could do not to fall to her knees and weep. She blew out a breath and walked from the room and to the ward's reception desk, clinging to its edge as a wave of weariness washed over her.

'Hi,' Jill said to the nurse who was sifting through papers. 'I was visiting Stuart? I'm ready to leave now.'

'Oh, OK. Hang on, I'll come and let you out.'

'Thanks. Actually, can I ask you something before I go?'

'Of course, ask away,' said the nurse. Now she'd moved Jill could see her name on the shiny white badge at her chest. Deborah.

'I was just wondering what's actually wrong with Stuart. I mean, to make him the way he is? This is the first time I've met him. I'm... kind of his sister-in-law, I suppose. Has he always been like he is now? And he mentioned someone called Anna; said she was his girlfriend. Do you know anything about her?'

'Stuart's schizophrenic. To cut a long story short, he lived with it for a long time and then it got the better of him, and now he's here. He's been with us for a few years now, and he seems happy, a lot of the time.'

'And Anna?' Jill asked. 'Do you know who she is?'

'Anna? I think she was his girlfriend, at one time. She comes every now and then to see him.'

They stood at the door. Deborah raised her pass to open it.

'I'm pregnant,' Jill said. 'Although you probably noticed.'

Deborah smiled as eyes went to the swell of Jill's belly. 'Yes, I did notice. You don't look as if you've got too long to go now. Congratulations.'

'Thanks. Just over five weeks to go. Not long at all, really. Stuart said something weird, though. He said Anna was angry about the baby. He got really agitated.'

Deborah frowned and ran a hand across her face. 'The thing is,' she said, 'with a condition like Stuart's... well, maybe it just made her think about how they can't be together and that they'll never have a family. Stuart's understanding of emotions is sometimes very simplistic, and he often gets worked up when he can't get things across. Maybe Anna was upset, and he mistook that for anger. I don't know. I wouldn't worry about it, though.'

She opened the door and Jill walked through. 'Bye,' said Deborah. 'Maybe we'll see you again? It's all they've got sometimes, seeing a different face, hearing some news. I think it does them good.'

'Thanks,' Jill said. 'Yes, I'll come and see him again. I'd like that. Bye, then.'

Jill leaned against the wall, unsure whether her legs would carry her back along the corridor and out of the door. She took a deep breath and walked away, desperate to breathe in some fresh air.

33

Two days after Jill had met his brother for the first time, Michael, still held in captivity by Anna, jerked awake. He felt as if he was falling from a cliff. He screwed his eyes shut against the sick, dizzy feeling that filled his head. He tried to cling on to the dream he'd been having, but it was floating away, just out of his reach.

In the dream, he'd been in bed, and Jill had walked into the room. She was wearing a dressing gown and her feet were bare. The sound of laughter – children's laughter – rang in the air. It was muffled, as if it were far away, in another part of the house.

She'd leaned over and he'd breathed in the orangey scent of her hair, still wet from the shower. He'd pushed the shaggy curls from her face and looked at her. Really looked at her. How many times had he done that, in reality? Not enough, he thought. Not nearly enough.

Now that he was awake, he knew Anna was in the room, even without opening his eyes. He could hear her breathing and humming quietly. The rustle of fabric told him she was moving around. It was funny, how quickly you got used to another person's presence. In the three weeks that he'd been here, he'd got used to her ways and routines. He knew how she smelled, the sound of her footsteps, and that she rarely wore any jewellery other than the pendant around her neck. Just yesterday, as they'd sat on the bed and watched TV together, he'd noticed the tiny, fair hairs on her face. He knew her nails were short and she never wore nail polish on her fingernails.

Not like Jill. So many nights, he had fallen asleep with that familiar, chemical smell filling his senses as she sat up in bed, painting her nails from the bottle balanced on a book on her lap. He'd asked her why she had to do it in bed. There'd been a reason. He couldn't remember it now. Why hadn't he listened to every word she'd said?

Even trivial stuff, like what to have for dinner, or arguments. Anything. Everything. So he could store it all, and play it back now. Break the monotony; hear her voice in his head. He'd woken up yesterday, sweat running down his face, sure that he'd forgotten what she sounded like.

He'd lain there, breathing deeply, thinking about when they'd met, what they'd said. Holidays they'd been on, trips they planned to take, the wedding they would have. Just before all this happened they'd talked about the places they would go, as a family. They wanted their son or daughter to have loads of amazing experiences.

Even though Jill told him she'd read somewhere that children don't really remember much of their first three years, that didn't matter. He wanted to build up a store of memories, right from the start.

He hadn't set out looking for someone to love. He hadn't wanted anything like that. But then they'd kissed and he realised he didn't want to stop kissing her, ever.

They'd both agreed to take things slowly, but he'd felt so restless on the nights they didn't see each other, that he'd spent the time planning what they could do next.

At Jill's suggestion, they'd dated 'like tourists'. After all, she'd said, they lived in Edinburgh but when had they last been to the Castle, or the Zoo? They'd had coffee in the café where JK Rowling famously scribbled down the words of her first Harry Potter novel, and they'd had lunch on the *Britannia*. They'd ridden the open-top tour bus and went on a ghost walk. They'd squeezed into pubs on the Royal Mile and fought their way to the bar through masses of stags, hens and birthday celebrations.

They'd been living in those heady, early days, when the wrong word or action could see off what could have been a blossoming relationship. Somehow though, it had all gone right. Jill had told him once that, when she was a teenager, she'd split up with a boyfriend because he had 'funny feet.'

'Does that make me terribly shallow?' she'd asked.

'Yes,' he'd said. 'But his loss was my gain.'

At first, the somehow ordinary, everyday feel to his relationship with Jill shocked him after the heady, dangerous times he'd spent with Anna. There were no complications; they were just two people who enjoyed being with each other. And it was a surprise to him, the way he felt.

He found himself wanting to know more and more about Jill. He learned that she liked to floss her teeth with an impossibly long string of floss. That she never went out without her toenails painted. How she wasn't remotely squeamish, which came in useful when he caught a horrible sickness bug, and she cleared away bowl after bowl of vomit, without complaint

He discovered that she loved old, musty-smelling second-hand books and loud musicals with as much singing and dancing crammed into them as possible.

The more he got to know about her, the more he loved her.

'Oh, hello,' Anna said now, glancing over at him and realising that he was awake. She was barefoot, in jeans and a white, fitted t-shirt, and had a yellow duster in one hand and a tin of furniture polish in the other. 'I'm just tidying up a bit. Why don't you go and have a shower while I finish off? We could watch TV for a while before I go to work. I feel terrible about leaving you alone so much, but I have to work, darling. You do understand, don't you?'

Michael nodded and pushed back the covers. He headed into the bathroom. The chain stopped him from closing the door completely, and he could see her, continuing with her chores as he stood at the toilet and urinated. He turned to the shower cubicle, reluctantly pulling his eyes away from her.

As usual, she had left towels and fresh clothes perched on top of the toilet cistern. He picked up the electric razor she had given him a few days earlier and started to shave. It wasn't as good as the shave she had given him, he thought with a pang. Not nearly as good.

Washed and dressed, he headed back towards the bed. Anna was already sitting on it, her back propped up on pillows against the headboard. She had the remote control in her hand.

'Look what's coming on,' she said.

Michael stared at the screen. They had discovered a shared love of British thrillers and Hitchcock movies. Their relationship in the past hadn't really extended to watching films. *The Man Who Knew Too Much* was just starting.

He sat down beside her on the bed.

'Are you comfortable enough, Michael? I should maybe have got a chair for down here. A small sofa, even. It's not really worth it now, I suppose. Are you OK? Do you need another pillow?'

'I'm fine. Really comfortable, thanks. Let's watch the film. This is one of my favourites.'

They lay, side by side, until the closing credits filled the screen. Anna stood and stretched.

'I enjoyed that,' she said. 'It must be years since I'd seen that one. I'll really have to go shortly, I'm sorry. I'll bring your lunch down first though. Back soon.'

Michael watched as she smoothed down her clothes and walked across the room. He fell back against the pillows, alone once again.

34

'Ben? It's Jill,' she said as the phone was answered. She had spent the couple of days since her visit to the care home trying to make sense of the fact that Michael had kept such a huge part of his life a secret from her. She was hoping that Ben, as one of Michael's closest friends, might have some answers.

'Jill, hi. How are you? Any news?'

'I'm fine, I suppose. No news. He's still missing. It's been three weeks; can you believe that? How can that even be possible? Anyway, sorry, how are you?'

'Me? I'm fine, thanks.'

'Good. Listen, I hope you don't mind me ringing, but I wanted to ask you something. You've known Michael, well, forever.'

'Yeah, well, almost forever. Certainly seems that way.'

'Something's happened that I wanted to speak to you about. I met his brother. I met Stuart the other day.'

She heard a deep intake of breath.

'Right,' Ben said slowly.

'So you know about him?'

'Like you said, I've known Michael almost forever. So, yeah, I know Stuart.'

'But why... why has Michael never mentioned him to me, do you think?'

It sent a little stab of pain to her heart, every time she thought about Michael keeping a secret like that from her. She'd thought long and hard before ringing Ben, torn between wanting to know more, and not wanting to admit to Ben that

Michael hadn't felt able to share this particular information with her.

Ben hesitated before he spoke. 'I don't know. I'm sure he had his reasons. Maybe he just never found the right moment? It's not something he talks about much. How did you end up meeting him, anyway? He hasn't been released from the care home, has he?' Ben asked.

'No. I was tidying up some paperwork, trying to clear out the spare room. There was some mail from that place, and I got in touch, then I went to see him there. Look, do you think we could meet up? Speak about this properly? There's so much I don't understand.'

'It's not really my story to tell, Jill.'

'Please. It's not like I can ask Michael, is it? I'd really appreciate it.'

Ben sighed. 'OK. How about we meet for a coffee? I could make it tomorrow, if that suits you. Langton's at Tollcross? I could be there at about 11.00?'

Jill agreed and hung up the phone. She was fizzing with impatience that she had to wait a whole day. She wanted to know as much as Ben was able to tell her, and she wanted to know now.

3 5

The next morning, Jill was already in the café, sitting by the window and stirring the foam on top of a cup of coffee that she didn't really want, when Ben walked through the heavy glass door and scanned the room.

He was tall and skinny, and dressed in his usual jeans and tweed jacket. His thinning dark hair made him look older than Michael, although they were the same age and had met in primary school.

Ben was one of her favourites amongst Michael's friends. He'd made her welcome from the start, always asking how she was, what she'd been up to, and appearing to be genuinely interested in her replies.

She'd spent many hours chatting to him at parties and on nights out. She'd even set him up on a date once, with her friend Julie. When it had ended disastrously, neither party had held it against her. Or at least Ben hadn't. She couldn't think of the last time she'd heard from Julie.

Ben had rang or sent texts daily when Michael first disappeared. He'd even put a lovely card through the door, telling her to let him know if he could help. Then contact had dried up. She didn't hold it against him. He probably didn't know what to say.

And, she reminded herself, he's Michael's friend; that's where his loyalties lie. Yes, he was her friend too, but purely by association. And if, like everyone else, he'd bought into the idea that Michael had up and left, well, he wasn't going to keep in touch forever, was he?

'Hi,' Ben said, bending to kiss her on the cheek. 'How are you? You look – what's the word – blooming?'

'I think you mean enormous.' Jill laid a hand on the bump that seemed to her to grow bigger every night.

Jill refused his offer of another coffee and waited as Ben went to the counter and came back with a double espresso.

'What a mess,' he said, sitting opposite her and taking off his glasses. He rubbed a hand over his eyes before putting the thick black frames back on and looking directly at her.

Jill shook her head and let out a bitter laugh. 'Yeah, you could say that. So, Stuart?'

Ben cleared his throat. 'Well, Stuart, as you know, is Michael's brother. They, well... it's complicated.' He tore open a sachet of sugar and tipped it into his cup, then stirred it and took a sip.

'Why would Michael keep him a secret? From me, I mean?'

'I don't know why he hasn't told you about him, but like I said on the phone, it's not something he talks a lot about. They... I don't know, Jill, it's really not for me to be telling you this.'

'Please, just tell me what you know. I need to understand, in case it helps me find him. You've got to admit that this whole situation just isn't right. Michael has vanished, seemingly into thin air. He was so excited about the baby. We hadn't argued or anything. There was absolutely no sign that he intended to leave. And now, I find out he's got a brother that he's never mentioned. So please, just tell me what you know. So I can try and make some sense of it all. I'm falling apart here.'

Jill felt her lips twist as she fought with the tears she was determined not to release. She was scared that if she started to cry, she might never stop.

Ben picked up his cup again, and then placed it back in its saucer without drinking from it. He ran a hand through his hair, leaving it sticking up on end. 'Stuart was always ill,' he began. 'Then when we were, I dunno, about fourteen, he was finally diagnosed with schizophrenia. He seemed OK, most of the time, once they got his medication sorted and stuff. He was fine, for years. Had a job, went out with his mates; just led a normal life, pretty much.'

'So what happened, to make him like he is now?'

'Stuart and his mates, they were into partying, taking a few drugs, you know? He had a girlfriend and they'd always be out, clubbing and stuff. Anyway, there was a bit of an incident, with the girl. And Michael. If you know what I mean.'

Jill nodded. She felt uneasy, thinking about Michael and another woman, which she knew was ridiculous, given that what they were talking about was all in the past. Ancient history.

They'd only spoken about their pasts in very vague terms – she'd always thought it best not to know details. She knew that Michael had been no angel before they'd met. She couldn't claim to have been one herself. It was what happened when you got together in your thirties; everyone had history. And sleeping with his brother's girlfriend? That was low, but, well, not the end of the world.

'Anyway,' Ben continued. 'She left Stuart pretty much as soon as she met Michael, and they started seeing each other. Stuart and Michael fell out, which isn't surprising, really. And then Stuart got more into the drugs. And the more he got into that scene, the less careful he was about taking his medication. His symptoms got worse, much worse. He didn't know where he was or who he was most of the time. I'm just telling you what Michael told me – I haven't seen Stuart for a long time.'

Ben stopped and took a deep breath.

'Stuart tried to kill himself, and that's when he had to go and live in that place he's in now. I can't even think of how long he must have been in there now. Years. I doubt he'll ever leave. Michael took it badly, blamed himself.'

Jill sat back in her chair. He'd obviously kept it to himself because he was ashamed. Even so, she felt a little stab of pain that he couldn't have shared this with her.

'He got really worked up when I visited him,' she said. 'He was talking about someone called Anna. The nurse said she was his girlfriend.'

Ben looked up. 'Anna. Yes, that was the girl, the one they fell out over. That's a name I haven't heard in a long time. She was a bit strange. I only met her couple of times, but there was something about her. I could never quite put my finger on it. She was very, you know, *intense*. They weren't together that long, her and Michael.'

Jill sighed deeply. She really didn't want to know any more of the details. The paper napkin she'd been fiddling with lay in shreds on the table in front of her.

'So basically, it sounds as if he didn't tell me about Stuart because he's ashamed of what he caused, or thinks he caused,' she said.

'I don't know. Maybe. He's never said anything to me about it. I know he visits him, pretty regularly, but it's not something he really talks about a lot.'

Jill looked out of the window. He had kept a massive part of his life secret from her. Let her think he didn't even have any family.

'And his parents? Are they really dead, or is there a whole clan somewhere, hidden away?'

It came out harsher than she'd planned. 'I'm sorry. It's just a shock. Another shock.'

'Don't be sorry. This must be a nightmare for you. And to answer your question, no, there's no other family. His dad died a long time ago, and his mother... she died too, not long after.'

'I just wish, I don't know, that he'd felt he could confide in me, you know.' She rested her face in her hands.

'Don't read too much into it. Men are good at putting stuff in boxes. Separate compartments.'

Jill rubbed her dry lips with her fingers. 'If he's always visited Stuart regularly and then suddenly just stopped going, surely something's not right? And even if he had left me, he wouldn't abandon his brother. Or that's how it sounds, from what you've told me. Is sounds as if Michael looks after him.'

Ben placed his palms flat on the table. 'I don't know, Jill. I really don't know what the hell is going on. No one knows where he is. Maybe that's what he wants, for some reason. I suppose we never really know people as well as we think we do. And you know what he's like. Things go wrong, he buries his head, walks away.'

'That's the thing, though. Nothing has gone wrong. Not with us. Not with anything, as far as I know.'

'Like I said, I don't know. Who knows what was going on in his head? Maybe he got cold feet.'

Jill bristled. What was it with everyone and cold feet? She stared at him. 'But we were – are – happy. Everything was good. Better than good.'

Ben shrugged. 'I'm sorry. I shouldn't have said that. There's no answer though, is there? He must have his own reasons.'

He glanced at his watch. 'I'm sorry, Jill, I'm going to have to get going.' He pushed back his chair and stood. 'Let me know if you hear anything, though. Keep in touch, eh?'

Jill stood and he pulled her towards him in a hug. He smelled of coffee and woody aftershave. She felt a lump forming in her throat.

'Take care,' Ben said, and headed for the door.

Jill watched him leave. A skin had formed on her barely touched coffee. She stirred it, then grimaced as she took a sip. It was cold.

The café was filling up, the lunchtime crowd, too busy to actually sit down and drink, queued to buy drinks in paper cups. Everywhere, people were going about their lives. Jill sighed and pulled on her coat. She was no further forward.

She pulled her phone from her bag and dialled Michael's number, like she did, countless times a day. The all-too-familiar voice told her to leave a message. She ended the call and was about to put her phone back into her bag when she stopped.

She scrolled through her contacts and found the number of Pear Tree Lodge. Moments later, she was on hold at the reception desk of Stuart's ward. She closed her eyes and mouthed *Thank you* when the phone was answered by a cheery voice she recognised.

'Deborah Vine speaking, how can I help you?'

Jill could hear herself spouting a jumble of words. She should have thought it over before she'd dialled, tried to make more sense. Made notes, even. But Deborah listened to her, murmuring kind words, and let her finish. She wished she could help, she said, as Jill felt her heart sink, but, she explained, the visitor records were confidential. All she could do, if Michael did turn up for a visit, was ask him to contact Jill. Jill thanked her and ended the call.

This time, she did put her phone back in her bag, then picked it up and headed out into the street. She needed to get home.

* * *

Ben pulled up his collar and hurried away from the coffee shop, not looking back. He felt like an utter shit. He'd always had a lot of time for Jill. He liked her, always had. She was good for Michael.

But, well, what could he do? Michael was his mate. His best mate. Despite the fact that it wasn't even midday, he walked into the King's Arms and ordered a large whisky, drank it straight down, then ordered a second one. He sat, nursing it, at a corner table and scrolled through the text messages on his phone.

He'd received the first text soon after Michael had gone, in his usual style. Short and to the point. Basically saying he had to get away, nothing to worry about, not to tell Jill. He must have met someone else, Ben thought. What other explanation could there possibly be?

Ben was pissed off with Michael for a million reasons, not least that he hadn't been able to confide in him, Ben, his best mate. Ben had been there for him through all sorts of shit. He'd been there for Michael when his dad died, and then his mum. And all the crap with Stuart over the years. Michael hadn't told a soul, other than Ben, when he started seeing Stuart's girlfriend.

Yeah, Ben had been there for Michael through it all. So why not this time? What could possibly be so bad that he couldn't share it? In the three texts Michael had sent him, he had said more or less the same thing, which was precisely nothing. Ben had sent replies. Whenever he'd tried calling him, the phone was always off. He could be anywhere.

Ben sighed and took a gulp of the whisky, wincing as it made its fiery route to his belly. He knew he had to respect his friend's wishes. Sometimes people just chose to disappear for their own reasons. And how well did you know anyone really, even the best mate you've had for thirty-odd years?

36

I must have fallen asleep yet again, Michael thought. He could feel her lips, gentle and feather-light, tracing a path down his chest and onto his stomach. And then, the warm, wet touch of her tongue. He fought to cling to the dream he was sure he was having.

Her tongue continued its path, down and down. He felt a sudden coolness on his skin as the shorts he was wearing were pulled down, over his thighs. He moaned softly as her hand, and then her mouth, touched his stiffening cock, then moved away again, teasing and arousing him. Her other hand rested on his hip and he moved his arms so that he could touch her. Her mouth was at his inner thigh now, keeping a rhythm with her hand and as she kissed and flicked his sensitive flesh with her tongue.

It felt so real, he was desperate not to wake up. 'Jill,' he muttered. 'Oh, baby.'

There was a sudden flash of light. Michael blinked furiously against the sudden glare. The tiny lamp, clipped onto the headboard, illuminated Anna's face. The last thing he remembered was her leaving for work after lunch.

'You know, Michael,' she said softly, 'it's extremely bad manners to say another woman's name when someone is in the process of doing this to you.'

'What... what the hell were you doing?'

'Come on, Michael. I don't really think you need an explanation, do you? Now be quiet and let me get on.'

'No, Anna–'

But then he stopped talking as she leant forward and took him deep into her mouth. She had left the light on, and he watched her head, moving up and down as she sucked harder and faster. His hand moved towards her, and he threaded his fingers through her hair.

He could hear her breathing heavily through her nose as she moved her mouth up and down, up and down. Involuntary moans slipped from his lips.

I should stop her, he thought.

But he didn't. He stroked the top of her head, feeling the movement of her jaw muscles in his palms. He lifted his hips and thrusted against her, and cried out as he came.

She stayed where she was. He felt the movement of her throat as she swallowed, then lifted her head slowly and looked at him.

A flirtatious smile played on her lips, as she ran her fingertips across them.

'You can't... you can't just creep in here and do stuff like that,' Michael said, when he felt able to speak.

'Why ever not? And I didn't notice you complaining.'

She shifted across the bed and lay on her stomach, propping her chin on her hands.

'It's important for a relationship to be exciting, Michael. It keeps things alive. And until it's the right time for us to actually have sex, we need to, well, you know... keep things interesting. And I know you always loved blow-jobs.'

Michael sat up on the edge of the bed and pulled the shorts up from around his thighs.

'I'm going to have a shower,' he said.

'OK. Take your time. I'm just going to lie here for a bit.'

Michael turned and walked across to the door.

'And Michael,' she said as he entered the bathroom.

'What?'

'You need to just let go. Enjoy *us*. Admit to yourself how you feel. I know, and you know, that you never stopped wanting me, did you?'

Michael squeezed his eyes closed. He'd always desperately fancied her, even at the end. It wasn't as if the reason they'd split up was because he didn't find her attractive anymore. She was an easy person to be attracted to. He'd had feelings for her, Of course he had. Not love, but something. Or maybe he *had* loved her, in some twisted way. And he'd missed her, for a while, after... after she went away. Maybe she was right; deep down, he did still feel something for her. It was too dark and too complicated to even begin to make sense of.

You couldn't just rekindle something that had ended a long time ago. His feelings for Jill – sweet, kind, beautiful Jill – far outweighed anything he had ever felt for Anna. Of course it did. That was what he kept telling himself.

37

As Michael lay in his bed thinking of Jill, she was also lying in bed, wide awake, thinking of him. She found it so difficult to sleep properly now; she wondered if she'd ever be able to again. Maybe when the baby came, she'd be able to, from sheer exhaustion.

She had been thinking about her chat with Ben the previous day, and then torturing herself, thinking of the night she had first met Michael.

That night, over two and a half years ago, they'd been at a party. It had been a great party – someone she vaguely knew was leaving to start a new life in Dubai and had rented a room in a pub in town. She was pleasantly drunk and in such a good mood; one of those nights you didn't want to end.

Jill had noticed Michael looking over at her. She'd pinched a cigarette from her friend Lisa and gone over to ask him for a light, even though she'd never really smoked. He'd made her laugh, and she'd stayed, chatting to him, long after her friends, and almost everyone else, had left. As they'd stumbled out into the street to look for taxis, they'd kissed. He'd tasted of beer and cigarettes, but all the same she'd had an irrepressible urge to never leave his side.

Now, Jill sat up in bed and pushed back the covers. She didn't know why she hadn't thought of it before. She pulled her towelling dressing gown around her and went down to the kitchen, blinking as she switched on the overhead light. She opened the laptop and switched it on, drumming her fingertips on the table as she waited for it to come to life.

One hand went to the small of her aching back. She'd finally taken the midwife's advice about exercise the day before and taken herself to the swimming pool. She had never particularly enjoyed swimming, unless it was to cool off from lying in the sun on a foreign holiday.

However, it was good for her, apparently, and it filled time. She'd made a detour to Marks and Spencer to get a maternity swimming costume after she'd almost burst the seams attempting to put on the one she already had.

She had to admit it had felt good, slipping into the cool water and feeling lighter than she had done in months. And she'd slept for two solid hours when she got back. She was paying for the previous lack of exercise now though; her arms and back ached and she longed to take a forbidden ibuprofen.

Jill filled a glass with water and then sat at the table and watched as the home screen finally appeared. She navigated to the folder holding their photographs; the photographs she was always going to print and arrange in albums.

Somehow, she'd just never got around to doing it. It was a rainy day job, she said. She'd had it on her list of things to do when her maternity leave started, in between watching films and dozing on the sofa.

She'd never have thought that she'd be spending her time trying to find her missing boyfriend. Her fingers hovered over the keys, knowing that when she clicked, she was going to open the lid on a whole box full of memories.

She opened the first subfolder, and gasped as a close-up shot of Michael's head and shoulders filled the screen. She squinted, trying to remember where they'd been when she'd taken it. Barcelona.

She and Michael had walked for miles to the Parc Guell, because she'd read in a guidebook that it was one of the top ten places to visit. It had been worth the uphill trek in the blazing heat, and they'd sat, mesmerised by the view, drinking red wine from plastic cups until the bottle was empty and their faces were pink from the sun. That had been one of their first trips away together.

Jill swallowed down the anguish rising up her throat and moved on to the next folder of photographs.

She clicked through picture after picture. She was still sitting there, lost in thought, when the sun came up. She glanced up at the clock as she heard the sounds of the day coming to life. A distant door slammed and an engine spluttered loudly into life. She needed to make a decision. She went back to the very first picture, and touched her fingertips lightly to the screen. 'Michael,' she whispered. 'Where are you?'

She copied the photo onto a new document and added the words, *Missing – Have You Seen This Man?* and her mobile number.

If he was here, no doubt he'd be telling her it was a crazy idea; she'd be leaving herself open to all sorts of nutters ringing her up. Nutters, she could deal with.

She groaned as she stood to switch on the printer, her body protesting at being in position for so long. The movement made the baby stir and she put her hand to her stomach as she felt a sharp kick in the ribs. Jill walked slowly up the stairs, her hand at the small of her back, and switched on the shower.

When she came back down the stairs twenty minutes later, dressed in loose grey trousers and a Lycra top that stretched over her belly, the printer was still whirring away. Jill picked up the pile of A4 sheets, and looked at the image of Michael.

She stared at it for a long time, as if she might find an answer in his eyes, then slipped the sheets into a cotton shopping bag and set it on the table. She peeled a banana and cut it into slices on a plate, then arranged the slices on a piece of bread and bit into it. It was a struggle to eat it, and she had to force herself to swallow every last bite.

When she'd finished she walked through to the hall and slipped her feet into the trainers that lay in their usual spot by the door. They felt loose. Seeing as bending to fasten the laces tighter was practically impossible, they would have to do, she thought, as she picked up her handbag and her bag of posters. She grabbed the denim jacket that was slung over the bannister. She needed to get going, now.

Jill headed in the direction of the town, planning in her mind the best route to take. It was slow progress; she stopped in every newsagent, shop and café that was open. She told each bored shop assistant, each harassed waitress the same story. They took her poster, promised to display it.

Her feet ached and her bladder was bursting as she stood outside a café on North Bridge and watched as the waitress brushed the sweaty pink fringe from her eyes and pushed the poster under the counter. Jill wanted to run back in and shake her. Tell her how important it was. Ask her how she'd feel if it happened to her. She didn't though. She just walked on.

38

It was early afternoon when Jill walked into the rear entrance to Marks and Spencer on Rose Street and headed for the Ladies. Thankfully, there was no queue and she sat down heavily on the toilet and leaned forward, closed eyes resting on her clenched fists.

As she washed her hands, she glanced at herself in the mirror. Her mouth seemed to have turned downward over the last few weeks; deep grooves marked out the route from her lips to her chin. Her cheeks were dry and sore and her eyes looked heavy.

She looked, well, just sad. So sad. It was as if every drop of happiness had been rung out of her. She dragged herself back out onto the street and leaned against the rough stone wall.

The music shop Michael liked, the one he always insisted he'd just nip in for a quick look, and always come out with a bag, was opposite. Her trainers, loose when she had left the house, now felt tight against her swollen feet. She closed her eyes, willing herself to find the energy to hand out the remaining posters. She'd take one into the music shop, she thought.

She opened her eyes and gasped as a wave of dizziness almost sent her to her knees.

'Are you OK, love?'

Jill turned to see a woman, maybe in her mid-sixties, looking at her in concern. Jill nodded, letting the woman take her elbow. She was suddenly too choked to speak. This tiny gesture of kindness was almost too much.

'It's just, well, you don't look it. Maybe you need to sit down. Tell you what, why don't I buy you a cup of tea?'

Jill opened her mouth to protest; she had so much still to do. The bars would be opening soon and she wanted to get to them before they filled up and the staff were too busy to take notice of her.

But instead she allowed the woman to steer her into the Rose Leaf Café, and into a window seat. She watched the steam rising from the white china cup in front of her as this kind stranger poured tea from a pot. The older woman lifted up the milk jug and offered it to Jill. Jill shook her head, then watched as the woman poured a healthy glug into her own cup and slowly stirred it.

The woman shrugged off her coat and unwound the silky blue scarf from round her neck, placing both items over the back of her chair. She was wearing a blue sweater, almost the same colour as her sparkly eyes. A waitress placed a plate with a toasted teacake in front of Jill.

The woman opposite her gestured towards the plate. 'You looked like maybe you could do with something to eat,' she said. 'How are you feeling now? It takes it out of you, pregnancy. We like to think we can just go on as normal, but sometimes, our body just says "No". And we have to listen to it, whether we like it or not. I'm Barbara, by the way,' she said, extending her hand.

Jill shook it. 'Jill. I'm fine, honestly. And thank you. This is really very kind of you. What are you, some kind of fairy godmother or something?'

Barbara laughed as she shook her head. 'Don't be daft. We should look out for each more, I think. Everyone's so busy these days, rushing about, full of importance. I think sometimes, people are just in the right place, just when they need to be. And anyway, I was a nurse for a long time. It's part of who I am, looking after people.'

Jill looked down as her eyes filled with tears. She sniffed and rubbed her face. 'Sorry.'

'Don't apologise. That's another thing about being pregnant. Your emotions are all over the place.' She leaned forward and patted Jill's arm. 'Although you do look as if you've got the weight of the world on your shoulders.'

Jill shrugged. 'I'm just having a bad time, at the minute.'

'Do you want to talk about it? I'm not being nosy. And I know it's not the done thing, talking to strangers. But sometimes, it helps, I think, to talk about things. Not bottle everything up.'

She sat back and took a long sip of tea. Jill tore off a piece of the teacake and chewed it slowly, watching as Barbara lifted the pot and refilled both of their cups.

'I don't know where to start,' Jill said. She lifted one of the sheets of paper from her bag. It looked pathetic, she thought now. Desperate. It was the kind of thing people did when they lost a cat. 'This is Michael. My partner. Father of my child.'

39

As Jill sipped tea with a stranger, Michael looked up from the TV as Anna came into the room.

'Hi,' she said. 'How are you?'

'Fine,' Michael replied. He picked up the remote control to turn the TV volume down.

'I've had a really crappy day at work. I'm so glad to be home.'

'What was so bad about it?'

'Oh, never mind about that now, I just want to forget about it. I thought we'd have a little fun.'

Michael shifted across the bed and sat up on the edge of it. They'd fallen into a routine, if she was home, of watching TV together. If she was around at teatime, they'd watch *Pointless* – a programme he'd not even been aware of a few weeks ago, but was now strangely addicted to – followed by the news. If she got back later in the evening, they'd watch a drama or movie.

He picked up the control, ready to look for something to watch. He'd recorded *Rear Window* earlier. Maybe she fancied watching that.

'Not TV, not tonight,' she said. She took the control from his hand and switched the TV off. She was holding the iPod again, and plugged it into the speaker. He didn't recognise the music; it reminded him of the background noise they played at his dentist's surgery.

Michael frowned. 'What do you mean then?'

Anna smiled as she reached into the pocket of her jeans and pulled out a long strip of silky fabric. Her hand slipped into the other pocket and drew out another, identical piece.

'No, Anna,' he said. He thought he knew exactly what she had in mind.

'Oh, come on. Where's your sense of adventure? It'll be fun, I promise.'

'It's bad enough having a chain attached to my leg, without being tied up as well.'

'Now come on. You know the chain is just a temporary thing. I want nothing more than to have you here, unfettered, out of this room and with me properly. But it's just a precaution, just for the time being. Anyway, enough about that. You're spoiling the mood. Just lie down on the bed.'

Michael shuffled across and sat up against the headboard. She moved towards him, then knelt on the bed and took one of his hands gently into hers. She lifted it and kissed his palm, then slowly wound the soft fabric around his wrist, again and again. She pulled his arm up behind him and tied the loose ends around the one of the wooden slats of the headboard. Michael pulled against the cloth but there was no give.

'Come on, Anna. I'm not really up for this, whatever it is you've got planned. Just untie me; we can watch a film or something.'

She looked at him and gave a tiny shake of the head, then moved to the other side of him and started the process over again.

He attempted to pull his arm away then stopped resisting and watched as she carefully wrapped the fabric, smoothing out any wrinkles and leaving herself just enough length to tie a tight knot. Despite himself, he could feel the stirrings of arousal. He'd always had a thing for tying or being tied. You had to completely give yourself over to the other person. Trust them. Jill was never keen; she hated the lack of control. And that was fine. But it had been a long time and–

'There,' Anna said, sitting back and admiring her handiwork. 'And now, this.'

She took a black, fabric eye-mask from her back pocket and placed it over his eyes, reaching around the back of his head and adjusting the elastic. It caught on his hair and he rubbed his head against the pillow to move it.

Blindfolded and bound, Michael felt a sudden rush of fear as he remembered first waking up at Anna's; the terror of not knowing where he was or what had happened to him. He could hear his breathing, shallow and panicked, and feel the prickle of sweat on his forehead.

'Relax,' Anna whispered. He heard her zip opening, followed by the sound of something – her clothes, he assumed – dropping to the floor. He felt the mattress move as she climbed onto the bed beside him. He tensed as she laid her hand on his thigh.

'I'm just going to lie with you,' she continued. 'You just need to calm down, and enjoy it.'

Michael shivered as she pulled up his t-shirt and laid her hand on the bare flesh of his stomach. She laid her head on his shoulder. The inability to see or touch had sent his other senses into overdrive. Her breath was warm against his neck as she nuzzled close to him. The rustle of the bedclothes was overly loud as she shifted her body closer to his. The heady, floral scent of her shampoo seemed to fill the air.

'Just because we can't have sex – and we really can't, it's still too soon – doesn't mean we can't enjoy each other, does it?' she said.

He gasped as she moved closer, brushing her lips against his, then taking his lower one between hers and sucking gently on it. She climbed on top of him. Thoughts of the massage she had given him sprung into his mind. This time, though, she wasn't wearing knickers. He could feel her, soft and wet against his skin.

'Jesus, Anna. What are you trying to do to me?'

'Ssh.'

Michael rubbed his head against the pillow, desperate to dislodge the mask from his eyes and look at her properly. He felt the brush of flesh against his face; soft and warm – her breast, he realised. He felt the inside of her mouth as she took his fingers inside, one by one, slowly sucking and biting them. He cried out as she slid her hand up inside of his t-shirt and twisted his nipple, hard, between her fingers. Then her hands were moving again, down towards his waist, and then under the waistband.

'I don't want to turn you on too much,' she said.

Michael could feel his erection straining against his shorts. His breath caught in his throat. 'It's a bit late for that, isn't it?'

'See how good we are together, Michael?'

She leaned towards him and pulled the blindfold upwards from his eyes. He blinked at the sudden light. She was still astride him, and she snaked her hand between her own legs now. He watched, mesmerised, as she touched herself, her eyes closed and a look of blissful concentration on her face.

She looked up suddenly and leaned forward, then deftly untied his right wrist. He flexed his fingers against the numbness then moved his hand down towards her.

Anna shuffled further down his thighs, just out of reach of his fingers and placed her hand back between her legs. Michael pushed his own hand down inside of his shorts and grabbed his cock. She rested her free hand lightly on top of his; he could feel the heat from it even through the fabric of his shorts. He cried out as he came. Seconds later, he heard her shudder and gasp as she did the same. She slumped onto the mattress beside him, and, breathing heavily, turned onto her side and curled up against him.

Michael looked down at her face. He felt dizzy and disorientated. Anna's face was flushed, and there was a faint smile on her lips.

'I told you,' she said softly. 'I told you we'd have fun.'

40

Barbara took the sheet Jill offered her and nodded. 'Nice-looking man,' she commented. 'Kind eyes.'

Jill smiled through her own swimming eyes.

'Yes, they are aren't they? And he is kind. Generous. Thoughtful. I'm not trying to make him out to be some sort of saint. I mean, he does all the rubbish stuff as well. Dirty clothes scattered about the house, toilet seat left up. Forgets to ring when he's had a pint too many. Sorry, I'm waffling. I'd give anything for his dirty socks and wet towels at the minute. I don't know where he is,' she said, her voice breaking.

Barbara tucked a strand of her short blonde hair behind her ear. Jill noticed she had tiny gold studs in her ears, and a stack of worn, gold rings on her left hand. She took in the pale, pearly gleam of her polished nails.

Jill tugged at her top, noticing a toothpaste stain on the front. What a sight they were, she thought. This glamorous lady, co-ordinated to within an inch of her life, sitting with this scruffy, tearful woman, who looked more than a little bit crazy.

People would think Barbara was one of those do-gooders who took homeless people for hot drinks. Barbara leaned forward onto her folded arms.

'Anyway, I'm sure you don't want to hear this,' Jill said, suddenly embarrassed to be opening her heart to a complete stranger. 'I'm sorry– '

'Don't apologise. I don't mind listening.'

'Well, he... he just didn't come home one day. He went out to work one morning – before I'd even woken up – and just didn't come back. I know, you're probably thinking what everyone else does. That he's got cold feet – honestly, if one more person mentions cold feet, I'll... well, I don't know what I'll do. It's just better not to speak to anyone, I think. I'm sick of everyone having an opinion, or thinking I'm mad. I don't think I can take another pitying look. I... I just miss him so much. I just want him to come home.'

Barbara shrugged. 'One thing I've learned, Jill, is not to worry about what people think. And I'm not here to judge you. You can tell me whatever you want. Leave bits out, make bits up. Or just drink your tea and let me enjoy your company for a while. It's up to you.'

She sat back and picked up her cup. Jill copied her. Her hand shook as she raised her cup to her mouth. The feeling of warmth in her mouth and down her throat was comforting.

'The thing is,' Jill said, plucking at the white cotton tablecloth. 'I know myself how ridiculous it all sounds when I say it out loud. But sometimes, you just know, don't you, that something isn't right?'

Barbara nodded and passed Jill another tissue.

'Nobody believes that he's missing. Not one single person. They don't think it's strange that he would just vanish into thin air, telling no one and taking nothing with him. I know. I know in here,' she tapped her chest. 'I know that he wouldn't leave me. Leave us.' She put a hand to her stomach, spreading her fingers wide as the baby shifted position.

Barbara frowned and carefully placed her cup on the table. A waitress appeared with a fresh pot of tea and filled both of their cups.

'How long is it since he went? And have you been to the police?' Barbara asked.

'He's been gone for three-and-a-half weeks. And yes, I went to the police almost as soon as he disappeared. I thought at first that they were going to help me; they asked loads of questions, wanted all kinds of documents, details about where he went, where, who with. But... they've lost interest. They think everything points towards the fact that he just decided to leave. Chosen to disappear, walk right out of his own life. Apparently a lot of people do that, according to one of their leaflets,' she said bitterly. 'They think I'm stupid, that I need to move on, get over it. I can't. Not until I know what's going on. And now, I've found out he was keeping some... some family stuff from me, that for some reason he didn't want to share.'

Barbara raised an eyebrow as she lifted her cup again. Jill shook her head.

'I've found out he has a brother. Michael has a brother, who he's never mentioned to me. Not once. And I'm trying to understand his reasons, but it's hard. It's all so hard. Nothing seems to make sense at the moment.'

'Families can be funny things. You know what they say – you can choose your friends. Presumably you've tried the rest of his family? And his friends?'

'As far as I knew, there was no family. One distant aunt, and that was it. I've been in touch with everyone I can think of. Even people he hasn't seen in years. I found a whole pile of business cards and rang or emailed the contacts on every single one of them. I've walked the streets, thinking I can find him if I just look hard enough. I even thought about ringing a private investigator. What's the point, though? They wouldn't believe me either.' Jill paused and looked at Barbara. 'I realise this all sounds ridiculous.'

'Not at all. When Ken – that's my husband – died, I used to go to the club he drank in, and the golf course he was a member of. I went to the betting shop he sometimes used, just in case I could catch a feel of him. As if he'd be in the air, somehow. I didn't wash his pillow case for months. I wore his jumpers around the house. You don't have to talk to me about ridiculous. It's funny what grief does to you.'

Barbara opened her navy leather bag and reached for another tissue. She dabbed delicately at the corners of her eyes.

Jill nodded. 'It took me three weeks to change the bedclothes; I only just did it the other day,' she said. 'And I've sat for hours watching his DVDs, just to feel closer to him.' She shook her head as she thought of the episodes of *24* she had watched. He'd been obsessed by it, ages ago, and had sat up half the night because he needed to watch *'just one more.'*

'So,' said Barbara interrupting her thoughts. 'What are you going to do now?'

'I don't know. Give these out in as many places as I can.' Jill gestured at the bag of posters. 'Keep looking. Keep ringing people, in case he's turned up somewhere. Call the hospitals, again, in case he's lying somewhere in a coma. And in the meantime, get prepared for the baby. I just feel so helpless.' She put her face in her hands.

'It's like...,' she paused, trying to find the words. 'It's like being in limbo. I can't move on, eat, sleep properly. Time keeps ticking away. I just feel that I have to do something. Does that even make sense?'

Barbara nodded and squeezed her arm. 'Don't give up hope, love. Sometimes it's all we have. And no doubt you're probably sick of hearing this, but you have to think about your baby. When's it due, anyway?'

'In five weeks. It feels like no time at all.'

Barbara nodded. 'I remember when I had my children; you think nine months is forever. And then, the time flies. And once the baby is here, it flies even faster. You feel like one minute you're giving birth, and the next you're buying a school uniform. I take it you're on maternity leave?'

Jill nodded. 'I haven't been able to think about work since all this started. I haven't been back since the day he disappeared. They've been really good about it at work. Although they probably just realised I'd be no use whatsoever just now. I have to go in a few days, to fill in some paperwork. I'm dreading it. I feel as though everyone will have been talking about me.'

'What do you do?'

'I'm a civil servant. Although I'd always thought I'd take a few years off. That was the plan anyway. Who knows, now? What about you, do you work? You said you were a nurse, didn't you?'

'I was, yes, but I've been retired for a good while now. I worked a lot with children. I loved it. But you have to know when to stop. I was getting too old.'

'So,' Barbara continued, as she reached into her bag and produced a pen and a tiny notebook, 'It looks as if we both have a bit of time on our hands. Here,' she said, tearing off a page after she finished writing and handing it to Jill. 'That's my number. Ring me if you want to chat or have a moan. We could meet up again, if you like. Just don't think that you have to be alone. And don't worry, I'm not some crazy old woman trying to worm my way into your life.'

Barbara stood and pulled on her coat then began wrapping the silky scarf back around her neck.

'Now you take care of yourself. And that baby.'

Jill swallowed down the lump that seemed to have lodged in her throat. 'Thank you. Really, thank you so much.'

Barbara stood up and picked up her bag. She reached forward and squeezed Jill's arm. 'Ring me any time. Don't worry if it's late. I don't sleep well. Take care, love.'

Barbara lifted her hand in a wave as she headed for the door. Jill waved back. Some people were just so kind. She stared at the number, written neatly in a curly script, then tucked the paper away into her purse.

Jill sighed and headed to the bathroom. As she washed her hands, she looked at her reflection. Her face was pale and her hair was sticking out at angles. She rummaged in her bag and found an elastic band. She pulled it around her hair, wincing as it caught on her thick curls.

I need to go home, she thought. She left the café and walked along to the end of Rose Street. She would come back tomorrow, start again. She would need to print off some more posters anyway.

She considered waiting for a bus and then abandoned the idea and instead climbed into the back of a taxi. She gave her address and leaned back on the leather seat. The tea sloshed uncomfortably in her stomach and the smell of diesel fumes from the driver's open window made her mouth flood with water. She breathed deeply through her nose, waiting for the wave of nausea to pass.

The roads were quiet, a lull before the rush that would come later, as children were collected from school and workers escaped for the day.

Her sickness passed as the cab pulled into the street. She paid the driver and walked up the path to the front door. As she opened the door, it felt like an empty shell. The place that had always been her sanctuary, her haven.

It didn't look the same, or feel the same without him here. It didn't even smell the same. She couldn't believe she used to complain about the heavy scent of the deodorant he used, or the smell of the kippers and curries he loved to eat. She'd give anything for a whiff of them now. Or to trip over a pair of shoes he'd left lying about.

Jill leaned against the bannister, trying to muster up the energy to climb the stairs. She dragged herself up and lay, fully clothed, on the bed, reaching across to the place where he should be. She hugged Michael's pillow towards her and buried her face in it. She sobbed and sobbed, until it was soaked through and she was asleep.

***

Michael shifted across the bed and opened his eyes. He was alone in the room again, but the small bedside light was on and he squinted against its glow. He propped himself up on one elbow as he noticed the note attached to a brown paper bag on the bedside cabinet.

'*Sorry I had to dash away,*' it read. *Had to get to work and didn't want to wake you. Thought you might be hungry after earlier. Enjoy! A x*'

Michael opened up the bag and found a large sandwich – bacon, with slices of avocado and tomato, between thick slices of granary bread – inside. He sat up, kicked off the covers, flicked on the TV and started to eat.

He suddenly realised that he couldn't work out whether or not he still hated her.

41

A few days later, Jill waited at the bus stop at the end of the road. The bus was on time, and she sat down heavily, grateful to have a whole seat to herself. She'd considered driving into town, but the thought of going into the office was bad enough without the additional stress of finding a parking space.

She felt thick-headed – if it hadn't been months since she last had a drink, she'd swear she had a hangover. She rested her hands on her bump. It felt lower and heavier; as if the baby was getting ready to be born. It weighed around six pounds now. The size of a melon.

According to the book, the baby could open and close its eyes. Eyes that were surrounded by eyelashes. Jill wondered if they'd be thick and dark, like Michael's. They were annoyingly long, the type no amount of mascara could replicate. He'd watch her, dying hers, or putting on false ones for a special night out, and shake his head in wonder, as he often did when he discovered some new aspect of female maintenance.

She'd forgotten he was gone, just for a few seconds, when she'd stirred awake that morning. She leaned across and stroked the sheets, reaching for him. The bitter disappointment she felt made her gasp.

Jill looked up as the bus stopped and a young woman wheeled her bright red pushchair on. From where she was sitting, Jill could see the baby's tiny rosebud lips, sucking gently even as it slept. The woman leaned forward and stroked its cheek.

Jill felt her eyes clouding over and looked down at her hands, twisted in her lap. She wondered if that baby looked like its dad. She wondered if she'd have to introduce their baby to Michael by showing it photographs of what he used to look like. Before he disappeared. The thought of it was unbearable. Never knowing how he aged, how he changed over the years.

As she'd told that lady, Barbara, the other day, she'd been dreading this, her first time in the office since the day Michael had disappeared. A month ago. A whole month. She'd deliberately chosen a Friday – it was always a quieter day, with people taking leave to extend their weekends, and most of the part-timers having finished for the week.

Still, she felt sick, her stomach in knots, as she typed in the security code and walked through the door. She wanted to turn and walk right back out again, and was thinking of doing just that when Helen from the office next to hers came bustling in behind her, clutching a Sainsbury's carrier bag.

'Jill!' she exclaimed, in her loud, grating voice. 'Lovely to see you! How are you? OK I hope. You're looking well. Sure it's just one in there?' She pointed at Jill's stomach, laughing at her own joke, and headed off along the corridor, without waiting for a reply.

Jill let her walk ahead and turned into the Ladies. She leaned against the sink unit, breathing deeply. You can do this, she told herself. Go in, do what needs to be done then leave. It would all be over within an hour.

She blew her nose and smoothed down her hair. She had a long-overdue appointment to get it cut later on. She should have had it done beforehand, so she didn't look quite so wild and crazy.

'Hi,' Christine said as Jill walked through the door. She was as immaculate as ever, in swishy black trousers and a long cream top. She fiddled with the gobstopper-sized beads around her neck.

Jill smiled, feeling guilty that she'd returned so few of Christine's calls and texts. It was just so much easier not to talk to anyone, no matter how well-meaning, how understanding they were. Everyone had their own ideas, their own opinions. What was it her friend Kate had said when they'd last spoken? *'Hasn't he made it obvious? That he doesn't want to be found?'*

'Hi,' Jill replied. She looked around the office. Steph and Margaret, the two admin assistants, looked up and smiled, quickly looking back at their screens in unison. They'd never been that conscientious before, Jill thought. Obviously been having a good chat about me.

'Come through,' said Christine, beckoning her into the private office that took up the end of the room. Jill sat while Christine tilted the blinds, obscuring them from the view of the rest of the staff.

'So, how've you been?' Christine asked.

Jill shrugged and tried to speak. Her lips felt rubbery and her throat tight. 'Sorry,' she said, as the tears started to flow down her face.

'No need to apologise. No news, I take it? I've rang you a few times – well, more than a few times. I guess you didn't want to talk.'

Jill took a handful of tissues from the box Christine offered and wiped her face.

'I'm sorry. I'm just such a mess. I couldn't face talking, or seeing anyone. I don't seem to be able to face anything really. Maybe I should just accept it, like everyone seems to think. Resign myself to life as a single parent. I don't know.'

'Don't talk like that, Jill. Things will sort themselves out, I'm sure. And I bet you need this like a hole in the head.'

Jill laughed through the tears. 'Yes, coming in here wasn't on my list of things I really wanted to do. Had to do it sometime though.'

They looked round as Jackie, the HR Manager, knocked and then opened the door. She was clutching a thick manila folder and a black manual. She placed both on the desk and turned her cool gaze towards Jill. 'Jill,' she nodded.

'Hello, Jackie,' Jill said, looking at her. Not a hair on her head dared to be out of place. She was wearing a silky, dove-grey blouse, tucked into the waistband of her expensively cut trousers. Jackie tapped her manicured nails onto the paperwork.

'Better get on, eh? Lots to get through.'

Jill sat as she quoted laws and rights, telling her what she could and couldn't do, what was expected of her.

'So that's clear, then?' Jackie said, standing and smoothing non-existent creases from her trousers. She gathered up the sheets and the fat reference manual and walked out of the door.

'Is it just me, or does the temperature drop ten degrees when that woman walks in the room?' said Jill.

Christine smiled. 'The Ice Queen. She knows her stuff though. And that seems OK, doesn't it? For you?'

Jill nodded. They'd agreed that her maternity leave would start in a couple of weeks. She'd take some holidays up until then. And the sick note she'd got from the doctor a couple of weeks ago would cover the rest of the time she had off.

'Yes, of course. Jackie was really helpful, actually. I'm so grateful I don't have to come back in here, trying to pretend things are normal. I'd be no use anyway.'

'It might help, you know,' Christine said. 'Having something to take your mind off things? A reason to get up and get dressed on a morning?'

'Maybe. But I couldn't face it. You saw how those two out there could barely look me in the eye when I came in. I can't stand the thought of everyone having an opinion, wanting to tell me what they'd do.'

Christine nodded. 'Whatever you think is best. Anyway, you need to have a rest, before that baby comes. I remember spending an entire fortnight lying on the sofa watching black and white movies and eating toast. It was bliss. I had Peter running around like a slave, fetching me this and that... anyway... sorry. You don't really need to hear about that, do you? Just... just take care of yourself. OK?'

'I will. I promise.'

Christine moved forward and embraced her. Jill hugged her back, her eyes filling with fresh tears, then picked up her bag and headed out of the door.

'I'll call you. We'll meet up for a coffee soon,' Christine said.

Jill nodded and headed back along the beige-painted corridor, with its familiar stains on the carpet, the same old posters on the wall. She hurried out of the building, desperate to be away before she bumped into any other familiar faces.

'Jill, wait.' She turned to see Jackie hurrying along the street towards her. Jill felt her heart sink. Maybe she'd made a mistake and was coming to tell her she had to come back to work after all.

'What is it? Did I forget to sign something?'

'Sign? No, no, nothing like that.' Jackie ran a hand over her face before she continued. 'It's just, well, it was all business in there. I wanted to tell you that I understand. What you're going through, I mean.'

'You do?' said Jill. So the Ice Queen had a heart.

'Yes. When I was pregnant with Alice, Chris... well, he left me. Just upped and left. So, I, I just wanted to tell you that I know how you're feeling. It does funny things to men, sometimes. Pregnancy, I mean.' Jackie patted Jill's arm, her face flushed. 'I just wanted to tell you. Anyway, better get on.'

Jill stood and watched as Jackie headed back into the office, where she seemed to spend most of her waking hours. Jill wanted to shout after her, point out that Michael hadn't actually left her.

And yet, standing there, rooted to the spot, as life went on around her, she wondered if maybe she was right. If what everyone else thought was a truth she needed to wake up and face for herself.

42

As Jill stood in the street, watching Jackie head back to the office, Michael was watching Anna unpeel the lids from the foil cartons she'd placed on a large white plastic tray.

'I know it's a bit early in the day for an Indian, but I thought we could have a takeaway together before I have to go back to work. I hope the food's still warm enough.'

She had come into the room just after Michael had finished watching the lunchtime news. The rich, spicy aromas had made his stomach growl, and he sat up, eager to eat whatever was on offer.

More often than not, when she was working through the day, she'd leave him a colourful salad, or a thick, chunky sandwich, in a cool-bag, with a yoghurt or some fruit.

'Thanks,' he said, as she handed him a plate, laden with rice and two different curries.

'I thought we'd share, is that OK?' she said.

He nodded and lifted a forkful of one of the dishes to his lips. It was hot and spicy; a Madras. The other dish was a bright red Tikka Masala.

They ate hungrily, the silence broken only by the ripping of naan bread or the crack of a poppadum being snapped in two.

They generally ate one meal a day together, when Anna's shifts allowed it. Michael sat on the edge of the bed and Anna on a folding chair she'd brought to the room.

She had readily admitted that her culinary repertoire was pretty basic and unimaginative, and that she was no great cook.

But he never went hungry – there was usually toast and cereal for breakfast, lots of salads and pasta and rice dishes, normally made with a sauce from a jar.

He ate what she gave him, without complaint. This was the third time she'd brought takeaway food – there had been pizzas one night, eaten while they watched back-to-back episodes of *24* on Sky, and a Chinese another time.

'I'm sorry I have to go out again,' she said. 'I'm doing another double shift today. It's a bit of extra money though – it'll come in handy.'

For a second, Michael felt his heart plummet. More hours alone in this room. He filled the time when she was away; he read, watched TV, showered, dozed. He had discovered programmes he'd not previously known had existed, and read more books than he had in years.

But she worked so much of the time. He wondered when she had time to do all the other stuff, all the plans she seemed to make. In a weird way he'd come to admire her skill at planning and at scheming, even when so much of it was directed against him and Jill. He also admired her for finding time to work out as much as she obviously did. She used to run, he remembered. She must still do something – she couldn't have a body like that without serious effort.

'Why don't you watch television?' she said, leaning towards the bed and switching it on with the remote control. 'Wait until I'm back before you watch any more of *24* – I don't want you getting ahead of me.'

A couple of times, she'd pulled up the table-football set and challenged him to a game. He'd thought he'd win easily, but she was remarkably good at it. She'd also given him a couple of puzzle books, but he'd put them on the bookshelf, practically untouched.

He took the control from her and started to flick through the channels. He settled on a quiz show.

'It's a month today, you know,' she said as she gathered up the plates and containers and stacked them on the tray.

'What is?'

'Since we've been back together. A whole month.'

'I'd sort of lost track of time.'

Watching the news usually kept him aware of the date it was, but still, with his erratic sleeping patterns and the lack of natural light, it was easy to forget what day it way. And whilst she'd replenished the magazines and added to the books, she'd not once given him a newspaper.

'Not long to go now,' Anna said. 'Before the baby arrives, I mean. My plan is to deliver at thirty-eight weeks, just in case Jill does something silly like go into labour early. It's perfectly safe then, and the baby will be fully developed and ready to be born. I can't sleep, I'm so excited. I still can't believe that in just two weeks, we'll be a family.'

Michael watched as she lifted her hands up to her flushed cheeks.

'There's something I wanted to ask you,' he said. 'Something I don't understand. It's been on my mind.'

Anna crossed her arms and frowned. 'What?'

'I don't understand why... why you went ahead with it. The abortion, I mean. Why didn't you keep the baby, if you were so keen to? You said I talked you into it, but surely, if you'd really wanted to–,'

'It's quite simple,' she cut in. 'A baby needs its dad. And you made it quite clear, back then, that that wasn't going to happen. You've got to give a baby its father. It needs to be part of a family.'

'But–,'

'There's nothing more to be said about that. Anyway, I'll have to get going.'

He remembered the prickle of unease he'd felt, back then, when she first mentioned settling down. When she told him she'd never felt like this before, and how maybe they could move in together.

But that wasn't what they were about. It was about excitement, fun, not knowing what she'd suggest they got up to next. But was it though? He had to admit, she was like an addiction. Thinking about her had made his heart beat faster, his stomach twist and turn. He had known what she was like; dark and complicated and exciting. Yet still he'd been drawn to her. Maybe *because* of what she was like.

It wasn't as if she even seemed the type to want to settle down. And then, the baby. It had terrified him, the thought of being tied to her – to anyone – like that. It had been a relief, he thought guiltily, when she'd agreed to an abortion.

He watched as she folded her chair and placed it at the back of the room, then picked up the tray and headed for the stairs.

'Right. That's me sorted. I'll have to get going now. I'll be late back, sorry.'

'Wait,' he called, as she started to walk out of the room.

She turned, frowning. 'What is it?'

He licked his dry lips. He didn't know what to say. The thought of being stuck alone in this room for hours was suddenly unbearable. He needed some company. Another human being breathing the same air as him. He said the first thing that came into his head, and the words shocked him as they left his mouth.

'Don't go.'

She turned back towards him, eyebrows knitted together.

'I... I'm not feeling great,' he lied. 'I think, I dunno, maybe I'm going to be sick.'

'Lie down and let me have a look at you. It can't be the curry – you've only just finished eating it.'

Michael lay, holding his breath, as she leaned close to him and laid her cool palms on the pale, bare flesh of his stomach. He felt an unexpected flip of desire at her touch.

'It feels OK, no swelling or anything,' she said. 'And it can't be your appendix. You had that out years ago, by the look of it.'

He shivered as she ran a finger along the faded pink scar. He'd almost forgotten about that. He must have been what? Nine or ten?

He remembered having a fortnight off school and being allowed to watch loads of TV. And comics. His dad had bought him comics on his way home from work. His mum would fuss around him, bringing glasses of orange squash and bowls of ice-cream. Vanilla. The only flavour he liked, even now.

It had been summer, and Stuart would come home, his face pink and freckled from a day in the sun, gloating about how he'd been to the outdoor pool after school.

'I'll get you something for the sickness,' Anna said, her voice bringing him back with a jolt.

Michael listened as she hurried up the stairs and unlocked the door. A few minutes later, she reappeared.

She popped two white pills from a blister pack. 'Here, these should help.'

Michael dragged himself up to sitting, his back against the pillows, and swallowed down the pills that he knew would do nothing for what he was really feeling with a gulp from the water bottle she held out to him. She stood over him, frowning and running her index finger back and forth along her top lip.

'I really need to leave soon, if I'm going to get there in time. I've got a clinic at the surgery this afternoon. Maybe I should ring in sick,' she said, placing a hand on his brow. 'I'm never off sick, though. In fact the last time I took sick leave was when... well, you know.'

Michael closed his eyes. No matter how desperately he craved her company, he couldn't bear another conversation about their past.

'You should go,' he said. 'I'll just sleep it off. Go. I'll be fine.'

She lingered at his side, then cupped his face in her hands and kissed him on the forehead.

'If you're sure.'

He nodded, sure he could still feel the imprint of her lips on his skin.

Michael listened to her footsteps on the stairs, the rattle of the keys as she opened and then locked the door. The creak of the floorboards above his head.

He was alone. Again. He understood now why solitary confinement was a punishment.

If anyone was going to find him, it would have happened by now. He'd watched the programmes. He'd read the books. They always said something about the first forty-eight hours. Panic slammed at his brain.

And what if something happened to Anna? If she died in a car crash or something? They'd find him here, or what was left of him, years from now. He kept the TV volume low, or read in silence, listening for the creak of a floorboard or the rattle of a key that would confirm she was back in the house. Only then could he relax.

Michael switched off the TV, rolled onto his side and pulled the covers up to his neck. He closed his eyes and set about waiting for her to come home.

43

Later that afternoon, as Michael dozed away the hours until Anna's return, Jill walked to the car, clutching the folder full of notes and with Elizabeth, the midwife's, caution that she must take care of herself still ringing in her ears. A watery sun was breaking through the clouds.

She took off her jacket and laid it on the back seat, then squeezed into the driver's seat of the car. Four weeks. Only another four weeks to go.

She closed her eyes and swallowed, leaning back against the seat. The thought of giving birth on her own, without him there... it was driving her insane. She gripped the steering wheel and took a deep breath.

The first antenatal class had been the previous week. She'd barely heard a word that was said; just sat, staring at the clock and counting the minutes until she could escape from the room full of couples, holding hands and smiling, nodding over leaflets and laughing as a midwife and trainee bathed a pink plastic doll.

She hadn't thought for one minute that she'd be the only one on her own. Where the hell were all the single mothers that the press never stopped going on about? No doubt that's what the rest of them thought she was – just another statistic.

Just let them think what they want, she thought. It wasn't as if she'd be going back. She'd just have to figure out for herself how to recognise a labour pain and change a nappy.

She'd never imagined herself pregnant, when she was younger. When they were kids, Louise always had a kid or two in tow. She'd knock at neighbours' doors, asking to take their babies for a walk in their prams. They'd always let her. People did in those days.

Not like now, when even the most innocent request had to be treated with suspicion. Louise used to carry a doll around, one of those that looked freakily like an actual baby. Their mum had bought her a little cot to put it in and everything. Molly, she called it. Or Milly.

Not Jill, though. She couldn't remember actually having a doll. Not a baby one anyway. She'd had a couple of Barbies, because she liked cutting their hair and getting them ready for their dates with Ken.

She'd never even thought of herself as maternal. She wasn't one of those women who clucked and cooed when someone brought a new baby into the office.

Not like Christine, who'd stand there, fingers twitching, until the baby was placed in her arms. Her face would soften and she'd gaze lovingly at the child. It didn't matter whose it was.

Jill had never imagined that she would actually want a baby, let alone be pregnant and close to giving birth. It wasn't that she'd been sure she didn't want kids; just that she hadn't given it enough thought to be sure that she did.

It was funny, how things changed. As soon as they'd decided to try for a baby, it had taken over her life. When it didn't happen the first month – which, she knew, would have been more than a miracle – she felt bone-crushing disappointment. She'd had tears in her eyes as she stood in the queue in Boots, buying tampons.

She'd been so sure. Her jeans had felt tight and she'd felt sick. It became a mission, even though she knew it was likely to take at least six months. A year even.

Still, she'd bought zinc for both of them, because she'd read that it was important for fertility. Folic acid, for her. Loose boxer shorts, for him. She'd remind him not to sit with the laptop actually on his lap. Gave up caffeine and alcohol.

Those enormous glasses of Pinot Grigio were far less of a miss than she'd expected. She'd find herself slowing down and taking a detour through the baby department in John Lewis, tracing her fingers across kitten-soft blankets and holding up perfect, miniature outfits. She bought baby powder, and secretly sniffed it in the bathroom, like some sort of deranged drug addict.

And then, suddenly, she was pregnant. Part of that elite club she'd been so desperate to join.

Before she was even twelve weeks, she'd gone back to that baby department and chosen two outfits. A pink one, with tiny frills across the front, and a blue one, embroidered with boats. Michael had shaken his head and looked at her as if she were mad, but later on, she'd caught him, taking them out of the bag and holding them up in front of him. 'They're so little,' he'd said. 'How can they be so little and actually fit someone?'

They were in a drawer at home, carefully wrapped in tissue. *I really should pack a bag,* Jill thought. She'd have to remember to put in those two little outfits. Overcome with a sudden need to do something, she switched on the engine and pulled out of the surgery car park.

44

Jill drove to Tesco and pulled into a parking bay as close to the door as she could. She eyed up the parent and child spaces, wishing she could use one so she didn't have to waddle quite so far. She collected a trolley, and leaned against it as she made her way into the store.

The baby aisle was huge. She stood, bewildered, in front of the nappies. There were mountains of them. Different brands, different sizes, different names.

She had no idea there would be so much choice. She didn't know where to start. How on earth was she meant to know which ones to buy? She supposed she could ring Louise. That would mean embarking on a friendly chat with her, and she wasn't ready for that yet. And anyway, Louise would relish the thought of Jill needing her advice.

No, she decided. I need to get used to doing things for myself. She picked up a packet with 'Newborn' scrawled across it and started to read the information on the back.

'Your first, is it?'

Jill turned towards the voice and saw a woman younger than her and with a toddler sitting in her trolley, slowly chewing a banana. The little girl stared at Jill and frowned. Even the child knows I'm clueless, thought Jill.

'Yes,' she said. 'It's a bit... overwhelming.'

The woman laughed. 'Just do what I do – get the ones on special offer, or stick with the own brands – they're just as good. And get plenty of wipes. You can never have enough wipes. You'll wonder how you ever lived without them.'

She walked away, shushing her child and removing banana skin from her mouth.

'Good luck,' she called, as she turned the corner. Jill watched her go, then took her advice and picked up the packs of nappies that were on a 'three for two' deal. She walked further down the aisle and found a twelve-pack of baby wipes. She gasped as the baby kicked her as she reached into the trolley to put them in.

It was funny, she thought, how being pregnant made it perfectly normal for people to want to speak to you. She'd taken the bus for years and hardly spoken to anyone, had gone unnoticed in shop queues and on the street.

Now though, it seemed as if every time she left the house, there was someone with a story. Or an old woman wanting to touch her stomach. Jill shuddered. There was something creepy about a stranger wanting to put their hands on you. Just yesterday, she'd jerked away from a woman at the Post Office as she reached out her hand.

And people seemed to be experts at predicting the sex of a baby by the shape of a bump, she'd discovered. It was as if you became public property overnight.

Although it wasn't always a bad thing, she supposed. She probably wouldn't have met that lovely Barbara if she hadn't been pregnant and had a funny turn. She'd rung her the day after they'd met, to thank her for being so kind. They'd texted a couple of times since. It was nice, Jill thought, to have someone to talk to.

When they'd known for sure that Jill was pregnant, and that all those tests weren't flukes, she and Michael had agreed not to tell anyone.

It would be their secret, until they knew that everything was all right, and they'd actually seen the proof, by way of a scan, that there was a baby in there. But Jill hadn't been able to keep it from Louise. And telling her sister didn't count, anyway – how could she keep something that big from her sister? And Michael had confessed he'd told Ben.

Michael had found her weeping one night, sitting on the bathroom floor, feeling bereft at the fact the baby would have no grandparents; that it would miss out on big family Christmases and summer barbecues.

He'd pulled her close and reminded her that it would have a fantastic aunt, in Louise. And they had friends with kids. And anyway, they'd have a whole houseful of their own.

He'd managed to make her laugh, at his enthusiasm. The next day, she'd taken flowers to her parents' graves, and told them her news.

What Michael had failed to mention, though, was the baby's Uncle Stuart. Her hand went to her chest as it occurred to her that Stuart's condition might be hereditary. She shook her head. No, she was *not* going to give herself something else to worry about. And she'd call the care home later, just to see how Stuart was.

Jill paid for her trolley load of purchases, trying not to listen as the girl on the checkout told her exactly how many stitches her sister-in-law had when she gave birth. She loaded the bags into the boot, one hand at the small of her aching back.

It occurred to her suddenly that she hadn't even bought a pram. Something else to do when she got back. She'd have to make another list.

45

Back at home, Jill parked the car and made her way to the front door of the house, laden with carrier bags. She saw a carrier bag hanging from the door handle, a bunch of purple tulips peeping from the top. She put her shopping on the doorstep and looked inside.

As well as the flowers, there was a *Marie Claire* magazine and a box of Maltesers. A yellow post-it note on the chocolates revealed the gifts were from Christine, who was letting her know that she was *thinking about her.*

Jill felt an irrational surge of anger. It wasn't as if she was ill. The anger was quickly replaced by guilt. She should ring Christine. Like she should ring a lot of people, and stop living in the bubble she had created for herself.

Once Jill had laid the last bag of shopping on the hall floor, a sudden pang of hunger sent her to the fridge. She should have bought food at Tesco and not just baby stuff, she thought, as she opened an ancient jar of olives and ate them where she stood.

It took three trips to carry all the bags up to the spare room. Although it wasn't the spare room anymore – it was the nursery, now.

The newly organised paperwork was hidden away in a tall, white filing cabinet. The delivery men had taken pity on her and carried it upstairs for her, even insisting on taking away the cardboard and plastic packaging. They'd brought the flat-packed chest of drawers up for her too. She looked over at the chest of drawers now, feeling a sad sense of pride that not only had she managed to build them, they were actually still standing.

She'd pored over the instructions, following them to the letter. Not like Michael – he'd have tipped all the bits out onto the floor and then spent hours cursing and trying to fathom it out. Even though he always managed in the end, there were always a few bits left over. Those, and a handful of screws that would sit on the windowsill in an old jam jar for weeks.

She ran her hands over the boxes and packages stacked next to her against the wall, the results of hours of nocturnal online shopping. The white wooden cot still needed to be built, but she was beyond that level of DIY now – and anyway, the baby would be in their room (*her* room, whispered a voice inside her head) in the Moses basket for a good few months.

A plastic bath, decorated with tiny yellow ducks, sat in the middle of the room, wrapped in cellophane. There was a car seat, changing mat and a little chair that rocked gently and played lullabies.

Jill had had no idea about the amount of stuff a baby apparently needed. She pulled her eyes away from the beautiful wicker basket, piled high with toiletries and tiny items of clothing. It sat there, releasing that lovely, new baby scent, with a tag tied onto one of the silky ribbons. *Love from Louise, Peter, Charlotte & Harry x.*

Jill hauled herself onto her knees. She'd put everything away into the drawers. Tidy up a bit. And then, sort that bag out. She really must make that list. She put her hand to the wall, attempting to pull herself up.

She still forgot, sometimes, that she didn't have a waist anymore, and could no longer bend in the middle. She smiled sadly as she looked at the room full of stuff. *I don't want to be doing this on my own,* she thought. *Why aren't you here to share this with me, Michael?*

An unexpected wave of dizziness almost sent her back to her knees. She leaned against the wall. Maybe I should lie down for a bit, she thought. I can tidy up later. She gasped as she felt a sudden gush of wetness between her legs. Oh no, she thought, Christine was right. I'm wetting myself already.

Mortified, she walked to the bathroom and stepped out of her trousers. It took a few seconds for her to register what the bright red on her thighs was, and what it meant. Her hands flew to her mouth.

'No, no, no,' she whispered as she tipped the contents of her bag onto the landing floor, searching for the leaflet with the emergency number that she'd kept meaning to save onto her phone. When she found it, her shaking hands meant that it took her three attempts to dial it properly.

Don't panic, the nurse said. Although it was a miracle she had even understood a word Jill said, she was sobbing so hard. She'd obviously been trained to speak in that calm, soothing voice. The sound of it made the panic rise even further. She asked if there was anyone who could bring her.

'No,' Jill wept. 'There's no one.' Jill told the nurse she would get a taxi, right away. That she lived close by and could be there in fifteen minutes.

She started to shake as she folded a facecloth and pressed it into a pair of knickers and pulled them, and a clean pair of black yoga pants, on. The she sat on the bottom stair, clutching her stomach and counting the minutes until the taxi arrived. The driver obviously realised that she didn't want to talk, and drove her in silence to the maternity wing at The Royal.

46

An Indian midwife, her long, dark hair plaited down her back, took Jill's details and led her to a room. She handed Jill a scratchy blue gown and told her to strip to her underwear and put it on.

'Try not to worry,' the midwife said, squeezing Jill's shoulder as she turned to leave the room. That small gesture of kindness made her cry again. Although she didn't think she had actually stopped. She sat on the edge of the bed and stared at the floor.

'Please,' she whispered through her tears. 'Please, please, please. You have to be OK.'

The doctor was a small, olive-skinned woman. She pushed her rimless glasses up her nose and worked silently. It was too quiet. As Jill lay there in the darkened room, being checked, scanned and probed, nobody said a word.

The nurse had turned the screen away from Jill's view and carefully positioned a box of tissues next to the bed. Tears slipped from Jill's closed eyes, running down her face and pooling at the base of her neck, as she prepared herself for the news they were about to give her.

As the room lit up, Jill opened her eyes. The doctor raised her head and looked at Jill. She fiddled with her glasses as she spoke.

'I don't think there's anything to worry about,' she said.

'But the blood...'

'I know, it's scary,' the doctor said. 'There's often absolutely no explanation as to why something like this happens. It can just be a random blood vessel, and it might have happened anyway, even if you weren't pregnant. We'll keep you here overnight, though. Just to keep an eye on you.'

Jill lay there, stunned, clutching at the sheet across her lap. The doctor peeled off the rubber gloves she'd been wearing and placed the box of tissues next to Jill on the bed. She strode across the room and put her hand on the door handle.

'I'll get a nurse to come and sort you out,' she said, before she disappeared out of the door.

Jill nodded. She couldn't speak. She lay back on the pillow, staring at the ceiling and stroking her stomach.

'Hello, love,' said the nurse as she came into the room. Her shoes squeaked on the floor as she came closer. 'I'm Pauline,' she said, handing Jill another tissue. 'Now, don't get yourself so upset. It's a shock, I know. Sometimes we just have no idea why these things happen. Funny old thing, the body. Now, is there anyone I can call for you?'

Jill shook her head and blew her nose. 'No, there's no one.'

'OK, no problem.'

The nurse picked up a folder of paperwork, and bent her head to read through it. Jill watched as she ran a hand through her wiry grey hair and then slipped the clipboard into its holder at the end of her bed. She must be used to this, Jill thought; women on their own.

'I'll get a bed sorted on the ward, get you up there and more comfortable. You just rest and I'll be back soon. You'll need a jab, just for the baby's lungs, in case he or she makes an early appearance.'

'Oh, OK.' Jill started to pull up her sleeve.

The nurse smiled, her eyes twinkling. 'The jab's not in your arm I'm afraid.'

'Oh. Oh, I see. Actually, would it be OK if I call someone? Can I use my mobile?'

'Yes, yes, of course, go ahead. I'll be back in a few minutes.'

She handed Jill her bag and helped her raise herself up the bed. Jill scrolled through the numbers, and dialled.

'Hi, Barbara?' she said, when the phone was answered almost before it had started to ring. 'It's Jill.'

'Jill! I was going to ring you today. I thought you might like to meet up, have a coffee and a chat. I'm so glad you called. How are you?'

'Well, I'm fine, I suppose. I've... I've just had a bit of a scare and needed to hear a friendly voice,' she said.

Barbara listened as Jill told her where she was and why, making sympathetic noises and assuring her that these things happened more often that she'd think.

'So,' Jill said. 'I'd love to meet up for a coffee, if that's OK with you.'

'Of course. Tell you what, why don't you come round to mine later in the week? Get yourself home tomorrow, have a proper rest – don't even get out of bed – and then come to me on Friday. I'll do a bit of lunch.'

Jill reached for her bag from the chair by the bed and scrabbled for a pen. She wrote down the address on an envelope. Then, exhausted, she lay back, hands on her stomach, and willed the baby inside her to stay where it was, and grow strong. To wait until its dad was home.

47

As Jill drifted off to sleep in her hospital bed, Michael lay in his bed at Anna's. It was dark; really dark. He couldn't see, but he felt she had tied his wrists with something, just slightly too tight, then covered his eyes with some silky fabric, knotted at the back of his head. His hair had caught in the knot and he pushed his head back against the headboard to try and free it.

He was aware, suddenly, of the weight of her body on his thighs as she straddled him. So she was naked now, he thought, as he shifted so he could rub against her.

They remained there, in silence, as she stroked and touched him, and then when he couldn't contain his desire for a second longer, she freed his wrists and he pulled her towards him, and they moved from the bed and stood, facing each other. He massaged her breasts with his hands and rubbed her stiff nipples between his fingers, then bent and took them in his mouth, one by one. Then he spun her around so she was facing the wall, and kissed the back of her neck, his hand trailing down through her pubic hair. And then suddenly, she was on all fours on the floor, ready for him. He was ready to explode as he entered her, hard, from behind. He gripped her sides and pulsated with her. She gasped and he cried out–

'Wake up, sleepyhead,' Anna said. 'You were calling out in your sleep. Were you dreaming?'

Michael opened his eyes, sticky with sleep, and tried to fight the feeling of disorientation. She'd put on the light, a small, clip-on thing that attached to the headboard. He blinked at the brightness and rubbed a hand across his face, then quickly crumpled up the bedding to hide his very obvious erection.

But he should have known. Nothing got past her.

'Pleased to see me, are you?' she said, a smile playing on her lips.

He felt the heat in his face as it flushed red, but he said nothing, just shook his head and looked down at the bedcovers.

'Were you dreaming about me?' she whispered softly into his ear. 'You know, men often reveal a lot about their true selves in their dreams. You shouldn't just write them off as dreams. Sometimes what you see when you sleep is what you really want. Your deepest hopes and desires.'

He looked at her properly for the first time since he'd woken. She was wearing one of her tight, strappy vests and was sitting up at the other side of the bed. Her hair was slightly messed up and she was rubbing her eyes with her knuckles in an almost childlike fashion. It still took him by surprise, how completely beautiful she was. It dawned on him that she had been asleep beside him.

Michael cleared his throat. 'Anna,' he said. 'What are you doing?'

She frowned. 'What do you mean?'

'Here. What are you doing here, in bed with me?'

'Oh,' she said. 'I see, sometimes I just can't resist getting in with you. I always come to check on you, before I go to bed.'

Michael shivered. He'd had no idea that she'd been in bed with him – apart from when she'd woken him with a blow-job, of course. But sleeping next to him? That was a whole different level of intimacy. *As intimate as sharing meals and wine and watching movies together?* his mind whispered.

'Anyway,' she said, 'stop changing the subject. Tell me what you were dreaming about, Michael.'

She reached under the covers and traced her fingers across his bare thighs, then reached into his shorts and took his cock in her hand.

'Was I doing this?'

'Or this?' she continued, climbing on top of him.

He made a half-hearted attempt to push her off and pull away, but she was too strong, and he knew that once she had her mind set on something, there was no going back. She lifted her hand and licked it slowly, without taking her eyes away from his. When she had lubricated her palm with saliva she took hold of him again.

Her stroke was gentle at first, then harder. She looked at him the whole time. He breathed out through his mouth, almost panting as her grip got tighter, almost too tight. Unable to hold back, he slipped his hands under the straps of her vest and pulled them down over her shoulders. He pushed the fabric down, until the vest lay, crumpled, around her waist. She wasn't wearing a bra, and he placed his hands on her breasts. They were warm to his touch, the nipples dark pink.

He arched his back and thrust into her hand. She cupped his balls in her free hand and massaged them gently, never breaking her rhythm. Michael groaned, then cried out as he came.

Michael lay back on the bed, gasping. Anna lay beside him. She took a tissue from the box beside the bed and wiped her hands.

'You liked that, didn't you? You don't need to answer; you look a bit worn out. I *knew* you were dreaming about me. I could tell. You don't even need to admit it. Just wait until we actually have sex. It'll be so, so good. Just like it always was.'

She smiled, showing her even white teeth, and snuggled under the covers. 'It's lovely isn't it? Being together, I mean. We always had such a connection, you and I.'

He opened his mouth to disagree, but found that he couldn't. He couldn't deny the connection. He closed his eyes and thought, for a moment, of the passion, the longing. Of having sex over and over again until the only thing that made them stop was the complete, delicious exhaustion. But that had been in a very different time and place from where they were now, he told himself.

He glanced over at her, nestled down on the pillow. She looked almost sweet. Innocent. Not like a woman who he'd once watched strut around a room naked, a short leather whip in her hands. He shivered at the memory. It ended with her on top, her favourite place to be. On top and in control. He rubbed a hand over his face.

'You're very quiet,' she said.

'It was just a surprise, waking up in the middle of the night and finding you here.'

He lay back and squeezed his eyes shut, too aware of the cold, wet patch on his shorts. He lay next to Anna in silence as his mind buzzed, full of long-forgotten details, creeping in from the corners of his memory and torturing him. Lying on the grass in the park with Jill, and then going to the pub for icy gin and tonics in sweating glasses. Stumbling home, arms around each other.

48

Michael's mind flashed to the night he'd first met Jill. It had been at a party, at someone's house. He couldn't even remember whose. He'd watched her, laughing and waving a very full glass of white wine around, so it slopped onto the carpet as she became more and more animated. He'd known, right away, that he had to speak to her. It had scared him, the urgency he'd felt.

He'd known that he couldn't let her leave without getting her number. He'd tried to ignore the feelings, and swallow them down with another drink. He'd been smoking a cigarette in the garden when she'd come over and asked him for a light. And that had been that.

Words, thoughts, memories – there was too much going on in his head. He forced his eyes open and let the images fade. All he could see was this room. His cell.

'I just thought it would be nice, sleeping with you,' Anna murmured now. 'It seems silly, me up there on my own and you down here.'

She pushed a hand through her hair and propped herself up on one elbow.

'Do you remember, one night when we were lying together, you described us as soulmates. I've never forgotten that, you know. Even when all the... horrible stuff was going on. We're meant to be together, you and me.'

Had he ever actually said that, Michael wondered? Maybe he had, drowsy from booze and sex. But now he knew what a soulmate really was. And this woman lying beside him was keeping him away from his.

'Anyway, we should get some sleep. Not long to go now before it'll be our baby waking us up in the night,' she continued. 'It'll be here before we know it. I've got some things for you to read. I'll bring them in later, leaflets and stuff about fatherhood. And we really must start thinking about names. I'm so excited, Michael. I can't believe it's nearly time.'

Michael got out of bed and made his way wordlessly to the bathroom, chain dragging after him. He sat on the closed lid of the toilet, elbows on his knees and his head in his hands.

Minutes later, he climbed back into bed beside Anna. And when she turned to him, and stretched her leg across both of his, and laid her head on his chest, he didn't pull away. He lifted his left arm and held her, until they were both asleep.

49

Jill eased herself further up the bed and stretched. She felt like she'd slept, properly, for the first time in ages. Maybe it was because, for once, she wasn't alone. It was ridiculous, she thought – taking comfort from a plastic-covered bed in a noisy ward.

The ward was designed for six. Only one bed, other than Jill's, was taken. The woman occupying it had pointedly pulled the curtain around when Jill was brought in. Jill could hear her now, moaning about the breakfast options on offer, as if she were a guest at The Ritz, and not an NHS ward.

'I don't do dairy. Or white bread. Urgh, no I couldn't eat that,' she was saying. A member of staff retreated, rolling her eyes. The woman's voice started up again as she embarked on a phone call, telling whoever it was she was speaking to how terrible it was and listing all the items they must bring in for her.

Jill put her hand to her stomach as she felt a kick in her ribs. She had to get her act together. Maybe she needed to accept that it might just be her and the baby for a while. Just until Michael came back.

'Breakfast.'

Jill looked up as a nurse, a young black woman with braided hair scraped back from her face, placed a tray on the wheeled trolley next to her bed. Flabby white toast, a plastic tumbler of warm orange juice and a mini box of cornflakes with a jug of milk. Maybe the woman across the way was right. But, she had to eat; from now on, she would do everything she was supposed to do, to the letter. She raised the bed up with the button at her side and set about clearing the tray.

Jill had barely finished when the tray was whipped away, and replaced with a cup of tea so stewed it was as if the teabag had lived in it for days. She leaned back against the pillows and watched as beds were changed, bins emptied and the floor washed.

Her eyes felt so heavy. A kindly nurse had brought her a pile of magazines. She barely had the energy to pick one up, let alone read it. Finally, at around eleven, a doctor came bustling in, a flock of juniors at his heels. He picked up Jill's chart without speaking to her and flicked through the sheets, then stared at the monitor attached to her belly for a few seconds. He nodded and detached the wires.

'Feeling OK?' he said.

'Yes, I feel fine,' Jill replied. 'Totally fine.'

'Good, good,' he said, already turning away. 'We'll have you off home then.'

Jill slowly sat up and lowered her feet to the floor. She drew the curtain and got her clothes from the cupboard next to the bed.

In her panic to get to the hospital, it hadn't occurred to her to bring a change of clothes or a wash-bag, so she was forced to pull on the trousers and top she'd arrived in. She was wearing a pair of papery, hospital-issue mesh knickers. She quickly pulled her trousers up over them so she didn't have to dwell on how hideous they were.

'Where do you think you're going?' a nurse said, peering around the curtain, her booming Irish accent stopping Jill as she attempted to lean over far enough to lace up her shoe.

'The doctor said I could go home. I'm fine, honestly.'

'I don't care how fine you are, you can't be discharged until someone comes to collect you.'

'But there's no one I can call. I promise to get in a taxi and go straight home.'

The nurse folded her arms and fixed her eyes on Jill, apparently about to deliver a lecture. Jill prepared herself to tell this woman that she was going home, and she couldn't stop her. Both women turned their heads at the sound of raised voices in the corridor.

'What the–,' the nurse said, turning on her rubber soles and heading out of the door.

'It's fine,' a familiar voice said. 'I just need to check she's OK.' Jill racked her brain, trying to put a face to the voice.

'Elizabeth,' she exclaimed, dredging the name of her midwife from the depths of her brain, as the woman dashed over to her bed, her face creased with anxiety.

'How are you? I came as soon as I heard. Is everything OK? Is the baby all right?' She picked up the paperwork at the end of Jill's bed and started flicking through, running her fingertip down the page and nodding. 'Hmm,' she said. 'Everything seems fine. What a fright you gave me.'

Jill watched as Elizabeth read. She was taller than Jill remembered. She fiddled with her necklace, a pretty silver knot on a chain, as she checked through the medication Jill had been given.

What a nice woman, Jill thought. To be so concerned that she would dash in to see one of her patients like this.

'I'm absolutely fine,' Jill said. 'I was just trying to explain that I don't need a babysitter and I can take myself home.'

'You really need to be more careful. You need to appreciate how precious that baby is.'

She shook her head, and Jill was sure she saw wetness in her eyes. That woman, she thought, really takes her job seriously. Although maybe that's how it was when what you did for a living was a matter of life and death.

Jill couldn't imagine what that was like – the worst that could happen in her job was a document being filed in the wrong place. A document that it was unlikely anyone would ever look at again anyway.

'It's so nice of you to be so concerned. Really, though, you don't need to worry. I have every intention of going home and doing nothing.'

'I'll take you.'

'What? No–,'

'I'm not taking no for an answer. I need to go to the surgery at some point today, and I can take you on my way.'

Jill realised that there was no point arguing. And if she agreed to a lift from Elizabeth, at least she could avoid another showdown with Nurse Battle-axe.

'Well, if you're sure,' Jill said.

She bent down awkwardly to finish tying her shoe, then stopped as Elizabeth gently pushed her hands aside and took over, resting Jill's foot on her knee as she tightened the laces.

'Er... thanks,' Jill said. She put her feet on the floor, and almost lost her balance.

Elizabeth caught her and pulled her upright with one hand. She seemed so strong and capable, Jill thought. She hoped she would be on duty when it came to delivering the baby.

Jill picked up her handbag and followed Elizabeth out of the ward. She stood to one side while Elizabeth spoke to the nurse at the desk.

'Right,' Elizabeth said. 'That's everything sorted. These agency nurses can be a bit bossy. Only on duty for a few days before they disappear to another hospital, so they like to make their mark.'

Jill nodded, and breathed a sigh of relief as they reached Elizabeth's car. It was a Volvo, huge and ancient, but Jill sank gratefully into the passenger seat, placing her bag on her lap and pushing a clutter of coffee cups to one side with her foot.

'You really do need to be more careful, Jill,' said Elizabeth as they pulled out of the car park. 'Don't take any risks, look after yourself properly. It's a lot for the body to deal with, growing a baby.'

Jill looked across at Elizabeth. Her dark, serious eyes were fixed on the road, and Jill could see a frown creasing her forehead, as if she were trying to solve a particularly troublesome problem. Jill knew she meant well, but she was starting to get on her nerves.

'I appreciate your concern, I really do,' Jill said. 'But I wasn't doing anything out of the ordinary when this happened. They said at the hospital that it was just one of those things, it could happen anytime, for no particular reason. And I am being careful, honestly.'

She looked down, not wanting Elizabeth to see the flush rising in her cheeks as she thought of the furniture she'd built and the bags of shopping she'd carried. Who else was going to do it, if she didn't do it herself?

'Hmm, well, make sure you are,' Elizabeth said. Jill glanced across at her. She was chewing at her bottom lip. 'Which way now?'

Jill directed her to her street. As they pulled up outside the house, Jill unfastened her seatbelt and turned to thank Elizabeth, but she had already turned off the engine and opened her door.

'I want to make sure you get inside and into your bed. I'm not leaving until you do.'

Jill thought about protesting, but then nodded. It was easier to just agree with her and let her in. The sooner she did that, the sooner the midwife would leave. Jill fumbled in her bag for her keys and opened the door.

'Come in,' she said, dropping her bag at the door and slipping off her coat. She hung it over the bannister and walked through to the kitchen.

'Not so fast. You need to be in bed, resting for a day or two. Take it easy. Really, you should be taking it easy till baby arrives.'

'At least let me make a cup of tea. Herbal, of course,' Jill said, turning on the tap and filling the kettle. 'Can I make you one? I don't know how anyone manages to drink that stuff they offer you in the hospital – it's like tar. I hope you take a flask when you're on duty there.'

'What? Oh, yes. Actually, we have our own kettle. You sit down, I'll make the tea.'

Jill found herself being steered into one of the kitchen chairs, while Elizabeth opened cupboards, pulling out mugs and teabags. She poured the boiling water into the mugs and placed one in front of Jill.

Jill closed her eyes, remembering Louise doing much the same, all those weeks ago. She'd ring her tonight. They needed to clear the air. She was going to need all the support she could get, soon.

Elizabeth was standing, gazing out of the window. 'Do you like living here?'

'Here? Yes, I love this area. I've always lived on this side of town. I used to live in a flat not far from here. And then my aunt died a few years back, and left me some money. I'd always wanted one of these houses, and, well, that helped me to get this place. It's quiet, and still close to town. Good schools, nice neighbours. I can't imagine living anywhere else, now. What about you, do you live around here?'

'Me? No, I'm more of a country girl. I like the peace and quiet. Anyway, let's get you upstairs.'

Jill stood, resigning herself to the fact that this woman was staying until she was under the duvet. She picked up her cup and headed along the hall and up the stairs, Elizabeth at her heels.

'I'll just get changed,' Jill said, as Elizabeth followed her into the bedroom.

'OK. Can I use your bathroom?'

'Of course, it's just along there.' Jill pointed towards the bathroom door.

Perched on the edge of the bed, Jill pulled off her clothes, grimacing as she balled up the hospital-issue disposable knickers and shoved them in the bin. She was desperate to shower, and brush her teeth. She'd do that later, when she was alone in the house. She pulled on a pair of pyjamas and sat on the edge of the bed. Elizabeth tapped on the door.

'Come in,' she said.

Elizabeth walked into the room. Get into bed, and no getting up other than to eat or use the bathroom. I'll be off now and I'll see you for your appointment next week. And if anything like this happens again, call me. Don't ring the switchboard; it'll take ages to get through the push two for this, three for that nonsense. Here's my personal number in case you can't get me on my work mobile.'

She handed Jill a page from a notebook, with both numbers written neatly on them. 'Now, do you promise to get into that bed and stay there?'

'Promise.'

Jill pulled back the covers and climbed into bed, relishing the feel of the cool sheets on her bare feet and arms. 'And thank you. It was really kind of you to bring me home like this. I've been having a rubbish time lately. You've probably realised I'm on my own just now. Michael, my partner, he's... well, not here.'

'I see. Right. You have to look after the baby though. Just remember, it's a gift, having a child. The greatest gift there is. I'll see you soon.'

She hesitated by the door, that frown clouding her features again.

'Bye, then. Can you just pull the door closed on your way out? It'll lock itself.'

'What? Mmm, yes, no problem.'

Jill listened to her footsteps on the stairs. She heard her walk into the kitchen, and the clatter of dishes. She was even washing up. At last, the front door closed.

Jill lay back on the pillow and sighed, glad, for once, to be alone. It was nice the woman was so committed to her work, but she was a bit over-the-top. Jill wondered if she had children of her own, and if she was as protective of them as she was of the ones in her care. Still, she thought as she drifted off, it's nice that she cares so much.

50

Later that afternoon, as Jill slept fitfully, Anna dashed down the stairs and stood next to the bed, where Michael lay reading a new James Patterson novel she'd brought him a couple of days ago.

'Guess who I saw today?' she said breathlessly. Michael looked up from his book. She was still wearing her coat and was bouncing up and down on her toes, clutching her hands together. There was something different about her, he thought. It wasn't the clothes, and she hadn't changed her hair; it was still in a dark, glossy bob. It was her lips, he realised. Instead of the usual, neutral-coloured gloss, she had painted them a bright, orangey-red.

'I don't know. Someone famous? Why don't you tell me?'

'Don't you even want to try and guess? Honestly, Michael, you're no fun. Jill. I saw Jill. At your house.'

'*What?* What the hell do you mean, you saw Jill?'

'Calm down, Michael.'

'How on earth... you must be mistaken. How would you even know what she looks like? I don't understand–'

'I think you need to take some deep breaths. She was in the hospital. I picked her up and took her home.'

'What the fuck do you mean? You really saw her? How come? And *why* you? And *why* was she at the hospital? Is she hurt?'

'She's fine. Stop worrying about her. Do calm down. More importantly, the baby's fine too.'

'But why–'

'Michael, aren't you listening to me? Jill was at the hospital, and I took her home. I gave her a lift.'

'How do you even know where our house is? You can't have... what have you done to her? What have you done? If you've hurt her –'

'Hurt her? Don't be ridiculous. I looked after her actually. You should be pleased.'

'PLEASED? But you don't even know her! Have you... have you been following her or something? How–'

'Don't be ridiculous,' Anna cut in. 'Don't you think I have better things to do with my time than follow Jill about? Look, she was in hospital because she had a bit of a scare, and they needed to keep her in overnight. It was nothing to worry about, like I said, the baby's fine. Michael, you really do need to calm down. It was nothing. There was a bit of blood, and she panicked. It happens more often than you'd think. She's at home in bed now, right as rain. I watched her get into bed myself.'

'*BUT WHAT WERE YOU DOING THERE?* It can't be just some crazy coincidence.'

Michael felt as if he could hardly breathe. He tried to gulp down a breath into his aching lungs. 'Please. Please... *tell me.*'

Anna fixed him with a cool gaze. 'There's nothing more to tell you. Like I said, she's fine. And I was there because I was checking her notes and saw that she'd been admitted to hospital yesterday.'

'I don't get it,' he said, but feeling a little calmer now. 'What notes? I don't understand how you ended up looking after Jill.'

Anna frowned. 'I'm *her midwife*, Michael.'

Michael just stared, horrified, at Anna. He could feel his blood beating a hammering pulse in his temple.

51

'I've told you this before, I'm sure,' Anna said, casually. 'I've been doing shifts at the surgery, so I could make sure she was reallocated to me. I have to make a living, to support us, Michael; or have you forgotten that? I thought it was for the best, so I could keep an extra special eye on the baby.'

'What? Of course you didn't tell me you were Jill's midwife! Don't you think I would have remembered something like that? Does that mean you've seen her, while I've been here? How often? Are you sure she's OK?

'So many questions,' Anna said coolly. 'I've seen her a few times. If you'd just listen to me and stop behaving like a madman, I'll tell you everything you want to know. I see Jill at the surgery, where I signed up for some extra shifts. I thought it was better that way; I could keep an eye on her. I looked at her records when I got there today, like I always do, and when I saw what had happened, I went to the hospital, and then I took her home. Like I said, she's fine. Now will you please stop going on about it. I'm beginning to wish I'd never mentioned it.'

Michael dug his nails into the fleshy parts of his palms and tried to breath. This could not be happening. He should be with Jill. He needed to protect her, look after her. She was going through all this on her own.

When had he stopped thinking about her, every minute of every day? His stomach twisted greasily as he realised he'd barely even thought of her that day until Anna had mentioned her. Anna had got under his skin and he'd let her. He'd got too used to being here, just like she'd said he would.

I can't bear this, he thought. *I really cannot bear it.* He squeezed his eyes shut, a silent scream filling his head. The pressure inside his head was unbearable. He thought it was going to explode. He felt the overwhelming need to be away from here, running at full pelt away from Anna and towards Jill.

'Anyway, I've got something to tell you,' she said, as she tore open a parcel then stood and placed two new towels on the end of the bed. 'Some really exciting news. When I was checking the records I saw some very interesting information. It's a girl, Michael. We're having a girl.'

Michael stared at her. He imagined wrapping his hands around her neck, choking the life from her. He couldn't believe she'd been meeting with Jill all this time, pretending to take care of her, when really she was plotting to steal her baby.

'What?' he said.

'I checked the records. It's on there, even if you don't want to know. I thought it would be better to find out. So we can get the right clothes and things. Paint the nursery.' She clasped her hands together. 'A girl, Michael. Our own little girl.'

Michael watched her, as she gazed off into the distance, her face flushed and a smile playing on her lips. He'd been adamant that he and Jill didn't find out the baby's sex. *There aren't many surprises in the world, baby. Let's make sure this is one,*' he'd said.

Jill had agreed. It would be the best surprise ever, she'd said. And now? Anna had spoiled it. She really believed that her twisted vision of the future was real. *And what if it was*, he thought?

'It's very nice though, the house,' Anna said as she walked to the bathroom clutching a tube of toothpaste and a bottle of liquid soap. 'I couldn't live there, it's too close to town for me, but it is lovely. You're very quiet. What's the matter?'

Michael shrugged. 'Nothing.'

Anna turned to face him. 'Oh, I meant to ask you, what do you think of this?'

Michael frowned, not sure what she was talking about. 'What do I think of what?'

She moved, so close that their noses almost touched. Without thinking, he almost leaned forward and met her lips with a kiss.

'This,' she said, licking and then pointing to her lips. 'Does it suit me? I don't think it does. There were loads of them in the bathroom cupboard, maybe I should have chosen another colour.'

His mouth fell open. 'No, you're wrong, it does suit you,' he murmured. He'd had a go at Jill so many times about those lipsticks. The lipsticks that lay in a messy heap and threatened to spill out every time he opened the cupboard door. He swallowed as Anna searched in her bag and took out a small compact. His stomach twisted at the thought of Jill's lipstick on Anna's lips. She peered at her reflection in the mirror.

'I'm glad you like it, but I'm not so sure myself I like it. Not really me, is it?' she said, wiping her mouth on the back of her hand. 'A bit too teasing, really.'

Oh, and I suppose you don't go in for teasing, Michael thought.

Anna turned back to Michael as she delved once again into her pocket. 'I brought something else as well.'

She held a small bottle of Chanel perfume in her hand. Coco. Just like the one Jill kept for nights out.

'Here, have a sniff,' she said, dabbing it on her wrist and then holding it under his nose. Michael turned his head, not wanting to smell Jill lingering on Anna's skin. He didn't trust himself to speak. 'It's not what I normally go for, I must admit,' she continued. 'And Jill didn't really look as if she'd been bothering with perfume.'

He felt something break, deep inside him. Knowing how close she'd been to Jill – she'd been in their house, their *home* – he felt something so black that it almost scared him.

'Anyway I'd better get back to work, they'll be wondering where I am. And those babies can't look after themselves! They need me. I know you need me too, Michael. I'll be back soon.'

She walked from the room. Michael watched her leave, waiting until the key turned in the lock before he let the hot tears spill down his cheeks. He felt as if a war was breaking out within his mind. Guilt, fear and uncertainty flew around in his head like bullets. And he didn't know how to win the battle.

5 2

Two days after Elizabeth had taken her home and forced her into bed, Jill stopped the car outside of Barbara's house and switched off the engine. This part of Edinburgh wasn't as familiar to her as her own area, and she'd got lost a couple of times as she navigated the streets. It was an usually warm day for May in Scotland, and she felt hot, flustered and uncomfortable.

She undid her seatbelt and reached over into her bag, her stomach grazing the steering wheel, to check her phone. No calls, no messages. The crank calls she'd got since she given out the posters had stopped now.

At first, there'd been a glut of them, claiming to know where he was, or worse, offering to come round and replace him. She shivered. It had turned out to be the ridiculous idea Michael would have said it was.

She sighed, picking up the bunch of yellow roses she'd stopped at a small branch of Tesco to buy, and climbed out of the car. Jill opened the wrought-iron gate and made her way up the path. The house was a red brick semi-detached. A neat patch of lawn was bordered with pale pebbles, and three flower pots sat under the front window.

As she approached the door Jill could see the backs of several photo frames, arranged on the sill. She raised a finger to press the bell on the wall next to the glossy blue door, then hesitated. She felt suddenly nervous. It was one thing sending a few texts, but going to Barbara's home? Maybe she'd been too hasty, too emotional when she Barbara from the hospital. Was she really that desperate to have someone else in her life?

She'd stopped returning the calls from her well-meaning friends weeks ago. She knew even Lisa would try to persuade her that she knew just what Jill needed, which would no doubt be a night out, sitting in a bar or restaurant she had no inclination to be in. Or worse, a night in, where she'd get the girls round and they'd end up glugging wine and telling her about their own troubles.

Jill knew she was being mean. An ungrateful cow. They only called because they cared. They wanted to help, offer company and advice. Sometimes it was the kindest words were the hardest to tolerate. She knew what they were really thinking. That she was crazy and needed to move on, pregnant or not.

And things with Louise were still so strained. They'd spoken a few times on the phone, but not properly. Not like they used to. Even Christine, who always meant well, would tilt her head to one side and look at her with such *pity* that Jill couldn't bear to face her just now. The door opened, startling her from her thoughts.

'Hello, dear,' said Barbara, beckoning her into the hall. 'I saw you coming up the path. Here, let me take your coat.'

53

'Hi,' Jill said, any doubts and nerves she had quickly disappearing at the sight of Barbara's warm, welcoming smile. 'It's so kind of you to invite me to your house. You look lovely, by the way.'

Barbara was wearing a pale green floaty blouse, with a long string of pale glass beads around her neck. They caught the light as she hung Jill's denim jacket on a hook on the wall. Her bare feet, the toenails painted a pearly pink, peaked out from the hems of her cream linen trousers.

Jill looked down at her own outfit of dark maternity jeans and loose cream top and felt instantly dowdy. She put a hand to her ear, wishing she had at least taken time to put in some earrings. And she really needed to reschedule that hair appointment, cancelled when she realised the last thing she could face after her visit to the office was sitting in the salon chair and making idle chit-chat.

'Thank you,' Barbara said. 'That's nice of you to say so. It's such a nice day outside that I thought I'd wear something summery.'

Jill thrust the flowers into Barbara's arms.

'For me? You shouldn't have. They're lovely, thank you. I do love having fresh flowers in the house.'

She beckoned Jill along the hall. 'It's funny, isn't it, when you visit someone for the first time? I just want you to make yourself at home. I'll put the kettle on. And the bathroom's at the top of the stairs. I remember when I was pregnant, I liked to be no more than twenty paces from a toilet at all times.'

Barbara led the way into the living room, gestured towards the sofa and left Jill there. Moments later, Jill heard the clink of crockery and the sound of cupboards being opened.

She looked around the room. Shamefully, she'd expected crocheted placemats and china ladies. Floral fabrics and net curtains. The definition of an older lady's living room.

This was nothing like that, she thought, as she sank into the tan-coloured buttery leather sofa. She could see the right side of the pictures she'd spotted on her way up the path now. One of them showed Barbara and a smiling, white-haired man, and an older picture, obviously her and the same man in their earlier years. Her late husband, Jill assumed.

Another of the frames held a shot of three perfect fair-haired children, laughing as they tried to hold onto a scruffy terrier. Next to it, a wedding photo; a tall, blond man gazing so intently at his slim, dark bride that Jill felt like she was intruding even by looking at it.

A dark wooden bookcase dominated one wall, its shelves jammed with books and trinkets. An ornamental elephant, painted in a rainbow of shiny colours, stood on one end of the mantelpiece, with more photographs and a trio of fat candles at the other. The walls were painted in soothing, creamy beige. Jill could feel the tension slipping from her shoulders.

'You have a lovely home,' Jill said, as Barbara came through the door, carrying a laden tray.

'Oh, thank you. We lived in a bigger house when Simon – that's my son – was young. We moved here when he left home. It was good for us, down-sizing, got rid of a lifetime worth of clutter. We planned to holiday away the money we made. And then Ken, well, he got ill and that put paid to that,' she gazed at the pictures on the window sill for a moment. 'Anyway, enough about me. Let's have this tea. You don't take milk do you?'

'That's right. Black, no sugar, thanks,' Jill said, feeling absurdly touched that Barbara had remembered that small detail.

Jill watched as Barbara busied herself pouring the tea from the teapot into chunky white mugs.

'I got a few bits in,' Barbara said, handing Jill a plate and gesturing towards the scones, pastel-coloured cupcakes and foil-wrapped biscuits. 'None of it's home-made, but you'd agree that was for the best, if you'd tasted my baking.'

Jill smiled, and took one of the scones Barbara offered. It stuck to the roof of her mouth, and she took a sip of scalding tea to wash it down.

'So,' said Barbara, settling into the armchair opposite. 'How've you been?'

Jill shrugged, her throat suddenly tight. 'You know... OK, I suppose. Physically, I'm fine, but...'

Barbara nodded, producing a box of tissues from the shelf under the coffee table and offering it to Jill.

'Good and bad days, I imagine,' Barbara said. 'Or maybe good and bad hours. Mostly bad, though. Mornings when you wake up and think, just for a second, it's all been a dream. Not wanting to eat, not being able to sleep. Wearing the same clothes, for days, because you think, *what's the point?*'

Jill dabbed at her eyes with the tissue. 'Yes. Yes, something like that.'

Barbara smiled, lighting up her twinkly blue eyes. 'And I imagine there have been a few times you've wanted to punch the next person who tells you that life goes on, time's a great healer et cetera, et cetera.'

Jill laughed, startling herself; the sound of it was so alien to her ears these days. 'I've stopped answering the phone. The only people I see are the midwife and the postman. A woman spoke to me in the supermarket the other day and I just felt like turning my back and ignoring her.'

'It's weird,' she continued. 'I just feel like I need to be on my own, thinking about stuff, working it out in my mind. I tell myself I've got so much to do, and then end up just sitting for hours, staring into space. But sometimes I need a bit of company. I feel as if I'm going crazy.'

She sat back, exhausted.

'Well, if you're crazy, then so am I. And so are millions of other people. I know you'll feel alone, like it's you against the world, sometimes. It doesn't have to be like that, you know. When Ken died, I just wanted to close the door on the world. But getting out and about... well, that's what's kept me going, really.'

Jill nodded. 'I know. Sometimes, it just feels easier to be on my own. I get sick of having to explain myself.'

'Then don't. It is what it is. What you tell people is up to you, but it's your business and no-one else's. More tea?'

Jill held her cup out and Barbara filled it up. She took a biscuit from the plate Barbara offered and nibbled the edge of it.

'I was always so independent,' Jill said, wrapping her hands around the mug then taking a sip. 'And then Michael came along. I hadn't really thought about settling down, not properly. I pictured myself without any ties, floating around the world and doing as I pleased. And look at me now. Pregnant and on my own.'

She placed one of her hands on her swollen stomach. 'It just makes you realise you can never take anything for granted. Never relax or get complacent. You just never know what's around the corner.'

She took another sip of tea before continuing.

'It's like, the other day I was driving along the by-pass, and on the other side of the road there was a huge traffic jam. As I got further on, I could see people, driving along, oblivious to that fact that they were about to be stopped in their tracks.

They were probably laughing, singing, thinking about what to have for their dinner. You know that feeling of utter frustration? If only I'd done this, or that? That's how I feel, all of the time.'

Barbara nodded. 'Well, the thing is, life gets in the way of even the best laid plans. And having a child – I know it's a cliché – but it really is the best thing you'll ever do.' Jill watched Barbara's eyes mist as she glanced over again at the gallery of pictures.

'Don't you see them much, your family?' Jill asked.

Barbara shook her head. 'They live abroad. Australia. Simon's a surgeon. His wife, Ashley, she's a doctor too. She's Australian. They met when she was over here doing some work at the hospital. Anyway, they've been away for over ten years now. Don't get me wrong, it's a great life, and brilliant for the kids. I miss them, though.'

'I bet you do. Do you go out to visit much?'

'At least once a year. And they come here, sometimes. Simon's always on at me to move out there for good. It's such a long way, though. And this is my home. I've always liked living in the place where I'm from. Maybe one day. I don't know.'

'It must be hard for you.'

'Oh, it's not so bad. I make the best of it. We Skype and email, so at least I see them. Keeps me young, using all this technology. It could be worse. And I've got plenty to keep me busy here. I work the Cancer Research shop every Tuesday. And I go to a couple of classes at the gym every week. Then there's the book group. And I see my friends a lot. You need your friends, otherwise life can get very lonely.'

Barbara took another sip of her tea. 'I've noticed you've not mentioned your own family. I don't mean to pry, though. Just tell me to mind my own bloody business if you like.'

Jill placed her cup down on the table and shook her head as Barbara raised the pot to offer another refill.

'My parents died. A long time ago.'

'I'm sorry to hear that. Like I said, I didn't mean to pry. I don't want to upset you.'

Jill shook her head. 'It's OK. I was just a teenager. It was a car accident. Dad had picked Mum up from work. She'd only had the job a few weeks; she'd decided to go back to work now that we – my sister and I – were "all grown up" as she put it. It was just a few hours a day in a shoe shop in town, but she loved it. Kept talking about the people who came in and the staff discount she could get us. Not that I'd have been seen dead in anything they sold in there. I thought I was far too cool.'

Jill paused and rubbed her hands across her face. It had been a long time since she had told this story.

'Anyway, another car didn't stop at the lights and... well. Mum died instantly. Dad hung on for a few weeks. Mum had a sister, and I always kept in touch with her. She died a few years ago. And my grandparents all died when we were kids. So my only relative now is my sister. Louise. She's married with two kids, lives near Newcastle. We've not exactly seen eye to eye recently.'

Barbara nodded and Jill continued. 'I think the hardest thing for me just now is that no-one, not even my closest friends, not even my sister, believes me when I say that Michael wouldn't just leave like that. Everyone just assumes that I've been dumped. Urgh, I hate that word.'

Jill leaned forward, hugging herself. 'I mean, I admit it doesn't look great, when you look at the evidence.'

She lifted her hands and began ticking off the facts on her fingers.

'One – he went out one morning and didn't come back. Two – he's taken nothing with him, as far as I can see. Three – no one's heard from him. Four – the police say his cards and phone have been used. I know these things don't sound great. And that's without his secret brother.'

Barbara raised her eyebrows quizzically and sat, listening as Jill recounted the tale of the letter and her visit to Stuart.

'The thing is, despite all of that, I know that he wouldn't leave me. I just know, in here,' Jill placed her palm on her chest. 'And the fact that no one else accepts that is almost as bad as him being away. Almost.'

Jill rested her head back and sighed heavily. 'But ask me to explain what's happened, and I can't. There is no rational explanation. I just know. Sorry, I'm going on and on. I haven't talked this much in weeks.'

She lifted her hands and covered her eyes, dreading seeing in Barbara that familiar pitying expression.

'The thing is,' Barbara said slowly, 'sometimes you've got to trust your instincts. Go with your gut. Me and my Ken, we had our problems. He got into... a bit of bother, when we were younger. His family disowned him; my family just about disowned me. I believed in him, though. Stood by him. So my advice to you, for what it's worth, is sometimes it's good to stick with your instinct. Have a bit of fire in your belly. Sounds to me like you love your Michael a lot?'

Jill nodded and Barbara continued.

'Then maybe, whatever's going on in his mind just now, he needs to know you're sticking by him. Haven't given up. Maybe he's got some unfinished business he's sorting out. Who knows? Sometimes, hope is all we have.'

Jill looked up, tears running freely down her face. 'So you don't think I'm mad then? You don't think I should just accept that he's upped and left, like everyone else seems to think?'

'All I'm saying is trust your feelings, Jill.' Barbara laid a hand over Jill's clasped ones. 'Who knows where all this will end? Who knows, really, what goes on inside someone's mind? I just think you can't give up on what you believe in.'

She stood up and started stacking the dirty cups and plates. 'Now, can I make you a sandwich or something? Or get you more tea? I'd offer you something stronger but I know they don't encourage it for pregnant women these days. Or maybe they do again now? These things seem to change from week to week. I'm afraid I'm a bit out of touch.'

Jill shook her head. 'No, honestly, I'm fine. I'll get going soon; get out of your hair.'

'Stay as long as you like, I've no plans until tea time. Pilates,' she said, standing and arching her back. 'Does wonders, apparently. Although I rather prefer the gin and tonic Muriel and I go for afterwards.'

Jill laughed as she watched Barbara retreat to the kitchen, tray in her hands.

They spent another hour, chatting and looking at photographs. Barbara told her stories of her life as a nurse, and how different it had been in her day. She spoke of the characters she came across in the charity shop where she volunteered, and the bargains she gleaned from the shelves.

When she finally put on her jacket and made to leave, Jill realised that she felt better than she had done for weeks.

'So, I'll see you again soon, then?' Barbara said as she opened the door.

'I'd like that.'

'Good.' Barbara moved forward and touched Jill lightly on the shoulder. 'I'll give you a ring. You take care, now.'

Jill nodded, swallowing down the lump in her throat. She longed to stay there, in Barbara's bright, warm house. But she had to get home. In case there was any news. In case he'd come back.

54

As Jill arrived home to the house, and her suspicions that it would, as usual, be empty were confirmed, Michael felt a warm sensation, close to his face, and then a mouth, so near his that they were breathing the same breath. He gasped as his bottom lip was taken between teeth and sucked gently. And then, a kiss, hard and deep, tasting of mint and salt. The heady scent of perfume caught in his throat. It was the sort of kiss you don't want to end. He felt a rush of desire.

Michael opened his eyes. Anna was sitting cross-legged on the bed beside him, her mouth swollen and red. She had pulled up the t-shirt he was wearing and was trailing her fingers gently across his bare chest, catching the hairs on her fingertips.

'What are you doing, Anna?' he said, sitting up and shuffling across to the edge of the bed, pulling down his top.

A faint smile played on her lips and she laughed softly. 'Oh, don't pretend you weren't enjoying it. You were, I could tell. Remember how we used to kiss, Michael? You used to say you could keep doing it forever.'

She crawled over to where he sat and ran her short nails across the bare skin at the back of his neck. He arched against her, cursing his treacherous body and trying to ignore the feelings stirring inside him.

'Do you remember,' she continued, 'how we used to lie for hours, kissing and touching one another? I loved having sex with you, have I ever told you that? I've never met anyone who made me feel like you did. You were up for anything. You said we were a perfect match. That's the word you used. Perfect. Do you remember?'

'Stop it. Just stop.'

He screwed his eyes shut and gritted his teeth.

Whatever might have been perfect back then – the way they just seemed to fit together; the insatiable need that burned constantly in his belly; the quest to explore and experiment to a degree that was both thrilling and terrifying – was history now. This situation they were in now wasn't anywhere close to perfect.

She moved her hand and pressed her palm between his shoulder blades.

'You're very tense,' she said, as her hand drifted down to his lap.

She stroked him gently, then stood and stretched. The vest top she was wearing rode up, revealing the pale skin of her flat stomach and the lacy edge of her black knickers. Michael looked away.

'Just going for a pee,' she said, heading to the bathroom.

Michael leaned back again the headboard. When she'd told him about her encounter with Jill, about going to the house, he'd vowed that he wouldn't sleep, so that he could stay awake, and stay in control. No more waking up to one of Anna's surprises. But it was impossible. The air in the room was so thick, and he spent so much time sitting or lying on a bed, that he couldn't help but nod off. Lately, he'd slept more than he had in his life.

Michael wasn't even sure what day it was. The only way of knowing was switching the TV on and he couldn't remember if it had been Thursday or Friday the day before. Maybe it was Saturday today. He would have to check. Half of the time, he didn't know if it was day or night; the lack of natural light meant his sleeping patterns were all over the place.

Or maybe it *was* a weekday. In another life, he'd be watching the clock and looking forward to a pint with Gary and Kev. He wondered where they all thought he was – his colleagues, his mates. Jill.

An overwhelmingly feeling of homesickness washed over him. He'd lived in different cities, worked in countries where he didn't speak the language or know a single person, but he'd never felt as lonely as he did now.

He hoped people were looking out for Jill. Ben would make sure she was all right. So would Christine. She had plenty of friends. And of course, her sister would be there for her.

He wondered where Jill was, at that minute. Was she at home, or out somewhere? Maybe she'd be asleep in bed, or on the sofa, watching one of the hospital dramas she loved. He hoped she wasn't alone, feeling as lonely as he was.

'Right,' Anna said, smoothing her hair with the palm of her hand. 'I'd better get ready. I've got to leave for work soon.'

Michael hadn't heard her come out of the bathroom. She bent over at the far side of the bed and picked up the pair of jeans that she must have dropped there. He watched as she slid them up her long, slim legs and over the lacy knickers and did up the zip.

Suddenly, he wanted nothing more than to grab her and feel something, anything, other than despair. He moved quickly from the bed and grabbed her by the wrists then pushed her against the wall, so that he was facing her, their bodies touching, their faces just inches apart. Anna resisted for just a second, her firm, sinewy body pushing him easily away, but then gave in and leaned back against the wall as he forced his tongue between her even white teeth and deep into her mouth.

He drew back, panting. Anna stared at him. The intensity of her gaze was intoxicating. He started to count inside his head, trying to slow his hammering heart. His whole body was trembling.

'That was a nice surprise,' she said. 'And as much as I'd like to continue, I really do have to get ready for work now. I'll be back later though. We can talk more then. Maybe watch a film. Or something.'

Michael slumped down onto the bed. He felt as if the life was draining from him, bit by bit. He was losing his mind, he was sure of it. He needed to see Jill. If he could just see her, everything would be all right. But the feeling that he might never get away, might never set eyes on Jill again, clawed at his brain and twisted his stomach into a knot.

55

While Michael lay on the bed, wondering when, or even *if*, he would ever see Jill again, she was hanging on the phone, waiting for someone to answer.

'Hello,' Jill said as the phone was picked up. 'Could you put me through to Stuart Stanton's ward please?'

'One moment please,' said the receptionist. Jill pictured her sitting there, at her shiny desk, with her glossy hair and perfect nails. She drummed her own chewed fingers on the table as a blast of tinny, classical music filled her ears.

'Hello, Balfour Unit, Deborah speaking, how can I help you?'

'Hi Deborah. It's Jill, Jill Talbot. I don't know if you remember, I came in to see Stuart Stanton about three weeks ago. I was just wondering how he is?'

'Oh, hello, yes of course I remember. How are you? Must be almost time for that baby to make an appearance now, is it?'

Jill put her hand to her swollen stomach. 'Oh, I'm fine. Yes, not long to go now. Less than three weeks, if everything goes to plan.'

'Put your feet up as much as you can, then. Believe me, there's no time for that once junior makes an appearance. Anyway, Stuart. He's much the same. That's as we'd expect, though. He's fine. Nothing to worry about at all.'

'I... I was just wondering if anyone has been in to see him, since I was there, I mean. I know you can't give me any specific details, but if you could maybe just tell me if there's actually been anyone. Anyone at all.'

'Hold on, I'll just get the visitors book. Give me a second.' Jill could hear the muffled sound of voices, some of them raised, as she waited.

'No,' Deborah said, returning to the line. 'There's been no-one. That's unusual, actually. Some of them in here, they never see a soul from the outside world, but Stuart normally has a visitor every few weeks or so. Maybe you'd like to come in and see him again, sometime? I know you'll have your hands full soon, though.'

'Yes, I'll definitely see him again, and soon. I don't think I dare risk a drive down to the Borders at the minute though. I'm scared my waters would break and I'd end up giving birth in a lay-by.'

Deborah laughed. 'It'd make a good story though. You're lucky you can still drive at all; I was so huge near the end, there was no chance I could fit behind the steering wheel. Anyway, if there's nothing else, I'd better go and round this lot up for their lunch. Ring anytime, and like I said, it would be great to see you.'

Jill ended the call. That woman seemed really nice. As if she cared. You read so many horror stories about care homes. She was sure Michael would have done his research, though. He wouldn't have his brother living just anywhere.

Still holding the phone tightly in her hand, Jill walked over to the fridge. The business card she was looking for was held in place by a magnet in the shape of a large black button. She stared at the handset, her fingers hovering over the numbers. She shook her head and dialled quickly.

'Morton,' a voice said, just as Jill was about to hang up.

'Hello, it's Jill Talbot.'

She was greeted with silence from the other end of the phone.

'Michael Stanton's partner? I reported him missing over five weeks ago,' Jill said. Even as she said the words, she could barely believe he had been gone so long.

'Ah, yes. Miss Talbot. Is he back then?'

'No, no, he's not actually. I've still not heard from him. And I found out a while back that he's got a brother. He's in a care home, I didn't know about him. Anyway, Michael normally visits him regularly, and he hasn't been to see him, since he disappeared.'

Jill heard the sound of liquid being slurped, and the thud of a mug being placed back on a desk.

'Look, Miss Talbot, I'm sorry, but that doesn't really mean anything. In terms of him disappearing, I mean. In fact, it makes sense that he cuts himself off from everyone, and not just certain people, if you know what I mean. The truth is, people have the right to disappear.'

'And,' she continued, 'did you say that you knew nothing about this brother? Doesn't that strike you as odd that the man you live with didn't bother to mention that he had a brother?'

'Not necessarily that odd. People also have the right to keep things to themselves, don't they?'

'Indeed they do, Miss Talbot. Indeed they do. Like why they've decided to do a flit and vanish.'

'OK. Right,' Jill said. Why had she expected anything else? 'Sorry for disturbing your tea break.'

She hung up the phone and threw it down on the table. She could picture the snotty policewoman laughing as she slurped her tea, telling her colleagues about this mad, delusional woman who needed to get a grip.

Jill sat, massaging her temples with her fingers, wondering what to do next. She pulled the laptop towards her and switched it on. Minutes later she was reading through the results of her Google search for missing people.

There were good news stories, of course they were. Her mind focused on the other ones, though. Of how sometimes days and weeks turned into years. And if the police couldn't help, what chance did another organisation have? She slammed the screen down then picked up her bag from where it lay in a heap on the floor, and walked from the house.

Jill walked as far as the Post Office at Blackford, then stopped as she saw a bus approaching. She scrambled in her purse for change, then got on and took a seat by the window.

The bus was heading for Cramond, a place she hadn't been for ages. She remembered coming one day with Michael; they'd got the bus then, too, because he said it was more fun than taking the car, and he'd insisted they sit on the top deck, in the front seat.

He'd told her how he used to do the same thing with his grandma, when he was small. He'd pretend to be the driver while Grandma would point out landmarks and peel satsumas for him.

Jill stared out of the window as the streets flashed past. As they got closer to the town centre, a thin woman in a long striped cardigan sat next to her and took a fat novel out of her bag. Jill stared out of the window.

She saw a man sitting cross-legged on the pavement, seemingly oblivious to the policeman and paramedic talking animatedly above his head. People walked around the scene without breaking their stride.

As the route continued into George Street, Jill gazed out at the shops and bars she'd always loved. A group of teenage girls, laughing and tossing back their identical ironed hairstyles as they walked along, looked like they hadn't a care in the world.

Although Jill knew that probably wasn't true. She remembered her teenage years well enough to know there would have been long minutes of anguish as they chose their outfits that morning, and decided whether to curl their hair or have it straight. And they would be worrying that so and so hadn't called them, and what picture they should put on Facebook.

She wanted to jump off the bus, stand in front of them and tell them to enjoy life. Before they grew up and had real worries and responsibilities. Although she imagined that if she did, they'd either give her one of those looks that teenage girls were so good at or tell her where to go. She leaned her head against the window and sighed.

It was almost an hour before she got off the bus at the terminus. She made her way down to the beach, and bought a coffee at the café so she could use their toilet. She looked at her face in the mirror. She was so pale, as if the life had faded from her skin.

She smoothed her frizzy hair back behind her ears and squeezed out of the cubicle that she was sure was normal-sized but felt tiny to her now. She felt like Alice in Wonderland, a giant in a world of tiny spaces.

She walked along the front. It was a warm day, a gentle breeze blowing in from the sea. She sat on a bench and watched as a couple dished out sandwiches and drinks to their two small children, the little boy refusing to remove his cycle helmet and the girl unwilling to relinquish the collection of sticks she'd gathered.

Jill stood, a hand in the base of her aching back, and contemplated walking further along. She suddenly felt a vibration coming from her bag, and she rummaged for her phone, heart racing, just as it did every single time it rang. The screen told her it was Barbara. She smiled as she answered the call, and sat back down on the seat. An elderly man sat at the next bench along, and set about lighting up a pipe.

'Hello, love. How are you?' Barbara asked.

'I'm fine. Just out for a walk. I took the bus down to Cramond. Although I'm heading back soon.'

'You be careful, out wandering about on your own. First babies are usually late, but you never know. Anyway, presuming Junior doesn't make an appearance, I was just wondering if you'd like to meet for lunch tomorrow. I thought we could go somewhere nice, no kids running about. Before your life becomes full of those awful noisy play places and children's meals.'

Jill sat down on a wall. No, not really, she wanted to say. The thought of finding something decent to wear, and sitting in a busy restaurant, surrounded by strangers, was exhausting. And she should really go swimming again. And pack a bag for the hospital.

'That would be nice,' she found herself saying, suddenly realising that seeing a friendly face was more important than all of those things. 'I'd love to. Where shall we go?'

'Leave it to me, I'll book somewhere. About 12.30. Let's meet outside the station. You can get off a bus there, can't you?'

Jill told her that she could. They said their goodbyes and Jill once again lifted herself up into standing position. Meeting Barbara was the one good thing that had happened to her lately.

As she set off back along the path, apple-scented smoke filled the air, and stirred up a distant memory of her grandad, sitting by the fire with her on his lap, puffing away.

It was starting to rain as she stood at the bus stop. Her bones ached and she was desperate to take off her shoes. She wished she could ring Michael, ask him to come and pick her up. Funny, he always moaned when she did that, but she'd give anything to hear him moan now.

The sky had darkened by the time the bus came, and as she stared from the window, the world looked grey and blurry. She wiped away a patch of condensation. Through her little porthole she caught glimpses of the city. Flashes of life, illuminated through the lighted windows of the houses she passed.

A woman, holding a bottle of beer, was talking to an unseen figure, waving her arms about wildly. Or maybe she was talking to herself, Jill thought.

A huge TV hung on the wall of another house, and as the bus pulled in to let some passengers on, the grinning face of Bradley Walsh stared out, as he presented some afternoon game show.

After what seemed an eternity, it was her stop. She got off and headed down the street. A middle-aged woman with a tiny dog on a lead scurried past, shielding the dog with her umbrella.

As she turned the corner, a Sainsbury's delivery van drove past, spraying an arc of water with its wheels. She stepped back, narrowly avoiding being soaked. She pushed her key into the lock and let herself in to the empty house.

56

There was no sign of the rain as Jill walked along Princes Street the following day. The bright sunshine reflected against the shop windows, making her squint and wish she'd brought sunglasses.

She glanced at her watch. She had forty minutes before she was due to meet Barbara, so she decided to kill time by doing some of the chores that were still on her list.

Minutes later, she stood at the rail in Marks and Spencer, looking at what there was to offer in the range of nursing bras. How come they were so *ugly*? She knew they had to be functional, but really?

Jill was standing in the queue at the till, idly wondering if the two bras she'd chosen would be enough, when she saw him.

'Ben,' she called. 'Over here.'

She gave up her place in the queue and walked slowly over to where he was standing. He was in his usual, all-seasons wardrobe of dark jeans and tweed jacket.

'Jill, hi, how are you?' He bent to kiss her cheek. 'You look really well.'

'Thanks, although I'm sure what you mean is really huge. She smoothed down the black tunic top she was wearing. She had reached the stage of pregnancy where her stomach seemed to arrive everywhere minutes before the rest of her. 'I'm OK. Just buying some glamorous mother-to-be underwear then meeting a friend for lunch.'

'Great,' he said, glancing at his watch. 'Actually, I'm on an early sandwich run. Getting some supplies in for a meeting that's likely to go on and on. So... no news I take it?'

Jill shook her head. 'No, nothing. The baby's due in just over a fortnight. I was so sure he'd be back by now. He's been gone almost five weeks now. Who knows where he is, or what he's doing? Maybe he's run off to Vegas and married some girl he's met. Or maybe he's lying dead in a ditch. You know, that's the worst of it – not knowing. It's just such a nightmare, being in limbo. I lie in bed at night going over all the possibilities. And this could go on for months. Or years. I might never see him again.'

Ben dropped his gaze and squeezed her arm gently. 'I'm really sorry, Jill. I don't know what to say. Look, I'm going to have to dash now, but it's really good to see you. You take care. And let me know if you hear anything. Or if there's anything I can do. Keep in touch. Enjoy your lunch.'

'Will do. Enjoy your meeting.'

Jill turned to re-join the queue, which had doubled in size since she'd left it.

Ben was standing at the main entrance as she headed back out of the shop and into the bright sunshine.

'Hello again,' she said, shielding her eyes as he approached her. The frown on his face was knitting his dark eyebrows together. 'Is something wrong?'

Ben twisted the handles of his carrier bag and looked down at the pavement.

'No, no, nothing's wrong. It's just... what you were saying in there. It's not fair on you–'

'What do you mean?'

'What you were saying, about Michael lying in a ditch, not knowing if he's alive or dead. It's not right that you should be thinking like that. Worrying about him. He... he texted me, Jill. Not long after he disappeared.'

'What? What do you mean? You said –' Jill gasped.

'I know what I said. Jesus, this is a nightmare. He's my mate. It's crap, what he's done. Just disappeared into thin air.' Ben ran a hand through his hair.

'What did he say? Do you know where he is? Who he's with?'

Jill put her hand to her chest. Her heart was racing and she didn't seem able to breathe properly.

'No, honestly. I don't know anything else, I promise,' Ben said. 'All I know is that he said he was OK. Not to worry. But not to say anything to you. I'm sorry, Jill. I really am. Can you see what a difficult position he put me in?'

'What? A difficult position? Do you know how worried I've been? I've been wandering around like a total *idiot*, sticking posters up in shops, going to the police. Telling everyone they're wrong, and I'm right. And all that time, you knew. You knew. You sat opposite me, drinking coffee, making sympathetic noises, and all the time you knew this?'

'But that's the thing,' Ben pleaded. 'I don't know. I don't know where he is, who he's with, if or when he's planning to come back. What was the point telling you? I had nothing to tell. I've tried to get in touch with him – I've rang and texted. He never replies.'

'Do you have any idea how long I've spent on the phone to hospitals, praying that just one of the men lying there was him? How sick is that? Wishing he was lying somewhere in a coma?' She put her hand against the wall and tried to steady her breathing.

Passers-by turned to look as her voice got louder. Let them look, she thought. She couldn't have cared less.

'You knew something, Ben. You knew that he was – is – alive and well. I feel so stupid.'

She turned to walk away. Ben reached out and laid his hand on her arm. She turned and glared at him. 'I thought you were my friend. I was obviously wrong.'

She stormed away, leaving him open-mouthed on the pavement. Barbara was already there when she reached the station.

'Jill, are you OK? Are you ill?'

Jill shook her head, unable to speak. Her teeth were chattering despite the warmth of the day. 'No, I'm not ill. I've... I've just had a shock, that's all. Can we go and sit down somewhere please?'

Barbara linked her arm and steered her in the direction of George Street. Jill let herself be almost dragged up the concrete steps that led into The Dome. She allowed herself to be guided in, under the glittering chandelier and past huge vases of flowers. Normally, whenever she came in here, she'd look up and admire it all, but now she took her seat in the corner without seeing any of it. A waiter appeared at the side of their table.

'Can I get you some drinks?' he asked.

'What I'd like is a large vodka and tonic,' Jill said. 'But just some water, please.'

'For both of us,' Barbara said. 'And if you could just give us a minute?'

The waiter gave a small bow. 'No problem, madam. I'll be back in a moment with your water.'

He smiled and moved away from the table.

'What's happened?' asked Barbara.

'Right,' she said, as Jill finished. 'Well. I can see why you wanted a vodka. I'm sorry, Jill. There's not a lot I can say really. Except surely there still has to be some sort of explanation.'

'I know, there's nothing anyone could say to make it better. It's just a shock, after all this time, to find out that everyone else was right, and I was wrong. I feel so stupid.'

She put her head in her hands. 'I mean, ranting on about how his phone must have been stolen, when the police said it had been used. Insisting that he would never leave me. Sorry. I've been behaving like a mad woman.'

Barbara waved her hand. 'No need to apologise. Just think about it though. At least you know he's OK. There's nothing to suggest he's left you. Nothing to suggest he isn't coming back. He could just be having some sort of crisis, a breakdown or something. I mean, you told me about his brother. Maybe there's a mental health issue that runs in the family.'

Jill nodded. 'You could be right. I just thought I knew him. And the Michael I know, he... he just wouldn't do something like this. Even if he felt he had to leave me, for whatever reason, he'd at least have the decency to tell me. I know he would.'

Barbara patted her hand. 'Then don't write him off yet. And don't be too hard on this mate of his. You know how it is, loyalty amongst friends. They've known each other since they were kids, you said.'

Jill nodded. 'Yes, I suppose you're right. If Louise told me something in confidence and asked me not to tell Peter, well, I wouldn't. But it's so hard. I just can't believe it.'

'What I believe,' Barbara said, 'is that things are rarely black and white. Just don't give up hope. You never know what's around the corner.'

The waiter reappeared, holding out two gold-embossed menus. Jill took it and pretended to read it. All she could see was a blur of black lines.

'Do you think you could manage to eat something?' Barbara asked.

'Not really.' She felt as if she would choke if she tried to swallow anything.

'How about if we just order you something, and you can pick at it if you fancy? You've got to try and eat, you know.'

Jill nodded. It was a relief to let someone else take charge. She felt incapable of making a decision, even one as small as choosing a meal from a menu.

They were ordering coffee when Barbara produced a beautifully wrapped box from a carrier bag at her feet. 'I got you a little something.'

'What is it?'

'Open it and see. I know we've not known each other long, but I just wanted to get you something for yourself. Before the deluge of baby gifts starts and you forget all about you.'

Jill opened the ribbon and peeled back the tissue. Inside was a beautiful pair of turquoise silk pyjamas covered in tiny, brightly-coloured birds.

'Oh, Barbara, they're lovely. Thank you,' she said.

'You're welcome. You'll spend a lot of time in your pyjamas in the first few weeks, so you might as well have glamorous ones. They're a bit practical too, though. Those buttons will make feeding easier.'

'That's so kind of you. I love them.' She felt tears pricking at her eyes as she carefully folded the pyjamas and placed them back into the box.

Jill waved as she sat down on the bus. Barbara had insisted on staying with her until it came, and promised to ring later, to see how she was. Jill had felt like asking her to come home with her, and curling up in bed while Barbara looked after her. She was being ridiculous of course. She checked her phone and saw three missed calls and an apologetic text from Ben. She put it back in her bag without responding.

She felt a sudden rush of anger. How could he just up and leave? Put his friend in an impossible position? Leave her to confide in a woman she'd known only a few weeks? Barbara was wrong. It *was* black and white. There was no excuse. No good reason. What a fool she'd been. What a total fool.

57

While Jill stood, feeling foolish and furious and a thousand other emotions, Anna was standing by the bed, shaking Michael's shoulder gently.

'Wake up, sleepy head,' she said.

Michael opened his eyes. He was groggy and lethargic and his mouth felt full of cotton wool. He barely felt fully awake anymore, just in some hazy limbo. Although maybe, he thought, that was for the best. He'd worked out the day before that he'd been here almost five weeks. He'd gone over it again and again, unable to believe that so much time had passed.

'What is it?' he said.

'I've got a surprise for you,' Anna said. Her eyes were shining and she had pulled the front of her hair back and fixed it in place with a clip. She was dressed in dark skinny jeans and a tight black V-neck top, low enough to show the edge of a deep-pink, lacy bra. The silver knot on the chain around her neck floated just above the gentle curve of her breasts.

'What's going on?' he said.

She smiled, her face glowing. 'Wait and see.'

His stomach lurched as she came towards him. She reached behind her and took a pair of shiny silver handcuffs from her back pocket.

'What are you doing?' he asked, but she just smiled and gave a little shake of the head.

She lifted his right hand and grazed the knuckles with her lips, then moved to pull both hands behind his back. He didn't struggle as she secured his wrists with the cuffs. She stood back and brushed her hands on her thighs.

'This takes me back,' she said.

Michael stared at her. It took him back, too. She'd had a bedside cabinet full of what she called her 'toys'. Everything from playful feather cuffs and satin blindfolds to a short leather riding crop and an assortment of clamps and tassels. In his head, he'd found most of it a bit too weird. That hadn't stopped him joining in though.

He watched as she walked over to the pipe and began the lengthy and complicated task of undoing the locks. Maybe she'd seen sense, he thought, a bubble of hope rising in his chest; she'd realised what a crazy idea it all was and was preparing to set him free.

'There,' she said, as the chain clattered to the ground. She came over to him and knelt as his feet, producing another key that released the manacle at his ankle. She pushed the chain to one side and eased his feet into the pair of white canvas slip-on shoes she had brought with her. She rested her hands on his knees and lifted herself up.

'Sorry about the cuffs. Just a precaution.'

She moved so that she was right behind him, and put her hand at the small of his back.

'On you go,' she said.

She guided him to the stairway and up the stairs. When he reached the top step, she squeezed past him, so close he could smell her fresh, just-showered scent, and opened the door. His heart was beating a drum in his chest.

'Where are you taking me?'

Michael looked around, drinking in the change of scenery. He was in a wide hallway, the walls pale and creamy, the floors polished oak. A slim wooden table stood to one side, a neat pile of post and some pens in a pot on its surface.

From where they stood, he counted four closed doors, all of them solid white wood, without any panes of glass to reveal what lay beyond them. She edged him forward, and when he turned, he saw the front door, tantalisingly close, but so far away. A staircase was opposite the door, leading to the next floor, and he could now see another door, a little further along from the cellar he'd just left. An under-stair cupboard, he imagined.

'I'm giving you a tour,' she said. 'I thought it was time you saw some more of your new home.'

58

Michael sagged forward and felt his heart drop like a stone. He had to stop doing this; hoping; thinking she'd see reason and suddenly decide to let him go.

She took his arm in her firm grip and steered him towards one of the doors. He thought briefly about bolting away from her, but she'd catch up with him in seconds. And how was he supposed to open the chained, and undoubtedly locked, front door with his hands behind his back?

Michael looked up as she opened one of the doors. He found himself in the doorway of an airy living room. He frowned. Something wasn't quite right. It looked strangely familiar.

'Do you like it?' she said. 'I only had a couple of minutes to look around your old place. I think it's pretty close, though, don't you?'

Michael felt dizzy and light-headed. That was why it looked familiar. Although the shape of the room was different, the décor was exactly the same as at home. The walls were painted the same milky coffee shade. His overwhelmed brain tried to remember the name of it. He could picture the stripes of paint daubed on the walls, all looking the same to him, but which were, Jill assured him, all different. Mocha something. Or cappuccino. He'd said it was more like the menu in Starbucks than a paint chart.

It was the paint he and Jill had slapped on the walls and on each other. He'd joked that he'd never seen anyone get in such a mess when they were painting. She rewarded his attempt at humour with a fat brush-full of paint smeared down his front. They'd barely been able to finish, they'd laughed so much.

A huge print hung above the simple white fireplace, with flashes of scarlet and yellow that drew his eyes so much it was a struggle to look away. Just like the print they'd brought back from Thailand.

It was the first picture they'd ever seen that they both agreed on, so they'd bought it on the spot, forgetting to haggle and probably paying well over the odds.

Cushions were scattered across the squashy beige sofa. A thick, knitted throw was folded over one end. He closed his eyes and moaned, as he remembered Jill's brief dabble at knitting. She'd given up after three days. He'd said nothing when he found the knitting needles poking through a bin bag, or when the throw from John Lewis appeared on the sofa. It was just like the one Anna had placed here, in this room, on this sofa.

'I'm so pleased with it,' she said. 'I took a couple of pictures, but like I said, I didn't have a lot of time. I think I've done a good job, don't you?'

She stood close to him and wrapped her arms awkwardly around his waist.

'I wanted to do it up in a style you liked, and I thought this would be a nice surprise for you.'

She laughed, a girly, self-conscious sound that made Michael wince. It unleashed a pounding above his eyes. He hung his head and squeezed them closed.

'Right,' she said. 'Onwards.'

She manoeuvred him further along the hall. Everywhere, there were plain walls and wooden floors. She pointed out the kitchen, a second, smaller living room and the downstairs cloakroom.

She guided him up the stairs, following close behind him with her hand at his back.

'I've saved the best until last,' she said. They stopped outside of a closed door, and she pushed it open with a flourish, then flung her arms wide.

'There! What do you think?'

'What the– ' Michael whispered. He looked around the big room. The windows were framed with almost transparent, silvery curtains, their hems lying in silky puddles on the floor. The bed looked to him to be at least king-size.

He took in the pale grey bed linen, the tiny sequins on it glittering in the afternoon light. Four cushions stood to attention, propped up against the pillows. Lamps with pleated grey shades stood on slim cabinets at each side of the bed. There was a shelf, above the leather headboard. On it stood four wooden letters, spelling out the word 'Love'.

He blew out a breath and screwed his eyes shut.

'Lovely, isn't it?' she said, as she adjusted the venetian blinds to let in a bit more light. 'Obviously, I had to use my imagination because she had her bedroom in a bit of a mess. I think this is what it should have looked like, if it was tidied up a bit? And I couldn't get the same wooden sign. That one looks just as good though, doesn't it?'

Michael thought his heart would explode from his chest. He remembered the shopping trip when he and Jill had bought the stuff for their bedroom.

He hadn't been aware that he had any strong opinions about bedding, but he'd found himself immersed in the task of choosing just the right set. Jill had teased him, as he stood, pondering about thread counts, begging him to hurry up so they could go and have lunch.

Anna stood in front of him, her hands clasped together, her cheeks flushed pink, bouncing on her toes as if she was barely able to stand still.

'Do you like it? It's lucky I have such a good memory. One of my tutors at college used to say it was almost photographic. Obviously we'll have the Moses basket in here as well, for the first few months at least. I'm picking that up later today. I can't believe it's nearly time. Our family. I can hardly wait. In less than a week, we'll have our baby'

Michael shook his head. He couldn't speak; he could barely breathe. He closed his eyes, trying to block out the image of her, creeping around his house – his and Jill's *home* – snooping, taking pictures, touching their things.

And while this, this *intrusion* was going on, Jill was probably lying in bed, thinking Anna was looking out for her, taking care of her. Being kind.

'It's probably a bit much to take in, isn't it? A bit overwhelming? I know it must have been hard for you, spending all that time in your room. But you must understand why, don't you? You were so unpredictable at first, always bleating on about getting away. And I needed to make sure you were safe, when I had to work. Once the baby's here, we can enjoy the house. I've had my time off at work approved; I told them I was going travelling, to do some nursing abroad. So we can spend our days here, all of us together. I'm so excited –'

She stopped as a shrill buzzing sound cut through the air. It was so long since he'd heard that noise, it took Michael a couple of seconds to place what it was. It was the doorbell. Someone was at the door.

'*Help–*' he began to shout. His head jolted forward as she roughly shoved him back out of the bedroom and into the room next door. She followed him in and eased the door shut behind them.

Michael opened his mouth to cry out and found himself choking as she shoved in a wad of tissue.

'Don't even think about it,' she said, pushing him roughly onto a desk chair. The movement jarred his shoulders, sending a shooting pain across his back, and he spluttered, eyes watering as he tried to spit the disintegrating tissue from his mouth.

Anna grabbed a roll of parcel tape from the desk in front of him and tore off a strip, slapping it across his chapped lips.

She moved towards the door and stood, ear pressed against the wood. The doorbell sounded again, cutting through the silence. Michael tried to slow down his breath, to stop himself swallowing. He pictured the tiny cotton fibres, drifting down his throat and clogging his lungs. Maybe I should just let them, he thought. I'm going to die here anyway, one way or another. Through half-closed eyelids, he looked around the room.

It was some sort of office. Cluttered shelves bowed under the weight of thick folders. Barely an inch of the desk's surface was visible under piles of notebooks and documents. Several pots jammed with pens lined the narrow window ledge. An unravelled tape measure lay draped across a neglected pot plant like a long yellow snake.

He tried to push the tissue to one side with his tongue. Maybe then he could push off the tape and maybe whoever it was at the door could come and help him. It could be the police. Surely they'd break the door down.

He'd hear them soon, using one of those battering rams he'd seen on cop dramas on TV. He poked at the tape at the corner of his mouth with his tongue.

The walls were covered in papers and cuttings, he realised. Some were pinned, others fastened with strips of tape. He tried to focus, to move his mind away from the shallow sound of the breaths he was dragging in through his nose.

They were lists, some of them. He squinted, trying to make sense of the words printed there. Names. Lists and lists of names. Baby names, he realised. Rage soared through him at the thought of her sitting there, at this desk, listing name after name for a baby that had nothing to do with her.

One wall was entirely covered in newspaper articles. He couldn't make out the black blurry lines of their content, just the bold headlines, screaming out their stories of missing children, neglect and abduction.

He turned his head and saw another section of wall, covered in articles about families whose offspring stretched into double figures, like those they made TV documentaries about. He could see sections circled, words highlighted in vivid yellow.

Michael felt a scream building at the back of his throat. Sweat prickled in his over-long hair and trickled down his temples. If he could just pull off the tape. He stood and moved towards where she stood, leg pulled back ready to kick out at her, at the door, at anything that got in his way. A pile of papers tipped onto the floor.

Anna spun around, eyes flashing. She pushed him, hard, and he fell back against the chair. He didn't even register the flash of metal until he saw the tip of the scissors plunging through the fabric of his shorts and into the flesh of his thigh.

He tried to shout out, but then he was gagging. His leg felt as if it was on fire. He felt another stab, less painful, and in his upper arm this time. And then his vision was fading, becoming more and more hazy until it was a pinprick and then... nothing.

59

Michael was lying on his back on the floor, his head propped up on a pillow. His hair was damp and he felt cold and shivery. His wrists were still cuffed, but in front of him now. His leg was throbbing, pulses of pain keeping rhythm with the beat of his heart. He opened his eyes and tried to focus.

Anna was standing over him, wiping at a short line of neat stitches on his left thigh with a piece of cotton wool. She had changed into her uniform and smoothed down her hair. He watched as she taped on a square of bright white gauze. She had switched on the fluorescent overhead light; her skin looked translucent in its harsh beam.

There was ice in her voice when she spoke. 'Oh, you're awake then,' she said, glaring at him. 'That was a bit stupid wasn't it? I was just starting to think that maybe, just maybe you could be trusted. I'm just so, so disappointed.'

She wiped her eyes with the back of her hand.

'Anna, you stabbed me!'

Michael coughed; his throat felt raw and tight.

'You're a fucking lunatic,' he spluttered.

She jabbed a finger at his chest. 'You made me do it! What choice did I have? You were about to spoil everything. Everything we've worked so hard for.'

She closed her eyes for a moment and when she spoke again, her voice was little more than a whisper.

'You know, Michael, I'd really looked forward to today. Showing you around our home. Letting you see what I'd achieved. I've stayed up all night, to get things finished. I've painted walls, chosen fabrics, to get the place just how I thought you'd like it. And this is how you repay me.'

Michael turned his head. The papers he'd knocked from the desk lay close to his head. He fixed his gaze on a bent paperclip and tried to block out her voice.

'I had a surprise planned for tonight,' she said. 'A special dinner. I'd set the table in the dining room, bought steaks and wine. And then we were going to watch a film together in the living room. Go to bed together in the bedroom. Start living like a proper couple.'

She sighed and crossed her arms, then nodded towards his leg.

'I expect that's sore.'

'Yeah,' Michael muttered. Despite himself, he felt almost ashamed.

'I expect you'd like something for the pain.'

He shrugged. She was right; it was killing him.

'I know you're being brave. I expect it feels like a hot knife twisting and turning in there. It was actually quite a deep wound. Hopefully it's not an infection building up. Anyway, maybe it'll give you something to think about. Give you an idea of how much you've hurt me. You've really let me down. You have to work with me, you know, if we're going to be together.'

She took his hands and pulled him up to sitting.

'You're going to have to get up and walk. We'll have to get you back downstairs.'

Gritting his teeth against the pain in his leg, he let her pull him up. Holding the side of the desk, he clambered up awkwardly until he stood in front of her. His face was damp with sweat and he raised his cuffed hands awkwardly to wipe his brow.

He limped after her as she opened the door. She stood, arms folded as he walked slowly down each stair and into the hall. She put her hand at his back and pushed him towards the cellar door.

He didn't even try to resist as she opened it and gestured towards the stairs. When he was back in the room and sitting on the bed, she pulled off his shoes and then turned and began to chain him up. When she'd finished, she undid the handcuffs and started to walk away, hands in her pockets and shoulders slumped low.

'Wait,' he called.

She turned back, frowning. 'What?'

'Who was it? At the door, I mean? A delivery? The postman?'

She stared straight at him, her gaze hard. He shifted uncomfortably and turned his head away. He'd known that question would annoy her.

'What? So you want to know who it was? Your potential saviour? Do you really think I would be so stupid as to have anything delivered here? I've made other arrangements for that sort of thing. It was just some pathetic old man, out walking and no doubt lost. I watched him out of the window, stumbling away with a compass in his hand. So that's who you were relying on, Michael. Some idiot who couldn't even follow a map.'

She wiped her eyes and blew her nose into a tissue.

'I'm so disappointed,' she said, as she turned again towards the stairs. 'You've made a fool of me. I thought we were happy together. I've worked so hard on our relationship, these last few weeks. I've so enjoyed the time we've spent together. I thought... I thought you felt the same.'

She turned to go then stopped. She wrapped her arms around herself and started to rock slightly on the balls of her feet.

'You can't possibly understand what loss like that does to someone. You can't even begin to know what it's like. One of the first memories I have is pushing a pram with a doll in it. I remember feeling so proud as I tucked her in and wheeled her up and down the path. I was meant to be a mother.'

'I would never even claim to understand what it was like for you, having an abortion and then being told you could never have kids,' Michael said softly. 'All I can say is that I lost someone too, back then. I lost the brother I'd known all my life.'

Her voice hardened. 'It's not the same. It's not even comparable. He's alive. You can see him whenever you want.'

He gestured down to his manacled leg. 'Hardly.'

'Yes, well, that's just the way it is at the minute,' she shrugged.

'What I'm trying to say is, it isn't easy seeing someone I grew up with, lived with, went for a *pint* with, locked up in in that place. Never needing a pair of outdoor shoes. You know, when we were young, he was obsessed with trainers. He'd go on waiting lists, queue up for hours, anything to make sure he had the latest ones.'

He lowered his voice, so it was barely more than a whisper. 'Haven't you thought what this is doing to him? No one going to see him, not knowing where I am? I'm all he's got. It's not fair. It's bad enough that he's in that place. You of all people should know what this could do to him.'

She pursed her lips. 'He'll get over it. Let's face it, he can't get any worse.'

'How can you be so horrible?'

Michael stared down at his hands. He clenched handfuls of the bedclothes in his fists. He knew it was best to humour her, stay calm, even though rage was bubbling up inside him.

'This is our chance, Michael,' she said.

You can't just steal someone else's baby, he thought. *How can you think that doing something that is so, so wrong could possibly make anything right?*

She continued to speak, staring at the wall, as if she'd forgotten there was even anyone else in the room with her.

'Imagine being told you can never have a child. Imagine the pain. It was unbearable. I hadn't done anything to deserve that.'

'You didn't deserve what happened to you. No one deserves something like that. But do you really think that makes all this stuff, what you're doing, what you're planning to do, right? You know how bad you felt. Why on earth would you want to make someone else suffer like that?'

'It's not the same! Why can't you see that? The baby... it'll be best off with us. This is our chance to be parents, a family.'

'Now,' she continued, 'we'll just put today down to some last-minute nerves and say no more about it.'

'But... but what about you? You're denying yourself the chance of a proper relationship, a real life.'

She frowned and pouted her lips. 'A proper relationship? But that's what we'll have. That's what we already have. Soulmates, remember?'

Michael searched for something to say, but she was gone, the familiar sound of the key in the lock marking her exit. He opened his mouth to call her back. And then closed it, clamping it shut and biting on his lip until he could taste the metallic tang of blood.

What's the point, he thought? A sense of despair came down on him like a thick fog. There was no point. No reasoning. No way out.

60

A couple of days after Michael had been treated to a tour of Anna's house, the ringing phone pulled Jill from sleep. She'd been dreaming, although it wasn't even a dream, really. More of a memory.

They had been walking, hand in hand, around a street market in Thailand, where Michael had bought fruit while she fingered silk scarves the colour of jewels. He'd laughed as she recoiled in disgust when he threatened to buy a paper cone full of deep-fried grasshoppers.

They'd made their way slowly back to the hotel, wandering along the beach in their bare feet as the sun faded; laughing at some story he was telling. Michael was always so good at telling stories; had a knack of remembering little details that made everyone want to listen to what he was saying.

They'd stopped at a tiny salon and had massages that cost barely more than a cup of coffee at home. She'd been happy, content, not bothered that her face was shiny and her hair limp with oil.

That's when they'd gone into the little gallery and bought the picture that hung, stretched onto canvas, in the living room now. Until she opened her eyes, it was if they were still there. How long was it since she'd felt happiness like that? And what if she never felt like that, ever again? She should never have taken it for granted, even for a second.

Reality hit her as she heard her sister's voice, coming to the end of her answerphone message '–so if you could just ring me, let me know you're OK.'

Jill sat up in bed, taking a deep breath to try and push awake the sickly, disorientated feeling she had from being startled awake. There was no way she could ring Louise at the minute. Even if she didn't say the words, Jill knew she'd be thinking them – *I told you so.*

The clock on the bedside cabinet told her it was just after ten. She hadn't slept for so long in weeks, but she still felt exhausted. As she pushed back the covers on the bed, Jill looked at her stomach. The vest top she was wearing had ridden up, and she ran her fingers over her bare skin.

Her stomach was like a huge, ripe melon, hard and smooth. Her belly button had been pulled flat by the growing baby and it felt strange and tingly when she touched it. Her body seemed to change every day; she barely recognised it as her own. The previous week, she'd woken up to find two damp patches on her pyjama top. She'd jumped out of bed in a panic, and had only calmed down when a hasty internet search had told her that leaking breasts were completely normal in late pregnancy.

She hauled herself from the bed, glancing over, as she always did, at the empty space beside her. She wondered if she'd ever stray over from her own side. Or would she always think of it as Michael's side, even if... She swallowed and headed for the bathroom. The shower ran cold at first, and she turned up the heat until she could hardly bear the scalding needles hitting her skin.

She dried herself roughly, leaving her skin pink and glowing, then attempted to wrap a towel around herself. It barely met around her swollen breasts, so she gave up and walked, naked, to the bedroom, relishing the air on her skin. The warm weather made her so sluggish, and she dressed slowly.

Everything took longer now. She couldn't just reach down and pull on a pair of socks, or fasten her laces. By the time she had awkwardly hooked a pair of knickers over her foot, and put on her stretchy grey trousers and a white t-shirt, she felt hot and breathless.

Jill walked down to the kitchen and flicked on the kettle. She ran her fingers over the shining worktops, the result of hours spent cleaning up the place yesterday. The blackened bananas were now in the bin, along with the pile of leaflets from the police. She'd collected up all the half-empty cups of coffee and dirty glasses that were littered around the house and put them in the dishwasher. Her arms ached with the effort.

It had been worth it though. She flushed with shame at the state she'd let the place get in. The wooden floor glowed and everything was in its proper place.

The heartburn that plagued her began to fire up, as it did every day. Jill rubbed her chest and reached into the cupboard for the box of peppermint teabags. It was the last one. *Must get some more*, she thought, throwing it into a mug and covering it in boiling water. Not that it really helped that much, and she struggled to get away from the fact that it tasted like hot mouthwash.

She took a swig from a bottle of Gaviscon and sighed with relief as it soothed the heat. Prior to pregnancy, she'd never had heartburn in her life, but now, it was so constant she could barely remember a time when it wasn't there.

Jill sat at the table and pulled the notepad in front of her. She ran a finger down the list. The last of many, she hoped. She'd found so many lists, in every pocket and on every surface, that she'd started then cast aside. But she was almost on top of things now. She'd got nearly everything she needed.

The pushchair had arrived yesterday. It was still sitting in its huge cardboard box in the hall. She'd taken one look at the instruction leaflet and quickly closed the lid. She'd do it later. Just not today. She pushed the pad away and ran a hand through her still-damp hair. Everything was organised, more or less.

It was all so wrong. She shouldn't be doing these things on her own. Building furniture. Choosing prams; a cot; bedding. They should have been doing them together. It had got on her nerves sometimes, how much interest he took in the house. She'd trailed back to shops with cushions, lamps and pictures more times than she cared to think about, when he'd given them a look that told her he definitely wasn't keen.

If only he was here now, giving his opinions and interfering. Jill felt her throat thicken with tears and shook her head. She had to pull herself together. She poured the remaining tea down the drain and put her cup in the dishwasher, then walked along the hall, grabbing her bag from the foot of the stairs. She needed to get out.

Minutes later, she was out in the street. Her feet looked pale and naked in the black leather flip-flops she'd put on, but the thought of wearing her uncomfortably tight trainers was unbearable. The air was so close and muggy that she could barely get her breath.

Teabags, she told herself. I need to get teabags. Now that she had a sense of purpose, she walked out of the street and headed up West Saville Road, crossing to the shady side of the street. Her face was soon damp with sweat and she wished she'd tied her hair back.

Jill slowed as she came to the church. It always looked so peaceful. The gardens were immaculate, although she'd never seen anyone tending them. Maybe they did it in the dead of night.

Jill wondered suddenly what it must be like to have faith. Did it help? Or was it just something else to worry about? She shook her head; any vague religious beliefs she'd had in her youth, drummed into her in those dire RE lessons at school, had evaporated instantly when she became an orphaned teenager. Surely no religion could believe that was fair?

As the lights changed, she crossed the road, then turned abruptly and headed away from the shop. It was suddenly too exhausting – the thought of making polite conversation, answering questions about when she was due.

That was the thing with having a bump the size of a small country – it was hard to go anywhere unnoticed. Instead, she walked on, glad of the sloping path. As she approached the entrance to Blackford Pond, she stopped and turned in through the gate.

It was quiet as she wandered around the pond. The water glinted in the sunlight. It was almost still, like a sheet of glass.

Jill sat down on one of the benches and watched as a distant jogger, dust at his heels, disappeared from view. Even the sight of him made her feel too hot, and she pulled at the short sleeves of her top, trying to generate a waft of air, and rummaged in her bag for a tissue to mop the sweat from her face.

An elderly man was showing a small, dark-haired boy how to tear up bread to feed the ducks. The child was nodding, then casually eating the bread as soon as his grandad's back was turned. The ducks here were so overfed that they rarely ate the bread anyway. It just lay, rotting, a feast for any lurking rats.

Jill watched as two swans took to the water, swimming serenely. No matter how calm they appeared on the surface, they were always paddling frantically underneath. She knew how they felt.

She'd always loved this place, a quiet haven in the middle of the city. In the days before she'd had a garden, she used to come here with a book and a bottle of water. Later, they'd come here together, and if they were feeling energetic, go for a long walk.

She told him, half-joking, that he'd better get a bench here, when she died, and come and sit, gazing at the water and looking sad. And no bringing your new woman here, she'd warned. He looked at her, his face serious, and told her he promised that no other woman's backside would ever sit on her bench. She'd punched him in the arm and he'd threatened to throw her into the water.

Her whole body ached as she let herself back in the front door, and the heartburn was back. And she'd forgotten the teabags. She kicked off the flip-flops and thought how blissful it would be to sit with her feet in a bowl of cool water. But that would mean finding a bowl. And filling it up. Instead, she sank down on the sofa and closed her eyes.

This time, it was the doorbell that woke her. She sat up, head spinning and slowly pulled herself to her feet.

'Barbara!' she said, opening the door. 'Come on in.'

'I just wanted to see how you were. You sounded awfully tired yesterday. Actually, you still look a bit weary now.'

Barbara followed Jill through to the kitchen and leaned her back against the worktop.

'I'm fine, honestly,' Jill said. 'I was just having forty winks. Actually, I had a bit of an energy surge later on yesterday. Cleaned the house a bit. It was in dire need of it.'

'Nesting, that's what they call that.'

'What? Oh, you mean preparing for the baby? I think in my case it was more about making sure this baby's not living in complete squalor.'

Barbara laughed, a deep, throaty sound that rang out in the quiet house. She slipped off her light padded jacket and hung it on the back of the chair.

'I hope you don't mind me dropping in. I thought you might like a bit of company. I was in town, waiting for the bus and the one that came was going your way. So, here I am. Your house is lovely, by the way.'

'Thanks. It's really nice to see you. I've been doing my own head in, actually. Went for a walk round the pond and ended up wallowing. And I only went out for teabags. Which I forgot.'

'That's another thing pregnancy does to you. Makes your mind go. I remember once losing my keys and finding them a fortnight later in the fridge. Anyway,' she continued, nodding towards the almost-empty antacid bottle on the table, 'how's the heartburn?'

Jill grimaced. 'Awful. It doesn't seem to matter what I eat or drink, or even whether I eat or drink at all.'

'Not a lot you can do about it really. It'll disappear the second the baby pops out. Although I do believe there's an old wives' tale that says it means the baby will have a good head of hair.'

'Hmm. Maybe it would be better if it was bald then.'

Barbara leaned against the table.

'When are you back at the midwife?' she asked.

'Tomorrow. Who knows, this could be the last time. Just over two weeks to go now. Two more weeks.'

'Yes. Nearly there now. You must ring me, the second anything happens. I'm looking forward to meeting this baby.'

'I will, I promise. Although hopefully not just yet.'

Jill turned away, reaching for cups and switching on the kettle. The thought that in just a couple of weeks she'd be giving birth to a child and raising it, on her own, just wouldn't go away.

61

The following day, Jill tried to hide her surprise as she walked into the surgery for her appointment with the midwife, only to be greeted by a very attractive Spanish man called Alberto, who introduced himself as a relief midwife from another surgery.

'Hmm,' he said now, as he released the Velcro and undid the cuff on Jill's arm.

'Is something wrong?' she said, rolling down the sleeve of her top and looking across at his furrowed brow, as he made note in the folder. She eased herself up onto her elbows, no longer able to see her feet.

'Well, your blood pressure is quite high.'

Jill stared. Her heart sank. Surely that wasn't good? Louise had mentioned Peter having high blood pressure and having to make loads of changes to his lifestyle. 'And?' she said.

'Your due date is the third of June. That's only two weeks, give or take a day. It might be an idea to admit you to hospital, keep an eye on you. Then the baby can be induced it it's necessary.'

'What?' Jill gasped 'No. I mean... it's too soon. I'm not ready, I–'

The midwife smiled broadly, showing even, white teeth. 'Calm down, you'll make it worse. How about if you promise to go home and do nothing – and I mean nothing – then come back in two days? If things are still the same then though, we'll really have to look at getting you into hospital for bed rest. So make sure your bag's all packed.'

Jill nodded, relief flooding through her. 'The baby's OK, isn't it? There's no risk, is there?'

'No, no. I wouldn't let you go home if there was a risk. It's only slightly raised. But you need to promise – home, feet up, doing nothing. Agreed?'

'Agreed.'

Jill picked up her notes and bag, and made her way to the door as fast as her swollen body allowed, before he could change his mind. No doubt if Elizabeth had been on duty she would already be in an ambulance.

Jill eased herself into the car. Every time she went to get in, she was sure that this would be the day when she could no longer fit behind the steering wheel and had to either stay home or walk to the bus stop.

They'd debated for ages about what to get, when they'd gone shopping for this car. She'd wanted something small and sporty, but he'd talked her into something bigger. And safer he'd said, for when they had kids. Precious cargo, he'd said, as he pored over safety features and airbags.

She shook her head and fastened the seatbelt. At least she had that to thank him for.

The midday heat had turned the car into a sauna. Jill opened the windows. The air that came in was thick and heavy, so she quickly closed them and put the air conditioning on full. She turned the dial to blast the cool air on her feet and pulled out of the car park.

She felt the familiar lurch in her stomach as the baby embarked on one of its kicking sessions. Jill suddenly felt starving. What she really fancied – no, more than that, *needed* – was a bag of chips. Fat, salty chips. Her mouth filled with water at the thought. There was no way she could go home now. She wouldn't settle until she had them in her hands. She'd go and rest as soon as she'd eaten, she thought, the midwife's words ringing in her ears. Anyway, she convinced herself, if she wanted something this bad, it must be because the baby wanted it too.

She headed through Craigmillar and Musselburgh. If she was having chips she may as well have them at the beach.

It was one of the things she loved most about Edinburgh. Coast, city and countryside practically on her doorstep. She liked the fact that one day, she could be in the centre of town, shopping or sipping a pre-baby glass of wine, and the next, wandering along the seaside.

Half an hour later, she had parked the car and was standing in a queue at the fish and chip shop on the sea front at Portobello, breathing in the moist, fragrant air. It was all she could do not to grab a handful of chips from the child standing in front of her, waiting as his mother paid.

Jill drummed her fingers against the shiny counter as the painfully slow assistant scooped up and wrapped her order. She grabbed the parcel, satisfyingly warm and heavy, and headed out into the sunshine.

Jill sat on a bench and opened up the package. The harsh cry of greedy seagulls filled the air. She ate quickly, staring out at the beach, watching families building castles on the sand, or unpacking picnics.

A group of small, naked children ran in and out of the waves. They were too far away to hear but Jill could tell they were screaming in delight as the foamy water licked their toes. She remembered going to the beach as a child and doing the same thing herself.

She smiled sadly, thinking of those times, of her and Louise at the beach, probably bickering over whose sandcastle was the best. Of licking ice-cream as if it was the best thing she'd ever tasted. When the worst thing in the world was being told to pack up your things because it was time to go home.

Or going to bed when it was still light outside, and feeling cheated of hours that could be spent playing in the sun. She thought of skin tinged pink and eating food that always tasted of grit. Her mother, basting herself in thick, orange oil and smoking cigarettes as she sat on a deckchair in the sun.

And later, she remembered coming down coming down to the beach with portable barbecues and plastic carrier bags full of cans of beer with a group of people whose faces, never mind names, she couldn't remember.

The remaining chips were cool and congealed, and Jill bundled up the papers and threw them into the bin next to the bench. A greasy film coated her tongue and she felt full and heavy.

She stood and walked slowly back to the car, dodging out of the way as a little boy on a bright red scooter zoomed along the promenade, his dad panting as he raced to keep up. Putting one foot in front of the other was suddenly an enormous effort. She'd never felt so exhausted.

When she got home, Jill walked straight through to the living room and sank down onto the sofa, dumping her bag on the floor beside her. She suddenly realised she'd left her pregnancy folder in the car.

It had been drummed into her from day one that she shouldn't go anywhere without it and now she'd left it outside, lying on the passenger seat. *I'll get it in a minute*, she thought, closing her eyes.

She woke up with a start, breathing heavily. Her hair felt damp and when she ran her hand across her face, it came away wet with sweat. She could feel her heart beating a drum in her chest.

Something terrible had happened to the baby and she had been screaming and screaming and no one came to help. She put her hands on her stomach. It was normal, she'd read, to have really vivid dreams, and to panic about the baby, thinking something terrible might happen.

It had happened loads in the early days, those weeks before the scan when they knew that everything could still go wrong. No matter how many times it happened though, it was still terrifying.

Jill knew she should go upstairs and lie on the bed, as she'd promised to do. But the dream had unnerved her. She felt jittery and wide awake, as if she'd overdosed on caffeine.

She hauled herself up from the sofa. Even now, it still felt strange, being so heavy and cumbersome – she'd always been an average weight, not fat, not skinny. She'd forget sometimes, for a second, and try to squeeze through a space the size of her pre-baby self. Or she'd start to turn over in bed and groan, feeling as if a huge melon was strapped to her front.

It was hard to believe that soon she'd be meeting the tiny person who she had carried around all these months. She stroked her belly. 'Not long know, darling,' she whispered.

She walked upstairs and into the spare room. She'd check over her bag again, make sure she had put everything in that she was supposed to take to hospital with her.

She took out pack of disposable nappies and tore open the plastic wrapping. The tiny nappy she held in her hand looked as if it would fit a doll.

She pulled out the freshly washed, white sleepsuits and vests, breathing in the clean, new scent of them, then shuddered at the sight of the huge pairs of knickers and enormous sanitary towels. She smoothed the beautiful pyjamas Barbara had given her and laid them carefully on the floor.

That's everything, she thought, as she zipped up her soap-bag after checking its contents. The only thing she still needed in the bag, according to the list she'd been given, was an *old nightdress or t-shirt to wear during labour.*

She got up from the floor, groaning as her legs protested. She walked stiffly through to the bedroom and opened the drawer where she kept nightwear. Then she pushed it closed and opened the next drawer down. She laid her hands on the pile of t-shirts neatly folded in there.

She picked up the top one and buried her face in it, hoping to catch a trace of his smell, but all she got was a faint whiff of fabric conditioner. She carried the t-shirt through and placed it in her bag.

When everything was neatly folded inside, she zipped up the bag and put it next to the door. 'All ready,' she murmured, glancing down at her stomach. Jill walked back downstairs, with the careful step of someone who can no longer see their toes.

In the hall, she took her phone from her bag. A quick glance at the screen told her there were no missed calls, no new texts. She checked her emails. Just junk, offers and discounts. She walked through to the living room and sat down on the sofa. She scrolled to his number and dialled, heart in her mouth. Let him answer, she thought. Please, just this once. Let him answer.

He didn't though. She took a deep breath as the answerphone picked up her call.

'Michael, it's me. I just wanted to ring to remind you. It's only a couple of weeks now, until the baby is due. You know that, don't you? And they're saying I might have to go into hospital; that the baby might be early. Wherever you are, whatever's going on, just come home. Ben told me that... that you've been in touch with him. You must have your reasons, for just vanishing like this. I can't begin to understand what they are, but... I need you. The baby needs you. And I love you, no matter what's happened. You should be here. With me. With us.'

Her voice cracked as she ended he call, and she sat, face in her hands and wept. She stayed there, leaning as far forward as her swollen body allowed, tears forming a wet patch on her dress. After a while, she rubbed her face with the back of her hand and then, through blurred eyes, she sent him a text, and then an email.

She went through to the kitchen and blew her nose on the last piece of kitchen roll, then plugged her phone into its charger and switched on the kettle.

'That's it,' she said out loud. 'There's nothing else I can do.'

Jill sat down at the kitchen table and flicked idly through the pile of leaflets that had grown monthly since she'd become pregnant. A wave of panic washed over her as she read about problems and defects. Things that wouldn't have shown up on the scans.

What if there was something wrong with the baby? It would be hard enough to cope with support, but on her own? How would she manage when her maternity pay ran out? Even though she'd been sensible over the years, squirreling money away in savings accounts, it wouldn't last forever.

And if she had to work to pay the bills and feed them, who would look after the baby then? They'd both been against the idea of paying a stranger to bring up their child, and the plan was that she would stay home with the baby. That wouldn't work if she was on her own.

She'd have to sell the house, buy a tiny flat and live off the rest of the money. At least she didn't have a mortgage on this place, but that was little consolation. This was her home. She wanted to bring up her baby here.

'It's not fair,' she whispered, aware, but not caring, that she sounded like a child. 'It's just not fair.'

She rubbed at the spot between her eyes, which seemed to throb, constantly. At least when the baby came she'd be able to take something stronger than the odd Paracetamol. Or maybe she wouldn't, if she was breastfeeding. Another thing to add to the list of things she needed to find out for herself. She flicked through the remaining leaflets. Maybe she would find some answers in there.

Jill knew she would do whatever it took to make sure this baby had a good life. A happy life. Someone, she forgot who, had once told her that no matter how much you thought you loved your partner, you would kill them in a heartbeat to save your children. Stand on his head and let him drown, if it meant you could push your child above the waves.

You would do anything to protect them, and happily die for them – after all, that would be easier than living without them.

But just now, she needed Michael here. Needed him to take her hand, tell her everything would be all right. She needed to feel that she wasn't alone.

This was a time in her life when she should be full of excitement and hope. Yet all she felt was empty.

She stood and dragged herself up the stairs. She wanted her mind to be so busy, there was no room for thought. Or she wanted to sleep and sleep. She lay down heavily on the bed, on her side, and hugged herself. She imagined the baby lying in the exact same position, feeding from her, listening to her. Relying on her for everything. Jill felt as if the very last bit of fight in her was fading away. She closed her eyes and longed for sleep.

62

But no matter how hard she tried, Jill couldn't get to sleep. She tried clearing her mind and concentrating on her breath, like she'd read in some magazine article. That's a joke, she thought. There was far too much going on in her mind for it ever to be clear.

She heard her mobile ringing from where she'd left it downstairs and dragged herself up from the bed. *Maybe*, she thought, not wanting to allow the idea to fully form.

When she checked the screen she saw it was a missed from Barbara. She really should call her back. Tell her about this problem with her blood pressure. She'd ring her in a bit, when she felt more capable of disguising the sadness in her voice.

Jill switched on the radio and Steve Wright's voice rang out, announcing that the next song he'd be playing was Bruce Springsteen's *Dancing in the Dark*. A vague memory of a drunken night at a gig, when she'd danced madly and hoped that Bruce would pluck her from the audience to dance, just like he had with Courtney Cox, came to mind. He hadn't of course, but it had been such a good night anyway.

She stared out of the window. It was still sunny. Maybe she would go and sit out in the garden for a bit. It would be nice to feel a bit of sun on her skin.

It had always been one of her favourite things, sitting outside in the sunshine. When she and Michael had first met, he'd lived in a flat near the Meadows, and she'd drag him out at the first sign of a ray. She hadn't gotten around to tackling the garden at this house back then, and it was still a jungle –

no room to lay down a handkerchief, never mind a blanket. They'd take beer and crisps and find a spot beside the hundreds of other people with the same idea as them. The air would be thick with sun cream and barbecues. And petrol fumes, but they'd ignore those.

They'd lounge about for hours, dozing, reading newspapers. Michael would laugh as she changed position hourly, chasing the last rays of sun. It was never a waste of time, though.

In fact, it was one of the best ways to spend time, she thought. You never knew if the good weather would last more than a day, so you had to make the most of it. When the sun did finally fade, they'd walk home, stopping to pick up an Indian or Chinese takeaway.

She'd say it was too nice a day to cook. He'd laugh and say that she would say that even if it was lashing with rain. She tried to be indignant, even though she couldn't argue. She'd just remind him of her other talents instead.

She'd take the baby up there, she thought. Have picnics. Their son or daughter would have their first ride on a swing.

Would he be back by then, she wondered? Would he walk back into their lives one day, leaving her to introduce him to his child as if he were a stranger? Would it be amicable, or would they embark on a series of battles about access visits and custody? Would he even want to know? Maybe he'd have another family. Another life. Or maybe she'd never see him again, ever.

Jill shook her head. She had to stop thinking that way. If she stopped believing in him, it was as if she really had given up. Barbara was right, she couldn't lose faith. Even though she lay awake in the dark hours when it was no longer night but not quite morning, admitting to herself that everyone was probably right, that he had just decided to leave her.

She had a sudden urge to speak to her sister and reached for her phone. She listened as it rang and then went to answerphone.

'Hi, it's me,' Jill said. 'Just ringing to say hello, but you must be busy. Anyway, I'll speak to you later.'

She ended the call and rubbed her face, then turned on the cold tap. When it was running icy cold, she filled a glass and gulped it down, grimacing as it made her sensitive teeth ache. Another symptom of pregnancy that no one had warned her about.

A thump outside the window made her jump. She looked out and saw the neighbours' cat strolling across the lawn. It turned and stared at Jill defiantly, then sat down and began the laborious process of grooming.

That's what I should do, Jill thought. Tidy myself up a bit. She'd shave her legs, cut her nails. Wash her hair. Maybe even paint her toenails, if she could reach them. This might be the last chance she'd get, if they did take her into hospital.

She headed along the hall and started to climb the stairs. The ringing doorbell stopped her as she reached halfway. She turned and headed down to the door. Maybe, she thought. Maybe he's lost his keys and...

'Elizabeth,' she said, the hope that had risen in her sinking like a stone when she saw the midwife at the door. 'What are you doing here?'

Elizabeth's hands fluttered to her face, brushing her hair back from her forehead. Her flushed cheeks stood out against her pale skin.

'Hi,' she said, clearing her throat. 'Look, Jill, I need you to come with me. Right away.'

'Come with you? Where to?'

Elizabeth walked past her and into the hallway, her eyes darting around the room.

'To... to the hospital. You're on your own here aren't you?'

'Yes, yes I am. What's wrong? Why do I need to go to hospital? I've just seen... ' she searched her memory for the midwife's name then gave up when it didn't come to her. 'The man, the midwife, he said it was fine. I'm to go back in a couple of days. He just said to come home and rest. And I have been, honestly.'

'No. There's been a mistake. He shouldn't have told you that. He's not as experienced as me. He's not as aware of the risks. I came as soon as I saw his notes on your records. You need to come with me. The baby could be in danger. We can't be too careful. Come on, we have to go.'

She tugged at Jill's arm.

Jill's hands flew to her mouth. 'I can't... I need to... it's too soon–'

Elizabeth turned and looked Jill directly in the face, her eyes flashing. 'Can't you understand how important this is? You have to come with me. Now.'

Jill's stomach clenched, thoughts of shaving her legs and conditioning her hair forgotten. If Elizabeth was as worried as she looked, maybe something really was wrong. She let herself be steered towards the door.

'Wait,' she said. 'My bag.'

She could hear the drum of Elizabeth's fingertips on the bannister as she walked as fast as she could up the stairs to get the bag. What if she'd forgotten something? It doesn't matter, she told herself. As long as the baby is OK. She headed back down to where Elizabeth was waiting, arms folded and her mouth set in a thin line.

'Come on, quickly,' Elizabeth said ushering her towards the door and taking the bag from Jill's hands. 'Oh, hold on, just a minute,' she said, placing the bag at her feet. 'There's something I need to give you before we leave.' She produced a syringe from her pocket. 'It's for the baby's lungs.'

'Oh. Can't it wait until we get there?'

Elizabeth was already pushing back the short sleeve of Jill's top. Jill recoiled as the needle pierced her skin. 'I though the lung jab went into my bottom? They said–'

'Don't worry about that now.'

Elizabeth took her elbow and almost pushed her out of the door, pulling it closed behind them. She hurried down the path to her car, Jill following behind her.

Jill stopped and turned to look at the front door of the house. Next time she walked through it, she'd very likely be carrying their baby. She hadn't even thought about getting it home. She'd need the car seat, and a blanket, and–

'Hurry up,' Elizabeth called, interrupting Jill's thoughts as she threw the bag onto the back seat.

Jill opened the passenger door and sat down, pulling the seatbelt carefully around her stomach. The car was just as much of a mess as the last time she'd been in it. Worse, even. She turned her head and saw her bag sliding across the seat littered with papers and bags. A baby seat was fitted at one side. She hadn't noticed that last time she was in the car.

'Do you have children, Elizabeth?'

'What? No. What makes you ask that?'

'Just the car seat...'

'Oh, that's just for work. In case I need to give someone a lift.'

'Oh,' said Jill, raising her eyebrows. Elizabeth must really live for her job, she thought. She could see the seat was an expensive one; it was the exact same one she'd chosen herself.

'Right, let's go,' Elizabeth muttered. She pulled out, almost into the path of a van coming in the other direction. 'Watch where you're going, you idiot!' she yelled.

Jill put a hand to her belly and tried to focus. Her head felt thick and fuzzy. She chewed at her dry lips. She wanted to ask what was happening, make sure the baby was OK.

She was so tired, though. It would be so nice just to close her eyes. She felt so relaxed; her limbs felt loose and floppy. She rested her head back on the seat and, forcing her eyes open, turned to look at Elizabeth. She was staring ahead, a frown creasing her forehead as she waited for the lights to change at the top of Mayfield Road.

Jill tried to shift in her seat and found that she couldn't. Her already heavy legs seemed to have turned to lead. *'Please,'* she thought, *'please let the baby be OK.'*

She watched as Anna drove on, and tried to speak, to tell her she'd missed the turn-off for the hospital, but her tongue seemed to have grown too big for her mouth. She'd close her eyes, just for a minute.

63

Barbara walked along the street, wishing she'd got a taxi instead of spending the last forty minutes sweating on a bus. Life was too short, really. And what else was she going to spend her money on? Surely at this time in her life, she could treat herself, now and then?

'Stop talking to yourself, Barbara,' she muttered, as she approached Jill's house.

It was nice, she thought, this side of town. She'd always liked her area, with the bars and restaurants, and the eclectic mix of characters you came across. It was nice here, though. Quiet. Lovely wide streets and houses full of character.

Barbara pressed the doorbell then took a tissue from her bag and mopped her brow. It was so stuffy today. Needed a good thunderstorm to clear the air. She smiled to herself. She was sounding more and more like an old woman every day.

She pressed again. Maybe Jill was asleep, she thought. Her car was parked on the drive though. She took her phone from her bag and dialled her number. As it connected, she heard a faint ringing start up in the house. She lifted her hand and rapped on the door.

'Excuse me, love,' a deep male voice called. A Glaswegian accent, she thought.

Barbara looked around.

'Up here,' the voice called.

Barbara looked up to see a window cleaner, up his ladder, at the house next door.

'Oh, hello there,' she said.

He climbed down and leaned on the wall. Up close, she saw that his skin bore the deep tan of working outside. His hands, she noticed, were rough and leathery.

'If you're looking for the girl that lives there, she went out, a bit ago. Got in a car with someone medical looking.'

Barbara frowned.

'Aye,' he continued. 'It was the car I noticed. Ancient old Volvo. My dad used to have one like that when we were kids. We'd all pile in the back and go down the beach. Those were the days, eh? We were easily pleased then. Anyway, you've not long missed her.'

'Oh, well, never mind. I'll try her later. Thanks.'

The window cleaner climbed back up the ladder. 'No problem. Well, I'd better crack on. These windows won't clean themselves.'

Barbara headed back up the path and out onto the street. That was strange. She hoped everything was OK. And it wasn't like Jill to forget her phone. It was rarely out of her sight. Maybe she'd give the hospital a ring. She'd find somewhere to sit down first. She was sure she'd seen a little coffee shop along the road.

Ten minutes later, Barbara was sipping a cappuccino and waiting to be put through to the maternity ward at the Royal Infirmary.

'Hello,' she said when she was finally put through. 'I'm trying to track down a friend of mine. I was just wondering if she'd been admitted?'

The midwife who answered asked her to wait while she checked her records. Barbara stirred the foam on the top of her cup as she listened to the sound of fingers tapping keys. Not like in her day. When she'd started out everything was on paper. There was so much of it. Of course, things had been computerised by the time she left nursing, but she'd still liked to have paper records in her hands. Times changed though, she knew that.

'No, she's not here, sorry,' the midwife said, when she came back on the line.

'Thanks for looking. I was just a bit worried, I've just been to her house and she's not at home, and the window cleaner said he'd seen her with someone medical. Although I'm sure if it was something to worry about, she'd have been in the back of an ambulance and not an old Volvo.' Barbara laughed. 'Anyway, I'm waffling on and you're busy. Sorry to have bothered you.'

'No problem.'

The midwife frowned and hung onto the receiver. She quickly jabbed in three digits and waited for her internal call to be picked up.

'Hi, Janice, it's me, Lucy. Listen, what time did Elizabeth finish up today?' she said.

'Umm, not sure. Sometime this afternoon though. She hung around for Baby McLean to be born. You know how she is, won't leave until she's seen a birth through to the end. Do you need to get in touch with her?'

'What? No. It's just, well, it's probably nothing but I just had a call from someone, looking for a pregnant mother, and she mentioned someone had seen her getting into a Volvo. I think she's up to her old tricks again.'

Janice groaned. 'Do you think so? I'll have a word with her tomorrow. I mean, it's not as if it does any harm, really, but she has to stop befriending these waifs and strays. I think she feels sorry for them – it's always the single mothers or the young ones who haven't got a clue. Anyway, don't worry, I'll sort it. We'll have a chat about the line between friendship and professionalism, or something. Leave it with me.'

Lucy hung up the phone. She was a funny one, that Elizabeth. She herself couldn't wait to close the door on work when she finished a shift. Elizabeth, though; it seemed as if she never wanted to be off duty. The talk in the staffroom was that she'd even come in to give someone a lift home the other week. And she did extra shifts at the clinic. Well, it took all sorts, she supposed.

Upstairs, Janice grabbed a biro from the nurses' station and scribbled a note on a scrap of paper. *Speak to Elizabeth.* She shoved it into the pocket of her blue cotton scrubs. She'd deal with it later.

Then again, it was only a couple of weeks before Elizabeth started her year off. It might be daft to part on a sour note. And as she'd said to Lucy, it wasn't as if she was doing any real harm.

She reached into her pocket and scrunched up the paper. As she headed towards the labour ward, she threw it into the first bin she passed.

64

Michael had known something was wrong, from the moment Anna dashed downstairs as he was coming out of the shower. She had urged him to dress quickly then cuffed him and released the chain, and draped a dark hood over his head. She'd seemed uncharacteristically flustered as she'd pushed his feet into the canvas shoes and hurried him up the stairs.

He'd barely seen her over the last few days – or at least not spent a great deal of time with her. She'd dashed in and out, claiming to be *so busy* and seeming distracted, as if her mind were elsewhere.

Now though, she was guiding him along what he assumed was the hallway. After a short walk, she stopped and guided him by holding his shoulders until he made contact with what felt like a hard wooden chair.

He felt the pressure of something being wrapped around his torso and then each leg. The ripping sound told him she was taping him to the chair.

'What's going on?' he asked. 'What are you doing to me, Anna?'

She didn't answer; he heard her muttering under her breath, then the sound of her footsteps, quick and light across the floor. He sensed he was alone in the room, and tried to move his legs; tried to shake off the hood.

And then, she was back. She was speaking again, louder but in soothing, crooning tones. He held his breath and tried to make out what she was saying, and then gasped as his eyes were flooded suddenly with light.

He blinked rapidly. Anna stood before him, the hood dangling from her fingers. And behind her, slouched on a metal-framed bed with her eyes closed, looking very pregnant, pale and so, so beautiful, was Jill.

65

'What have you done to her? Why isn't she awake?' Michael said through gritted teeth.

'Calm down, I just gave her something to help her relax on the journey. You getting agitated isn't going to help. We need to just... just calm down. Everything will be fine.'

Michael tried to convince himself that there was a tremor in her voice. She won't go through with it, he told himself. She can't.

'I must be dreaming,' Jill thought. She could hear Michael's voice, she was sure of it. She'd worried that she would forget what he sounded like, and cursed herself for not having saved his answerphone messages, just so she could listen to him.

But she hadn't forgotten, of course. *That* was what his voice sounded like. He was here, with her. Or was she dreaming? Her eyelids felt so heavy; it was if there were weights dangling from her eyelashes. She focused on her breath; if this was a dream, she didn't want it to end.

Michael sounded tired. And angry. He didn't often get angry. Life was too short, he'd say. She wondered what could be wrong.

Jill was hot. Too hot. The air smelled like some sort of cleaning fluid. Disinfectant, maybe. Hospital, she thought. It smelled like a hospital. That was right. She remembered now. She'd got into the car with Elizabeth the midwife, and now she must be at the hospital. Maybe something was wrong. And the baby, what was happening to the baby?

She screwed her eyes tighter shut, not wanting to wake up. There was another voice now. She knew it but her mind was so foggy. She couldn't quite place it. Who was it? Elizabeth, she realised, relief flooding through her. It's Elizabeth. She gasped as a bright light shone into her eyes.

'What –' she said, trying to pull away.

'Hush now, it's fine. I'm going to take good care of the baby for you. You just rest. It'll all be over soon.'

Jill let her eyelids slip shut again. It would be nice to rest for a while. She was in safe hands with Elizabeth. And maybe she would dream about Michael again. She felt herself drift off towards a deep, velvety sleep.

'Wake her up!' Michael roared, spittle flying from his dry lips. 'Think about what you're doing. You have to stop this.'

Anna turned to face him and raised her eyebrows. 'Like I said, you need to calm down. And anyway, you're hardly in a position to be making demands.'

Michael clenched his teeth and glared at her.

66

Michael dug his nails into the flesh of his palms and strained against the tape that held his legs. He watched, speechless, as Anna opened the drawers of a metal cabinet, taking out sealed packages and laying them down on the trolley beside her. They were in a room he hadn't seen before. The walls were painted white and the blinds were closed. There was no furniture other than the bed, cabinet and the chair he sat in.

He pulled and stretched, feeling the edges of the tape digging into the bare flesh of his calves. The pain brought him to his senses. Do something, he told himself. Just do something. This was his only chance. He opened his eyes and looked across at Anna and Jill. Anna was staring past him, her face alive and her eyes sparkling.

'Not long now, Michael. And then our family will be complete at last,' she said. 'It's a few days earlier than I planned, but that's how it is with babies. They come when they are ready, not when it's convenient.'

She tuned to look down at Jill on the bed. 'I wonder what Jill would have done differently if she'd known what was going to happen today. Would she have worn a different outfit? Tidied up her hair? Who knows? Anyway, you might want to take a few moments to prepare yourself. Birth is amazing and beautiful, but it can be brutal.'

She was preparing for some sort of operation, Michael realised. When he spotted the little plastic cot tucked away in a corner, he could no longer convince himself that she was bluffing. It was real. It was really happening.

'Anna,' he cried, 'I beg you, please don't do this. Kill me, do what you want. Please, please don't hurt her. Don't do this.'

'Michael, can you just be quiet? This is stressful enough. I thought you should be here, at the birth. I assumed you would *want* to be. The baby will be with us very soon. A natural birth would have been nice, but it's too risky. It's better this way. It's time. At last, I'm having my baby. We're going to meet our daughter. Everything has worked out. Didn't I tell you it would?'

Michael stared at her. 'I'll stay with you. Forever. I promise. Just don't hurt her. Please. Please, just take her to hospital. You don't have to go through with this. You know it's wrong.'

Anna still didn't look at him. She kept her eyes on the metal tray in front of her, her lips moving as she silently counted the instruments. Then she frowned and walked from the room.

'Jill,' Michael whispered urgently. 'Jill, wake up, baby. Wake up. You have to wake up and help me get free. It's not safe here.'

He heard a soft moan and the rustle of fabric as Jill moved. She sat up slowly and looked at him. She tilted her head to one side and frowned.

'Is it really you?'

'Yes, yes, it's really me, and I know there's so much you want to ask and there's so much I have to tell you, but for now all you need to know is that we're in danger and you need to cut this tape. Quickly.'

'But we'll be fine. Elizabeth is here. She's my midwife.'

'Elizabeth? Is that what she calls herself? Her name isn't Elizabeth. It's Anna. And she's been keeping me prisoner here, Jill. You need to move, come on. This is our only chance.'

Jill hauled herself up from the bed. 'You have so much explaining to do.' Michael watched as she swayed on her feet and almost fell.

'Be careful. And I'll explain everything, I promise. Just grab something from that tray. Something sharp.'

Michael winced as Jill came towards him clutching a scalpel, his mind flooded with images of what Anna intended to do with it. Jill knelt down in front of him, supporting her stomach, and began to cut carefully through the tape on his legs.

'Do my waist first,' he said. 'Quick.'

It seemed like hours before the Jill cut through the tape, leaving it, as he instructed, stuck to his legs and t-shirt, so that Anna wouldn't notice it was missing.

By the time she finished, Jill's hands were shaking and Michael could see her eyelids beginning to droop. But he was free. Or as free as he could be with his wrists in steel cuffs.

He gripped Jill's hands in both of his. 'Baby, go and get back onto the bed and lie down, just like you were. Be careful. I need to take her by surprise. This will be all over soon, I promise.'

Jill mumbled agreement and staggered back across the room. As she collapsed onto the covers, Michael could hear her shallow, ragged breaths. He'd meant to take the scalpel she had used from her, but it lay forgotten next to her limp fingers.

The sound of footsteps on the wooden floor told him Anna was on her way back. She came into the room, carrying whatever it was she had forgotten and walked towards where Jill lay on the bed.

Michael waited until she was almost at the bedside, then launched himself from the chair. He took a lurching step forward and lashed his cuffed hands towards her face.

She turned her head as his attempt at a punch merely glanced her upper arm, unbalancing her but only for a second.

She recovered quickly, and, eyes bulging, grabbed a handful of Michael's too-long hair and pulled. Hard. His neck jolted and he was sure she was going to rip the skin from his scalp.

He hit out again, and this time his hands punched the firm muscles of her stomach. She gasped, releasing her grip, then pulled back her fist and punched him in the face.

Michael staggered backwards, determined not to fall. He tasted blood in his mouth and felt warm wetness on his chin. He shook his head, trying to stop the ringing in his ears and the pain that seemed to have taken over his entire head. Drops of blood spattered onto the wooden floor.

Anna grabbed the waistband of his shorts and slid her hand down them.

'You can't win this, Michael,' she said breathlessly. 'You might as well sit down and shut up or you're going to end up hurting yourself.'

Her face was so close to his that he could see the flecks of gold in her irises, the long, dark lashes framing her eyes. He could smell mint on her breath and the fresh scent of her hair.

'Fuck you, Anna. Fuck you.'

Michael closed his eyes. He tilted his head back and as he brought it forward to meet her forehead, he lifted his leg and kneed her as hard as he could in the crotch. She moaned, one hand flying to her head, the other grasping between her legs. He lifted his arms and swung them to one side, catching her in the ribs and sending her reeling backwards. As she fell, her head caught the edge of the metal trolley where she had so carefully laid out her tools.

Michael looked at Anna, lying motionless on the floor, then sat heavily in the chair and wiped ineffectively at his mouth. His head was pounding. He stood and made his way to the bed.

'Jill,' he said. 'Wake up. We have to get out of here.'

She gave no indication of having heard him. He shook her shoulder, gently at first, then harder.

'Come on, baby,' he said.

She was lying perfectly still. Her pale, bloodless lips moved in a silent murmur and a crease formed between her eyes. Michael clumsily took her hand between both of his and squeezed.

Her nails were bare and the skin around them red and raw looking. She'd always painted her nails, before. Seeing them so pale and naked unleashed a fresh wave of despair. He wanted to climb onto the bed and cover her like a blanket. Keep her safe.

'Think, Michael,' he said out loud. 'Just think.' The pressure inside his skull was unbearable. He thought his head would explode.

He couldn't possibly carry her, not with his hands cuffed, and anyway, he might hurt the baby. He groaned as he watched the sheets beneath her darken and realised that that her waters were breaking.

'I'm going to go and get help, OK? I'll be right back. Anna's out of it. You just lie there and rest. I won't be long, I promise. And when I get back I'll tell you everything. Just hold on, baby. Hold on.'

67

Michael stepped away from the bed and pushed Anna out of the way with his foot. He stopped as he heard a low, keening sound. Then he realised it was coming from him.

He needed a phone. He charged out of the room, his cuffed wrists making him feel unstable and vulnerable. His eyes roamed the hall. No sign of a phone. He checked every room, looking away as the passed the door to the cellar that had been his prison for all these weeks.

There was nothing in the living area or the kitchen. He hurried up to the bedroom, but there was no phone there either. The door to the office was locked.

As he ran back down the stairs, he slipped, and landed, face-first, on the floor. Stunned, he lay there, painfully aware that the minutes were ticking by. Her pockets. He needed to check her pockets.

Everything was as he had left it in the room, both women still unconscious. He got down on his knees and searched Anna's pockets. His hand touched on something metal. A key.

He pulled it out and held it before him. It was small, too small for a door. Closing his eyes and muttering a silent prayer, he held it awkwardly between his fingers and guided it into the hole on the handcuffs.

'Fuck!' he yelled, as he realised it wasn't the key that would open them. He threw it aside in frustration and rested his forehead against the side of the bed. He buried his face in the covers and took a deep breath. He thought his chest was going to explode. He felt the pressure building up inside him like a balloon being inflated. He eased himself up to standing and flicked his head to stop the beads of sweat from running into his eyes.

'I'm going to get help, Jill. I promise you, I'll sort this out. We'll be fine. Everything will be fine. I'll be back soon.'

He wanted to take her with him, or stay next to her. He didn't want to leave her side, ever again. He forced himself to move and hurried out of the room. He paused to look back at her, just once.

He was sure Anna must have a mobile, but searching the house would eat into the valuable time he had. There was no sign of a handbag.

The smooth, teak surface of the dresser by the door was empty, apart from a ceramic bowl. He reached for it, sending it skittering across the polished wood and onto the floor. Coins and receipts lay amongst the broken china, but not the car key that he had hoped for. Not that he'd really have been able to drive with his hands as they were, but he would have tried.

'If anything happens to her, I swear I will kill you,' he whispered as he reached the front door. He released the chain, but his damp fingers slipped on the latch. He wiped them on his t-shirt and tried again. Finally, it clicked open.

The door creaked towards him. He put a hand to his eyes against the sting of the bright, lemony light that streamed in. The still, clammy air tasted fresh and delicious to him. The trees were motionless; it was as if they'd been painted into the landscape.

Fear knotted his stomach as Michael raced down a flag-stoned path. He swallowed the feeling that he would never see Jill again and pushed the wrought-iron gate. Flakes of rusted black paint came off in his hand as it opened.

The Volvo was parked in front of the gate. He tried the door, in case by some miracle, she'd left it open with the keys inside. She hadn't, of course.

Michael shouted out in frustration as he looked left and right and saw a long road, stretching out before him like a grey ribbon. If you could even call it a road – it was barely wide enough for even one vehicle, and there were no paths at its sides – just bushy green hedges and thick stone walls.

He hurried on, all the while conscious that if a car did come, it would have no chance of avoiding him on the narrow, twisty highway. His progress was slow, so slow. The weeks of solitary confinement had made him weak and sluggish. The thoughts of sit-ups and press-ups had remained just that – nothing more than thoughts.

'No!' he yelled, as he tripped over a muddy ridge and went spilling to the ground. He pulled himself up onto his knees and squinted against the fields of bright yellow plants. In the distance, he could see sheep, dotted across the green like clumps of cotton wool.

Maybe there was a farm nearby. But around every turn, there was just more of the same. The trees had grown together over the road as he got further on, forming a thick canopy and giving him some relief from the sun that burned into his eyes. He heard a rustling sound and turned, praying for a dog, its owner nearby, mobile phone in hand. But it was just a cow, leaning over the fence, chewing idly and staring blankly at him.

In another time, another place, he might have appreciated this place. The air was so still, and so quiet. Now though, all he could see was a road leading to nowhere.

He stopped at a passing-place and leaned forward, gulping down a breath into lungs that felt on fire. He really was in the back-end of nowhere. It was like one of those rubbish horror movies that Jill loved, where idiot teenagers turned off the beaten track and ended up dead, or worse. He half-expected an old hillbilly in faded denim dungarees to appear out of the trees.

'Help!' he called out. 'Somebody. Please help me.'

As he steeled himself to set off again, a sudden noise stopped him in his tracks. It was an engine, he was sure. A car engine. It was coming from behind him, if he turned around, they'd see him and surely stop. He stood at the edge of the road and leaned out as the noise got closer.

And then it was close, close enough for him to see the Land Rover badge on the bonnet. Close enough to see the mud splattered against the sides. Close enough to see the driver was a lone woman with dark hair pulled back from her face by the sunglasses on top of her head. Close enough to see the puzzled look on her face as she accelerated and zipped past him.

He watched as the car turned the corner, the bike attached to the back also covered in mud. He was sure, so sure that she would stop. She was just finding a place to turn around. She couldn't just drive past. Could she?

He imagined this nameless woman, congratulating herself on avoiding a scam which would have, at best, ended up with her car being stolen. He'd read about things like that loads of times – conning drivers into stopping. No one in their right mind would stop in the middle of nowhere to talk to a stranger. Especially one who looked like an escaped convict, with his face covered in sweat and dirt and handcuffs around his wrists.

He had to move; he'd wasted too much time already. Michael put his head down and pushed himself forward.

It felt like hours before he glimpsed the flash of red at the side of the road, through the trees. As he got nearer, he saw that it was a phone box. An old-fashioned, red phone box, the type he didn't even think existed anymore.

Sure he was hallucinating, he tried to move faster. It wasn't until he had the heavy metal door in his hand, pulling it open and retching at the stench of decay that poured out, that he believed it was real.

A dead blackbird lay in the corner, its wings open as if it had surrendered to whatever had eaten away most of its body. Breathing through his mouth, Michael pulled the door wider.

The relief he felt was immediately eclipsed by the certainty that the handset, snaking down loosely towards the floor, wouldn't work. 'Please,' he muttered, over and over. 'Please'. He leaned forward to take it in his hands. It was firm and heavy. And, he realised, as he held it to his ear, lifeless.

'No!' he shouted, slamming it against the keypad. A noise cut through his laboured breaths. It wasn't an engine this time. It was a faint beep, and then, a ringtone. He jabbed at the nine key three times and grabbed the swinging handset once more.

68

What's wrong with me? Jill thought. She couldn't think straight. She wondered if the baby had been born. She couldn't feel it moving. And normally it did when she lay on her back. Or maybe she wasn't lying on her back. She felt damp and uncomfortable. She needed to sit up, pull herself together and find out what was going on. But when she tried to lift her hand to feel her stomach, it fell back onto the bed like a stone.

'Are you feeling a little confused?' a soft, breathless voice asked.

Jill tried to nod. The effort was just far too much, so she concentrated hard on her eyelids instead, trying to lift them.

There was a figure. A blurry figure dressed in blue. And a box. A clear, plastic box, at the same level as the bed. That's what they put babies in, she thought. She remembered that from visiting Louise in hospital when she'd had the kids.

This box was empty, though. She tried to move her head, to see more. This must be a labour room, she thought. The strong smell of antiseptic or disinfectant in the air made her nose itch. She should really make the effort to scratch it. Maybe in a minute. Her eyes slipped closed again.

A sharp slap on her cheek brought her back. She forced her eyes open and looked around. Her cheek stung and her eyes were watering. Her mouth felt so dry, and the air was thick and heavy.

'Where am I?' she said, and then stopped as she remembered. She pulled herself up straighter. Elizabeth, or Anna, as Michael had called her, was holding herself up against the side of the bed. It looked to Jill as if she was in pain.

'Where is he?' Jill said. 'He was here, I know he was. What did you do? Where's Michael?'

Anna laughed, a harsh sound that cut through the air. Jill noticed her eye looked swollen. There was blood on one side of her face.

'Hmm,' Anna said. 'He seems to have run off. He's good at that, isn't he?'

Jill felt an icy chill spreading through her bones, and noticed the wetness on her trousers and the sheets.

'I think maybe I need to see a doctor.'

'You're fine. Now, this is what's going to happen. In a few minutes, I'm going to sedate you and then I'm going to deliver the baby. You... you won't be around for much longer. But don't worry about the baby. Michael and I will take good care of it.'

'I don't understand. What do you mean? You can't deliver my baby, not here. Not now. This place isn't even a hospital, is it?'

'You've nothing to worry about. I've got everything here that a hospital would have. And I'm a very experienced midwife. You probably have a lot of questions, I understand that. Michael and I, we've got a lot of history.'

'What do you mean "a lot of history"?'

'Michael isn't the saint you probably think he is. He hurt me, a lot, and because of him, I can't have a baby myself. But we're good together. Really, really good. It's just one of those things that's meant to be; do you know what I mean? We're going to be a family, and we're going to raise this baby together.'

Jill recoiled and stared at Anna. 'I don't what kind of sick dream world you're living in, but there is no way I'm going to allow that to happen.'

Jill tried to get up from the bed. Anna's firm hand on her chest pushed her back down.

'Oh, Jill, please don't take it personally. And you've been a very important part of my plan, but you're, well, you're not part of our future. It's just the way it has to be. Try to understand. I really need to get on now.'

Anna turned to the tray of instruments at her side. Jill tried to pull herself up, as she did, a sharp pain darted up her body, so fierce that she cried out. She felt fresh wetness between her legs and put her hand to the crotch of her trousers.

She lifted her fingers in front of her eyes. They were red. Bright red. She tried again to sit up and moaned again as another spasm of pain gripped her.

'Help me,' she said, her voice fading to barely more than a whisper. She couldn't hear properly; it was as if she was in a tunnel or on a plane and her ears needed to pop.

'Please. Please. Somebody help me.'

***

'Sir,' the operator said. 'Sir, are you all right? Try to calm down and tell me which service you require.'

'All of them,' Michael said through gulping breaths. 'All of them. You don't know what she's capable of. Please. Come quickly.'

'What's the nature of your emergency, sir? And at what address?'

'I... I don't know. I don't know where I am. I was kidnapped, and now she's got my partner. Jill. She's pregnant. She was going to deliver the baby. Please you have to find us. Please.'

'What's your name, sir?' the operator asked.

'Michael.'

He thought he might choke with emotion at the sound of her kind voice. He could barely speak, but there was so much to tell her. So much he needed to say, even though he knew he was barely making sense.

'Michael, I'm Karen. I'm going to stay on the line with you, and we're going to trace the call. Are you in a house? Are you hurt?'

'No, I got away. I needed to find a phone, get help. I'm in a phone box. I need to get back. I've walked for ages, you have to hurry. And Jill–'

His voice cracked.

'Michael, listen to me. It's going to be all right.'

'How do you know?' he said. 'How can you possibly know that?'

* * *

Tears spilled down Jill's face. She lifted her arm to wipe them away and cried out as pain slammed again at her abdomen. She watched, helpless, as Anna turned back to face her. She was wearing thin latex gloves and holding a syringe in her hand.

'How can you do this?' Jill gasped. 'All those times I've seen you and you pretended to care, when really you were planning to steal my baby? What kind of sick fucking person does that? What's *wrong* with you?'

Anna was staring ahead, facing the far wall. Her voice was a low monotone and it was a struggle for Jill to hear what she was saying.

'The baby has always been for us. I care about it more than you can ever know. It's for me and Michael,' Anna said. 'You don't even deserve it. You've spent weeks barely even looking after yourself when all you should have been thinking about was this baby. You're just like the rest of them. Selfish. You don't deserve to be mothers, any of you.'

Jill could barely hear her now. She pulled at the sheets, trying to drag herself up. It hurt. It hurt so much. She spoke slowly, gasping for breath, fighting the growing urge to just close her eyes and sleep.

'What are you talking about? Who? And who are you to decide who should and shouldn't be a mother?'

Anna didn't reply; she just placed her right hand onto the swell of Jill's stomach. Jill watched through half-closed lids as Anna bent to the floor and picked up scissors and blades and laid them in a line on a folded blue cloth on the bed.

Jill tried to open her mouth, tried to speak. No words would come. She stretched forward, almost passing out with the pain. Her fingers brushed against the handle of the scalpel that she'd used to free Michael.

'I promise I'll look after her,' Anna said. 'You sleep now. Goodbye, Jill.'

Jill watched as Anna leaned towards her, the sharp pointed blade of the syringe she held in her hand catching the light. Then, with a strength she didn't know she could muster, Jill plunged the scalpel blade into Anna's abdomen, as far and as hard as she could. The handle slipped from her fingers and clattered to the floor as Jill closed her eyes and everything faded away.

69

Michael stood, clinging to the receiver, until finally, the emergency services traced his call to a country road, outside of Peebles. A place he'd always liked, he thought, bitterly.

They told him to stay exactly where he was. They asked if Anna was armed, and if she kept any weapons in her house. They had traced the house once they had established where he was calling from. It had been pretty easy, apparently. It wasn't somewhere that was very populated.

Michael waited until Karen stopped asking questions, and promised him, over and over again, that help would be with him soon. Michael didn't hear her. He leaned out of the telephone box and vomited onto the grass. And then, leaving the receiver hanging where it was, he set off back the way he had come.

70

'Jill,' Michael called as he ran up the path to Anna's house and approached the open front door. 'I'm back, baby. Help's on its way. Just hang on. They'll be here any minute.'

He took a deep, gulping breath as he prepared to cross the threshold, as if preparing himself to dive deep underwater.

Despite the open door, the air in the hall was thick and soupy. The sound of his own ragged breath filled his ears. His hands felt numb and spasms of pain jolted through them like electric shocks.

'You had to spoil things, didn't you,' Anna whispered. She was slumped in the hall, her back against the wall, her legs out in front of her and her hands resting limply on her lap. The white plastic apron she was wearing over her clothes was pushed to one side and the front of her tunic was stained dark. Blood, Michael realised. It was blood.

'What have you done to her?' he hissed, dropping down and drawing level with her on the floor. Close up, her eyes were dull and blank. A tear rolled slowly down her cheek.

'We could have been so happy,' she said, closing her eyes. 'We still can be, you know. We can start again, somewhere else. There can be another baby. I can find us another one, I know I can.'

She opened her eyes again and fixed him with her deep brown gaze. She reached out a bloody hand.

'You're crazy,' Michael spat. 'If you've hurt her...'

He pushed Anna aside. She didn't even try to protect herself; just toppled, like a skittle. He left her lying on her side on the floor and headed further along the hall.

'Jill,' he called. 'Hang on, help's on its way.'

He clung to the metal side bars at the side of the bed, blood roaring through his head.

'Oh, sweetheart,' he muttered. Her skin was bone-white; it was almost translucent, and the dusting of golden freckles across her nose, usually barely visible, stood out starkly against their pale canvas. He could see the blue veins on her closed eyelids; her eyes looked as if they were sinking into her head. He dropped his head closer to her and listened to the faint sound of her breath.

'Wake up, baby. The ambulance is coming. They'll know what to do. Just hang on.'

Her dry, colourless lips parted slightly and she let out a soft moan.

Michael felt his stomach twist. He gripped her hand and squeezed it, three times. Their secret code for when they couldn't say those three words aloud. She didn't squeeze back. Her hand just lay there, within his own, limp and lifeless. He tried not to focus on the blood on the sheets and instead looked at the swollen dome of her stomach, where their baby still lay. Their daughter.

His throat was thick and tight. She had to be OK, she had to be. They still had so much to do.

While he'd been here, locked away, Jill had continued to grow this whole other person inside of her. He should have been with her. He edged down the bars and lifted her top gently up, revealing the firm ripe skin. He kissed her stomach, stroking it gently with his fingers.

'*Please,*' he thought. '*Let them be all right. Both of them.*'

Michael clung to the side of the bed with his cuffed hands, then lifted them to wipe away the tears that were running down his cheeks. 'Just keep listening to me, babe. Listen to my voice. Do you remember the day you told me you were pregnant? How excited we were?'

It had just about taken his breath away, when she'd shown him those white pregnancy test sticks and he'd realised the implication of those little blue lines. It had shocked him, just how much he wanted it; this chance to build a proper family. He'd buried the hot flush of shame that washed over him as he remembered his very different reaction the last time someone had told him they were pregnant. He'd told himself that was all in the past, and this – Jill and their baby – was the future.

For years, any sort of commitment beyond a first name totally scared Michael. He'd seen first-hand what love and commitment could do to a couple. When his dad had died, ridiculously young, from a heart attack, his mum hadn't been able to live without him. At least, that was the only reason they could think of to explain why she'd washed down three packets of painkillers with a litre of vodka a fortnight after his funeral.

He thought suddenly of Stuart, sitting in his room at the care home, or reading one of his books in the common room, without any contact from the outside world. Even though Michael knew that it was unlikely that Stuart had even noticed his absence, he still longed to visit him, reassure him. He vowed to do that, as soon as all of this was over.

He'd tell Jill about Stuart and take her to see him. And he'd tell her how his mum died. It had been so much easier to just say nothing, and let Jill fill in the blanks. He'd tell her everything. No more secrets.

71

Michael grasped Jill's hand. She had to be OK. She was the strong one. The one who made the decisions. The one who booked the tickets, and rang up to complain about bad service.

He screwed his eyes shut and pictured her, curled up in the armchair, feet tucked beneath her and twirling a strand of hair around a finger as she read a newspaper from cover to cover, frowning or shaking her head, and giving him a running commentary on every article she had an opinion on. He'd often laughed and told her he'd never needed to read the news since he'd met her.

He grimaced as his eyes fell on the blood staining the sheets between her legs. He looked around for some sheets or blankets to cover her with, but he could only find a towel, so he pulled that over her. He knew how much she hated being cold.

She was always saying she was meant to live somewhere hot, and would move like a shot if only she didn't love Edinburgh so much. At the first sign of the sun, she'd be out in the garden, or sitting on a beach. He thought of the times she'd dragged him up to the Meadows. He could almost taste the sun lotion, the barbecued food, the petrol fumes.

Where the hell was the ambulance?

'Won't be long, now,' Michael said, hoping that he was right, and that the emergency services would turn up any second now and fix everything. He stroked Jill's cheek and brushed her hair back from her face. Why were they taking so long?

Michael leaned forward and rested his forehead against hers.

'Everything will be fine, baby,' he said. 'Just hang on.'

The silence was broken by the sound of distant sirens. Michael went out into the hall. It was empty – there was no sign of Anna. He'd assumed she had passed out on the floor. He quickly looked behind him, sure she was going to appear and overpower him. But there was no sign of her.

Then he noticed. There was blood on the floor, tiny crimson splashes leading towards the open front door.

He found her halfway along the path, stooped almost double and making her way towards the open gate.

'Where are you're going?' he said. 'The police will be here any minute. Just lie down and give up.'

Michael knew he had to stop her. She couldn't get away, not now. He broke into a run, but as he lurched forward, his foot caught on the step and he sprawled face down onto the concrete, his cheek grazing the stone. He heard her laugh through a ragged, panting breath.

When he lifted his head he saw that she'd made it to the end of the path and was out on the street, dragging herself into the Volvo.

'Come back, you crazy bitch,' he called, dragging himself up onto his knees. He willed the engine not to start. But then, after a long moment of silence, he heard the growl as it turned over.

Michael sank back down to the ground and rolled onto his back. He stared at the pale blue sky as the car engine faded away, and, at last, the sound of sirens drew closer. Anna had left. Jill was unconscious. Defeat settled over him like a thick grey blanket.

72

'She got away,' Michael said to the round-faced paramedic who helped him up and guided him down the path. 'She got away.' He shivered despite the warmth of the late afternoon sun.

'Tell the police, mate. We just need to make sure you're all right.'

'Please, just leave me,' Michael said. 'Go to Jill. Please.'

'Don't worry,' the paramedic replied, as he helped Michael up from the ground and onto the step. 'She's in good hands.'

Michael jumped as the radio at the paramedic's waist crackled into life, the sound like a jab to his ears. He tried to scramble to his feet, almost sending the paramedic flying.

True to her word, the woman on the phone had sent all of the services, and a fireman had cut the chain between the handcuffs with a pair of bolt-cutters, promising to cut off the cuffs as soon as he could.

There was so much commotion going on in the house – he needed to get in there. He felt the paramedic's gloved hands on his shoulders, gently pushing him back down. Michael sat, as the man dabbed his scraped cheek with antiseptic liquid and shone a light into his eyes.

They were taking so long in there with Jill. Too long. Surely she should be in the ambulance now, siren on and racing towards the hospital? Why were they hanging about? Unless… unless there was no point in hurrying. Unless whatever damage Anna had done was so great and–

Michael turned his head at the sound of voices in the hallway. Jill was being carried along on a stretcher, motionless and covered with blue blankets pulled up to her chin.

He stood helplessly as they loaded the trolley into the back of the ambulance. The only sign that Anna had been there at all was the blood on the path and the fluttering plastic apron on the lawn.

'Sir?' a female voice said behind him. Michael turned, facing the pretty white house in its picture perfect setting. 'There's someone here that would like to meet you.'

The voice belonged to another paramedic, a woman dressed from head to toe in green, and she was walking towards him, a white bundle of fabric in her arms. He stumbled over to her, puzzled, and then gasped as the tiny pink face came into view.

'Say hello to your daughter,' the woman said.

Michael followed her as she carried the baby into the back of ambulance. He slumped down onto the seat, and placed one shaking hand on top of the blankets covering Jill, the other on his baby girl's cheek, and started to weep.

Epilogue

It was a bright, sunny day and Princes Street Gardens was filled with the annual August influx of Edinburgh Festival tourists.

The gardens offered some peace and serenity from the chaos and heat of the city streets. The noise of buses and trams filtered through from the road, but the air smelled fresh.

Workers sat on the grass or on benches, hands clutched around takeaway coffee cups, eating sandwiches, reading books or newspapers, or just taking in the view and enjoying the freedom from the confines of offices and shops, even if it was just for thirty minutes.

Tourists stopped to take pictures of the Castle, resplendent against the bright blue sky. Mothers stood chatting while their children amused themselves in the play park. Parents and grandparents pushed buggies. People threw scraps to brazen, fat pigeons.

A tall woman in a skinny jeans and a white t-shirt walked stiffly along the highest path, and sat down on an empty bench. The large sunglasses she wore covered most of her face, and the golden highlights in her short, dark hair glinted in the sunlight.

She crossed her long, slim legs and reached into the large tan leather bag she wore across her body. She took out a small folder and grasped it tightly in both hands, then laid it on her lap and began to slowly leaf through the pages.

Down below, people continued to come and go. Some wandered slowly, taking in the view, admiring the flowers. A tall, skinny man hurried along with a tiny dog, barely bigger than a rat, on a red leather lead.

One of the pram-pushing women stopped by the fountain. She reached forward and arranged a pink knitted blanket over a sleeping infant, then lifted her arm to glance at her watch. A slim, dark-haired man walked towards her.

When he got close enough, he took her elbow, drawing her to him, and kissed her cheek, then bent and looked in at the baby. He straightened and together, they started to walk, his hand at the small of her back, whilst both of hers clutched the pram handle.

As they headed off along the path, the man turned his head suddenly, and looked up towards Princes Street and the row of benches. He lifted his hand to shield his eyes against the sun, then shook his head slowly and turned back towards the pram containing his daughter.

The woman on the bench sat perfectly still. An elderly woman, laden with carrier bags, approached her and stopped.

'Do you mind if I sit here, dear?' she said, as she sank down without waiting for an answer, and placed her bags at her feet.

The woman gave a tiny shake of the head and looked down at her folder.

'What a beautiful baby,' the older woman said, nodding towards the photograph in the clear plastic wallet.

The younger woman nodded as she turned the page, a smile playing on her full lips.

'Yours, is she?'

She nodded again. 'Yes. Yes, she is.'

With that, she closed the folder and slipped it back into her bag. She stood and smoothed down her clothes, and walked away into the bright afternoon.

THE END

Acknowledgements

Baby wouldn't have happened without the endless support of my partner. Thank you, Steve.

I'd also like to thank my wonderful agent, James Essinger of Canterbury Literary Agency, for his continued belief in me and this book. And my friend, the brilliant editor Anne Hamilton, who has given me feedback and advice since the book was nothing more than a few chapters and a vague idea of how it would end.

Thanks to all at The Conrad Press, and to Charlotte Mouncey for her fabulous cover design.

And finally, thank you so much to my family and friends for your support and enthusiasm. You all helped to make this possible. And no, none of the characters are based on any of you...